They were playing cards, Cass Calbraith and the others. As Kinstrey walked up to the table Cass's eyes flicked toward him, hard with resentment.

"We'll be leaving at six, Cass. You'd better come now."

Color burst in Cass Calbraith's youthfully smooth face. "I don't have to take orders like one of your damned bull-whackers."

The man with the flat face spoke to Kinstrey, his voice thin with arrogance.

"You heard what the kid said. Roll your freight, mister."

Kinstrey's eyes, usually a mild blue, now suddenly chilled. His glance traveled deliberately to the holster tied to the man's skinny shank.

"I haven't got my gun," Kinstrey said, "but if you're hunting a bloody nose I could fix you up."

The screw-head eyes of the small man remained on Kinstrey, malignant.

"Wear that gun, mister. That's my advice to you."

Also by
Clark Brooker

LONE GUN

Published by Ballantine Books

FIGHT AT SUN MOUNTAIN

Clark Brooker

BALLANTINE BOOKS—NEW YORK

© 1957 by Clark Brooker

All rights reserved.

Library of Congress Catalog Card Number: 57-8245

SBN 345-23488-X-095

First Printing: March, 1957
Second Printing: September, 1973

Printed in the United States of America

Cover art by Frank McCarthy

BALLANTINE BOOKS, INC.
201 E. 50th Street, New York, N.Y. 10022

1

OUTSIDE THE road ranch the rain was coming down now in tumbling sheets, lashed by a November gale that leaked innumerable cross currents through the big drafty structure and blew dipping tongues of flame against the bar's blackened lamp chimneys. Inside there was hubbub, confusion and a potpourri of smells, all noisome. Blue fog wreaths of tobacco smoke swirled above the bar, blending noxiously with strong fumes of coal oil and the damp stink of drying wool. Occasional hoarse laughter welled above a steady drone of voices. Glasses clinked, silver jingled, boots shuffed and scraped in unceasing monotony.

This was Tiny Tipton's. This was Sportsman's Hall, euphemistically named, cavernously bleak caravansary for man and beast astride the route to Virginia City out of Placerville, California. Here came the hungry to eat, the weary to sleep and the low in spirit to drink before plunging on to the passes that would lead them over the gray Sierras and on to the Promised Land. Or to lonely, unmarked graves beside the trail. . . .

From his post at the window end of the bar, Boise Kinstrey stared out through dripping panes with a tense uneasiness, then turned his glance back slowly on Big Matt Calbraith, standing spread-legged beside him.

"Quit worrying," Calbraith growled at him. "We had a busted axle. So what if we don't make Berry's tonight?"

"I'm thinking about you," Kinstrey said.

"Well, don't. A little back-bending's good for a man's gizzard. Come on, drink up!"

Kinstrey, toying with his whiskey glass, was silent. He was remembering Matt Calbraith's stubborn refusal to leave his drivers until they had finished replacing the Espenshied's broken axle an hour ago, at the height of the storm. And he was remembering the way Marna Calbraith had fussily herded her brother Cass off to the shelter of the ranch, forgetful of her father out there in the wind and wet.

1

A frown indented Kinstrey's forehead. It wouldn't have been so bad if Big Matt hadn't suffered pleurisy once, leaving him with a weakened lung. Matt Calbraith's trouble was that he had to have his finger in every pie, come hell or high water. He had to, or he wouldn't have been Big Matt Calbraith.

Now, looking back at the man beside him, Kinstrey said, "You ought to take things a little easier, Matt."

"Take things easy? *Me?*" Matt Calbraith was used to making himself heard above the snarl of a gash-saw, and his booming voice carried to every corner and cranny of the barroom. His cool, granite-gray eyes fastened on Kinstrey, then glinted with a mordant humor. "Boise, the day I start taking things easy I'll be six feet under."

He glanced up at that moment to find the eyes of Tiny Tipton on him from behind the bar. "And if anybody can put me there it'll be you," he informed the road ranch owner. "Serving a man this lye-and-brimstone gut wash!"

Tipton, a huge man with a shaggy red beard, grinned. "Thanks for the compliment," he said. "What this really is, though, is red pepper juice and paprika mixed into a base of Old Sachem Bitters and Wigwam Tonic."

"Well," Calbraith said, "just so long as you keep your own damned red whiskers out of it." He chuckled, interestedly watching Tipton refill their glasses, then downed his drink and glanced at Kinstrey.

"What's wrong, Boise? Sink it! It'll only kill you."

"Matt, you ought to be in bed. I'm surprised Marna didn't pack you off early."

"Pfah! Nobody packs this beaver till he's ready to be packed. You know that."

"I guess so."

"Guess, hell! You know it. So stop beating around the damned bushes. Don't be like Cass."

Kinstrey gulped his whiskey, grimaced. "Cass is young. Give him time, Matt."

"Only seven years under you. He's nineteen."

"You ride the kid too hard, Matt."

"Sure, sure. And what good does it do?" Calbraith flung up his hands as he cited, "Look what happened up at Puget, when I was mill boss for Moore-Fogarty. Cass couldn't even make it as a road monkey. Couldn't even grease a chute right!"

"Give him a little more responsibility, Matt. He'll make it. Let him have a little more rein and he wouldn't resent me so much."

"Damn it, he's got no cause to resent you or anything else!" Matt Calbraith's big-knuckled fist smote the bar top so hard that bottles jumped. Other drinkers turned to stare at him. Glowering, he lowered his voice to Kinstrey, continuing, "He's got to be seasoned, Boise. I wish you'd talk to Marna about it. She's only a year older than he is but she coddles him like an old-maid aunt!"

Color seeped through the weathering in Boise Kinstrey's cheeks. "Why should Marna mind what I say?"

"Why shouldn't she?" bluntly demanded Calbraith. "Ain't you two over the stage of sparking around in the dark yet?"

Kinstrey's flush deepened. "I've never spoken to Marna, Matt."

"Why not? Afraid she'd peck at you too? Hell, that's just a phase that all women go through!"

"Marna's used to the best, Matt, and I haven't got anything except what you've made possible for me. I've got to pay some of that back before I—"

"Damn you, Boise, you're foreman of this outfit right now and you'll be mill foreman when we reach Washoe and get our saws set up. Man, do you realize what lumber's bringing today in Virginia City? A hundred dollars a thousand! We'll all be nabobs. Fancy, high-chinned, solid-silver nabobs!"

"Then," suggested Kinstrey mildly, "let's wait till I am one, Matt."

"All right, Boise." Calbraith's voice was thin. "But don't wait too long. You do that you'll wake up some morning and find the parade's passed you by. Besides, before I get hauled off to the boneyard I'd like to have a grandchild or two to dandle on my knee." Suddenly he turned and looked around the room. "I wonder what the devil's happened to Cass?" he muttered peevishly.

"I'll find Cass. You get to bed, Matt; you could use some sleep."

"Reckon you're right. I do feel sort of played out."

"I'll hunt up Cass right now," Kinstrey promised. He hesitated. "And Matt? Tomorrow—if you could just give him a little more to do—some definite job he could be responsible for——"

Calbraith cut in, "Sure, he can pound sand in a rathole. But he'll get his foot caught in it." He stepped angrily away from the bar and Kinstrey again was aware of how unnaturally bright his cheeks looked. "Just look around till you find a high-stake poker game," he told Kinstrey with controlled bitterness. "That's where you'll find the misunderstood genius—losing his shirt!"

Kinstrey glanced uneasily across his shoulder, conscious of Calbraith's voice having grown loud again and people staring. "Don't worry. I'll see Cass gets to bed early," he said.

Calbraith's voice softened, "I know I can always depend on you, Boise." His hand reached out, gripped Kinstrey's arm. "And don't think you've got to own the Bank of California before you speak to Marna. I think I know how she feels about you, whether you do or not."

"Thanks, Matt."

"Thanks my foot! You've earned anything you ever got from me ten times over."

Kinstrey grinned. "All right. Then to hell with you."

Matt Calbraith grinned back. "Hell of a way for a man's future son-in-law to talk to him." He swung around. "Wake me up early in the morning; we'll shove off about six. Good night, Boise."

" 'Night, Matt."

The grin was gone from Boise Kinstrey's mouth now as he watched Matt Calbraith bull his way through the noisy crowd still pushing into the barroom. Not quite up to Kinstrey's own six-foot-three, Calbraith nevertheless was a solid six-foot, a powerful man with thickly muscled shoulders and a rocky jawline. Everything he'd ever got he'd earned by fight or sweat. But tonight something was wrong. The big slablike shoulders sagged. The head with its bristly iron-gray hair hung forward, limp.

He's got a fever, Kinstrey thought worriedly. His gaze ran to the left, where a deep alcove opened off the bar area. The sucker room. Kinstrey's eyes narrowed. Then he was elbowing his way out from the bar and into the throng pressing toward it. He reached the entrance to the alcove and halted.

Here, the smoke haze seemed even more dense than it had been in the barroom. In the center of the room the paunch of an iron stove glowed flame-red. Spaced on either side of it, chain lamps hung from crude beams spread a garish light on the intent faces of a score or more of men gathered around card and dice tables.

Kinstrey easily picked out Cass Calbraith's thin-boned frame and slightly angular face at a table not far from the stove. Next to Cass a tall, sparely built man wearing a gray wampus shirt was negligently riffling a deck of cards. Kinstrey noticed a deep cleft in his chin that had almost the appearance of a scar; otherwise the man's features were of a normal and even handsome regularity.

The two other men at the table, however, appeared less prepossessing. One had a low saddle of nose on a flat face and small, tinselly eyes. He was short and wiry, while the third man was inclined to stockiness and was jowled of jaw despite an oddly scrawny neck that lifted out of thick shoulders like a chicken's stretched to follow a worm.

As Kinstrey walked up to the table Cass Calbraith's eyes flicked toward him, hard with resentment.

"What do you want, Boise?"

"I don't want anything," replied Kinstrey. "But your father does. We're pulling out early tomorrow. He thinks you should get to bed."

"To hell with him!"

"Sure. You got that off your chest. Now come on."

"Leave me alone, Boise. I've got this game to finish. Then I'll be along."

"We'll be leaving at six, Cass. You'd better come now."

Color burst in Cass Calbraith's youthfully smooth face. "No!" he shouted. "And don't try and lead me by the nose, Boise. I don't have to take orders like one of your damned bull-whackers!"

Kinstrey looked down impassively at him. The man with the flat face spoke to Kinstrey, his voice thin with arrogance.

"You heard what the kid said. Roll your freight, mister."

Kinstrey's eyes, usually a mild blue, now suddenly chilled. He said, "I'll skid you out of here on your banty behind if you don't stay out of this. Come on, Cass!"

The wiry man jerked to his feet. Simultaneously the eyes of the man in the gray shirt reached him. "Let it go, Jack," he said.

The screw-head eyes of the small man remained on Kinstrey, malignant but hesitating. Kinstrey's glance traveled de-liberately to the holster tied to his skinny shank. "You've had good advice," he told the man. "I haven't got my gun, but if you're hunting a bloody nose I could fix you up."

"Wear that gun, mister. That's my advice to you."

Kinstrey was aware that the room had gone very still. The fire in the pot-bellied stove flared under a down-gust from the chimney, subsided. The eyes of the man in the gray shirt were a cool and lusterless gray-blue fixed on Kinstrey's taut face.

He said in an equable tone, "I'd ignore that suggestion if I were you, friend."

"I didn't ask for this trouble," Kinstrey said.

"There won't be any trouble." The speaker idly flicked a speck of lint from the wampus shirt as his gaze swerved to the man with the flat face. "Sit down, Jack," he ordered quietly.

The gunman's face darkened. Then with a glowering glance around the room he slid into his seat. "Too damned many bosses around here," he mumbled under his breath.

The man in gray ignored him. He told Kinstrey, "My name's Frank Ganahl. Forget this. It never happened."

"Boise Kinstrey," Kinstrey responded curtly, but made no offer to shake hands. His eyes dropped to Cass Calbraith's sullenly tightened face. "Let's go, Cass," he repeated quietly. "The old man's sick. The earlier we get started tomorrow the better."

"I didn't know he was under the weather." Cass spoke al-most reasonably, but now his oblique glance toward Ganahl told Kinstrey that fear probably had motivated his reluctance to quit the game at this point.

"Ganahl was thoughtfully stroking his chin. He eyed Cass and said, "You get right on along, friend. Get up early enough and you might make Berry's tomorrow."

"We'll make it," said Kinstrey.

Cass's eyes made an uneasy circuit of the table, putting in, "Sorry I have to quit. I wouldn't have let it get started if I'd known the old man was sick."

"Forget it!" Ganahl made a dismissive gesture before ei-ther of the others could speak. He said, "Maybe you'll give us revenge some other time. We'll see you in Virginia City."

"Sure—any time," Kinstrey recognized the false heartiness

in Cass's voice, his eagerness to appear before these gamblers as a hail fellow, well met. He took another look around the table, but his second impression of these men only confirmed his first. They were trail toughs. Ganahl had surface manners and a certain engaging air. He, therefore, was probably the most dangerous of the lot.

Kinstrey tugged at Cass's coat sleeve. "Ready?"

Cass twitched his arm. "All right! Let's go." '

"Good luck, Calbraith," Ganahl said. "Nice meeting you, Kinstrey."

"Thanks," Kinstrey said dryly, and was taking a last memorizing look at the man with the flat face as he turned his back. The man's eyes were like polished stones; his mouth resembled a string of blue gut on a piece of curing hide. Away from Ganahl, that fellow would kill, orders or no orders.

Kinstrey felt the strained silence behind them as he and Cass walked from the alcove. In the barroom they turned into a short corridor and in another moment were in a long room lined on three sides by tiers of bunks. About half were already occupied. Kinstrey halted at the first vacant one and shucked off his mackinaw. Then with a sidelong glance at Cass he began pulling off his boots.

"Well," he said, "how big a pot did you rake in?"

Cass looked smug. "Nearly a hundred. I only had twenty to start with."

"Lucky Calbraith." There was sarcasm in Kinstrey's voice. He drew off his pants and flung them down on the bunk. "Lucky hell!" he said.

Cass blustered. "What do you mean?"

Kinstrey's jaw was rocky. "I mean those sharpers wouldn't have let you win if they hadn't been setting you up for something."

"You're crazy; they're no sharpers. They're headed for Virginia City with a couple of wagonloads of store goods."

"Traders?" Heavy skepticism tinged Kinstrey's tone.

"Frank Ganahl owned his own store in Sacramento," rejoined Cass defensively, "and the stocky one—Al Moss—used to freight his goods to the mining camps up on the Feather."

"And Flat-Face?" asked Kinstrey.

"His name's Jack Raimo." Cass was sullen again. "Used to placer-mine on the Feather, he told me."

"*He* told you. *They* told you." Kinstrey couldn't suppress the rancor in his voice. "So what did you tell *them*—that we were rolling our wheels to Washoe to set up a sawmill? And that if we don't make it to Franktown by the thirtieth it blows our contract with Ophir higher than a kite?"

"What's Ganahl got to do with that?"

"Nothing, maybe." Kinstrey spoke meagerly. "But how do we know what they're carrying?" he pointed out. "It could be a donkey engine and a couple of gash saws."

"Hogwash! They're traders all right. Ganahl wouldn't know a gash saw from a muley."

Kinstrey drew a breath, sighed it out resignedly. "All right, Cass. Grab a bunk and get some shut-eye."

"*Now* what's gravelling you?"

Kinstrey flopped down on his bunk. He turned his face wearily to the wall.

"Nothing," he murmured. "Nothing at all—I hope." Every muscle in his body felt sore and drawn, and within the space of a minute he had dropped off to sleep.

2

KINSTREY was up and out at five-thirty, contemplating the morning's bleak grayness and not liking it. The day was damp and raw, cold and going to be colder, and already its chill was in Kinstrey's bones as he stood outside the road ranch buttoning his mackinaw and peering through sleep-bleared eyes toward the faintly discernible line of five massive Espenshieds.

Those wagons were his responsibility now; wholly. Yesterday he'd been only token boss of the outfit, under Big Matt. But Matt Calbraith wouldn't fork a horse today. He'd even been too sick to protest when Kinstrey had told him he'd have to ride with Marna in the bunk wagon. He had simply groaned, cursed and rolled over on his side, putting Kinstrey's somber face away from him.

Good Lord! Kinstrey worried. If it's his lung again, we're in for real trouble.

Distantly, the sound deadened by muffling woolsacks of mist that hung over everything, Kinstrey now could hear the brawling shout of his teamster boss, Pat Manogue, lustily exhorting his drivers to come out of their blankets.

"All right, ye lazy, shirking spalpeens! Roll out and yoke up! Cattle in the corral!"

Kinstrey moved out into the mist, only vaguely aware of the mingled shouts and oaths of the bullwhackers as they lunged around in the semidarkness hunting for their lead oxen. He dimly made out the thick-set figure of Charlie Creath, one of the drivers, hurrying toward the melee with an ox-yoke canted from his left shoulder, a bow in his right hand and the key in his mouth. Farther on, Geehaw Jenkins, another of their outfit, already had dropped a bow over the neck of his leader and was heading him to a wagon wheel to chain him there. Afterward he would search for the mate and yoke him with the ox already in hand.

The heavy air was tinctured with the strong smells of droppings and urine damp. The sluggish oxen bawled fitfully as the men worked among them. Kinstrey walked on, preoccupied, wanting to talk with Pat Manogue. Something touched his arm and, turning, he was startled to see a girl standing beside him.

"Mr. Kinstrey?" she asked diffidently.

"That's right." It was surprise that caused Kinstrey to stare longer than he ordinarily would have; the girl, at first glance, didn't strike him as pretty. "Something I can do for you?" he asked perfunctorily.

"I'm Effie Mannerheim. I understand you're bound for Virginia City. I'd like to join your train."

Kinstrey blinked under her quaint directness and then for a long moment stared again before shaking his head.

"Sorry. We don't have any room."

"But I can pay my way."

A slim girl, medium in height, with a fresh, clean-cut look and air of quiet competence about her. Kinstrey now saw her a little more favorably but still shook his head.

"It's not that. We've only got two wagon bunks and they're in use. One's for Mr. Calbraith, the other for his daughter. He's too sick to ride his horse."

"Then maybe I could ride it. I wouldn't need a bunk. I've slept on the ground before."

A voice from beside Kinstrey applauded, "A colleen after me own heart! Go on, Miss; break him down. 'Tis only on the outside he's as tough as a Kilkenny *Geancach!*"

Kinstrey felt irritation he couldn't wholly account for. He turned and laid cold eyes on Pat Manogue's blunt Irish face.

"Never mind the blarney," he said. "How soon can we roll?"

"Any time. The bastes av burthen are all yoked an' ready to do me biddin'."

"Then tell the men to get breakfast and we'll roll in half an hour."

Kinstrey turned. Effie Mannerheim was watching Pat Manogue stalk away, a big, dogged man with the lumbering gait of a bear. With a light laugh she looked back at Kinstrey.

"What on earth is a Kilkenny *Geancach?*"

Her brown eyes searching up at him held a lively interest and Kinstrey grinned in spite of himself.

"Pat likes to hooraw people. *Geancach* is Gaelic for Yankee."

"Then you must be from New England."

"I don't know where I'm from" Kinstrey's voice was abruptly dismissive.

"I wasn't trying to pry."

"It's all right," said Kinstrey harshly. "I'd tell you—if I knew myself."

"I'm sorry." She was turning, then, when he blurted, "Just a minute!"

She swung and faced him. "Yes?"

"Mr. Calbraith's horse is a buzzard-head; it gets a little mean sometimes."

"I've ridden buzzard-heads before." It was a simple statement, not boastfulness, and he studied her, aware again that her face was too thin and sharply boned to be exactly pretty. But it did possess an expression of alert intelligence and there was a strangely compelling interest in the contrast between her blond hair and large sepia-dark eyes.

"Why do you want to go to Virginia City?" he asked.

"My uncle runs a mercantile there. His name is Jules Mannerheim. I'm to work for him."

"What happened to the outfit you came here with? You didn't come from the Coast alone, I hope."

She smiled faintly. "No. I was traveling with a small outfit freighting in some lumber."

"What happened to you?"

"We were waylaid a few hours out of Sonora Canyon. Two wagons were stolen and one of our drivers was killed. They were only after the lumber. There was a third wagon with some household goods. They didn't touch that."

"Lumber's the big thing at the mines right now. How did you make it here?"

"I got a lift with a party that was coming as far as Sportsman's Hall."

"Who owned the outfit you were with?"

"Some friends of mine—Mamie and Jim Gerrity. They'd planned to sell the lumber in Virgina City; then Jim was going to get a job in the mines. But now they've gone back to Sacramento."

"That's what you should have done."

"They wanted me to. But Uncle's expecting me."

Kinstrey said dryly, "So you had no choice," but his irony seemed to escape her completely.

"That's right."

Kinstrey said, "Did you get any kind of look at the men who held you up?"

"No, it happened after dark. I just remember a lot of noice and confusion. And Mamie Gerrity screaming. It wasn't very pleasant."

Kinstrey's voice was grim. "These trails aren't meant to be pleasant. Especially for women."

"Women usually aren't long after going where men go." Effie Mannerheim smiled, then in a matter-of-fact voice added, "Why worry about where the next high wind may be coming from? It takes all the joy out of living."

"Won't your folks worry?"

"I haven't any, except Uncle Jules. He was my father's half-brother."

It was again a simple statement of fact, offered at face value and not a bid for sympathy, but Kinstrey's face darkened oddly. He said abruptly, "Had your breakfast yet?"

"No. I got up early so I'd be sure to catch you. Mrs. Tipton told me you'd be the one to see."

Kinstrey said gruffly, "All right. Go eat. Then meet me back here in twenty minutes."

She seemed to hesitate. "I'm beholden to you, Mr. Kinstrey. But I wish you'd let me pay something. I can——"

"No!" Why did they always have to keep pounding at a thing? Ashamed of his brusqueness he swung around. "Twenty minutes," he repeated across his shoulder and strode away, leaving her standing alone.

For a moment he walked purposelessly, moving past the dripping tilts of the Espenshieds into fog that momentarily seemed to have grown thicker. The girl had irked him, for some reason, but the truth was he was ripe for being irked these days. Suddenly he stopped and fished in his mackinaw pocket. After much scrounging he found his half-empty sack of Bull and a bent packet of papers and impatiently took a moment to build a cigarette.

Worry put tenseness into the deceptive mild blueness of his eyes as he jabbed the finished cylinder of tobacco between his lips and lighted it. This girl would be just one more responsibility to add to his load. Why had he been such a damned fool? Why hadn't he just said no to her and been done with it?

His face, running to length and leanness, tautened dourly as he drew on the cigarette. The haul from Placerville over the Sierras and on to Virginia City wasn't too risky as long as the weather held good. But almost from the beginning nothing about this expedition had seemed to go right.

He puffed absently, his eyes squinted against the smoke of his cigarette. First had been the delays in transshipping their saws and other heavy equipment from Sacramento to Placerville, where their new Espenshieds had been waiting. Then at the last minute Marna had decided to make the trip—to help keep down the friction between her father and Cass, she'd said. And now the *last* straw. Big Matt flat on his back. And weather likely to worsen any day now. And another female with the outfit, to be indulged and humored and become a drag on it...

Abruptly Kinstrey threw down his cigarette. Beyond the Espenshieds other wagons loomed in pale host, their Osnaburg tilts mounding out of the mist like spectral mosques. Quite close by, a pair of Murphys stood axle to axle, silent and deserted-looking in the bleak dawn light. Suddenly Kinstrey was linking something Cass had told him last night with information given him just a few minutes ago by Effie Mannerheim. Ganahl had two wagons. And two wagons had been stolen from the Gerritys. Suppose these Murphys were the ones? If they held lumber—

Kinstrey chopped off the thought. Even if they did, it wouldn't prove it was stolen lumber. But it would prove Ganahl was a liar. Store goods, he'd told Cass, made up his cargo. But suppose the cargo *should* turn out to be lumber?

Kinstrey hesitated. Probabilities were strong that Ganahl and his men had spent the night in the bunk room of the road ranch. But suppose Ganahl had left a guard? Should he chance a look anyway?

Kinstrey answered the question with an impatient stride forward. The poke bonnet hoods of the Murphys loomed before him. He swung past the nearer wagon and moved in stealthily behind it.

The perimeter of the fog was about twenty feet from him. Between him and it nothing visible stirred. A canvas curtain hung from the wagon's front down over its tailgate. The gate was too high to see over. Kinstrey unfastened its chains. He started lowering it gingerly.

A hinge shrilled and Kinstrey tensed, jerking his head around. The pale skirts of the mist seemed to have drawn back slightly; otherwise everything looked the same. He listened. A puff of wind fluttered the draw curtain. A horse's whicker faintly touched the stillness, the sound far away.

Kinstrey eased the gate down, pampering it. Then his hand was up to the curtain. He parted it with a jerk.

The familiar pungency of fresh-sawed pine swept out to him. Then he saw it—the pimpled butts of dressed timbers and boards, stacked rank on rank. The freighter was crammed from bedboards to tilt with lumber.

Leaving the endgate dangling Kinstrey wheeled toward the second wagon. One load of lumber might be a coincidence. But two ...

He reached the tailgate and had his hand up to the chain pin when an obscure sound pulled him taut. Simultaneously a muffled football squished in the wet grass and he whirled. A figure with an upraised gun leaped at him.

He had no chance of fending off the blow; he instinctively ducked and the gun barrel's sight ripped down his cheek as his head tipped away and he absorbed the blow's heaviest concussion on his right shoulder.

Dazed, he felt his knees go slack under him as he staggered and bumped violently against the tailgate. Luckily the impact jarred him alert and at this moment he recognized the man with the flat face, Jack Raimo.

The recognition seemed mutually instant and aversive. A hot malignancy shone in Raimo's eyes as he backed, sighting deliberately down the gun.

Sighting was his mistake. His bullet splintered wood where Kinstrey had stood a split-second before. The suddenness of Kinstrey's throwing himself down caught Raimo by surprise. He fired twice again as Kinstrey rolled toward him.

The small gunman shouldn't have missed but now panic was at his throat and his slugs kicked turf behind Kinstrey's barreling body. Then Kinstrey grabbed for his ankle and got it. His savage jerk flung Raimo onto the grass beside him, thrashing like a pinned rattler.

It was hopeless and the wiry gunslick knew it. He nevertheless made one wild, abortive effort, lunging up off his back and clawing his dropped gun back into his hand. Then Kinstrey's big hand flopped over it and tore the weapon free.

Kinstrey lifted to his knees, straddling the writhing figure under him and balling a fistful of Raimo's checkered wool shirt in his left hand. Then with his free right he swung up the heavy Navy Colt.

Raimo stared up at it with frozen fascination, his little feral eyes only at the last moment dilating as Kinstrey's hand blurred down.

Kinstrey heard the whimpering sound as his victim's head jerked and sagged. He released his grip on Raimo's shirt then, letting the spindly figure fall back supine. With that he stood, breathing hard and a little fast now, and for the first time aware of a feeling of primitive hatred and revulsion toward this little man made big and venomous merely by token of a seven-and-a-half-inch steel tube worn in a leather holder along his right pants' leg.

Kinstrey felt a rising pressure in his throat and knew that if Raimo had been a mad dog he would now finish him without compunction. Yet he could not finish this animal that walked on two legs. He couldn't because he wasn't like Raimo, and luckily there were few men in the world who were. Only another two-legged animal as vicious and rabid as this one could do the deed, at least in cold blood and without warning.

So now I won't sleep, Kinstrey thought bleakly, and I'll be afraid to walk alone at night.

He absently stroked blood from his gouged cheek, still staring down at the flat, ugly, nondescript face of the man on the ground. Then as he sighed and looked away a low wrangle of voices reached him and he swiveled abruptly, pulling the Colt up again.

Almost at the same instant he relaxed and lowered it. In the vanguard of three figures emerging out of the fog he recognized the burly shape of Pat Manogue.

"Are ye all right, man?" Manogue panted as he came up. He went on, "We heard shootin' and——" He stopped, staring down. "Holy McFoley! And who is this relict with th' face av th' divil?"

Kinstrey was terse. "His name's Jack Raimo, Pat. Ever hear of him?"

"No! And from th' ugly North-of-Ireland puss av him I'll not be displaised if I never see him again!"

"Did you say Raimo, Boise?" From behind Manogue, Geehaw Jenkins stepped forward, followed, to Kinstrey's surprise, by Effie Mannerheim. Jenkins was a grizzled old-timer with a seamed jawline and thinning gray hair. He said, "I knew of a Jack Raimo from up Placerville way—supposed to have killed a couple miners and had the vigilantes out chasing him. Reckon he was too slick for 'em, though." His glance squeamishly skirted Raimo's still body, then pulled back quickly on Kinstrey. "Why'd he go for you, Boise?"

Kinstrey succinctly explained what had happened, inquiring of Effie Mannerheim as he finished, "Maybe you'd know. Were the Gerritys' wagons Murphys?"

The girl shook her head and in an apologetic way looked troubled. "I wish I knew. I think Jim Gerrity did mention something once. But it didn't seem very important at the time."

"It's important now." Kinstrey's tone was thin. "Maybe you'd remember what kind of lumber Gerrity was carrying," he pressed.

"I'm afraid I wouldn't." Suddenly she seemed to sense his dissatisfaction with her and said, almost humbly, "Now I wish I'd asked. I guess I am just not a very curious female."

Kinstrey bit down on his lip. He realized that he didn't know much about women but this one seemed to have rubbed him wrong from the start. He tried to suppress his annoyance and failed. "You were curious enough to come running to see what all this excitement was about," he pointed out.

This brought the reaction some needling meanness in him seemed to require. He saw anger whiten her still face.

"Why, that's not so!" she blurted tensely. "I've been a nurse and I just wanted to be of help in case anybody——"

"Av course, av course," Pat Manogue nodded understandingly, then glared at Kinstrey. "A sweet colleen *bawn* wants to be an angel av mercy and ye've th' bad manners to talk to her like an uncivilized Orangeman!" He turned and snapped, "Come on, Geehaw! Standin' here listenin' to this *Geancach* Brian Boru won't be gettin' our work done!"

Kinstrey gave Jenkins a wry smile as the teamster looked inquiringly at him. "Go ahead, Geehaw," he said. "Get the teams lined up. Pat'll cool off."

Then he looked at the girl. She had not moved.

"Was there something else?" he snapped.

Her only reaction to the curtness of his tone seemed to be the way her clasped hands tightened together. Her voice was quiet, composed.

"I wondered if you still wanted me along, that's all."

"Did I say I didn't?"

"Not in words."

He scowled at her and said, "You know the danger now. It's up to you."

"Then I'll accept your offer. I know you think I'll be a burden. But I promise you I won't be."

Her restrained quietness of manner rebuked his own quick proneness to spleen and sent a sudden feeling of shame through him.

"I touch off too easy," he grumbled. "You'll do all right."

She smiled at that. "Thank you. And maybe I do have just a little tiny bump of curiosity."

"I thought all women did. Well, I'll see about Mr. Calbraith's horse if you're ready."

She was wearing a navy blue cape and blue sock hat with a jaunty tassel. She drew up the cape's collar around her throat. "I'm always ready." Then she fell unobtrusively into step beside him.

3

Boise Kinstrey rode his big skewbald dun well forward of the outfit of five heavily loaded Espenshied wagons, his eyes knifing through steely grayness into the late November's quick-gathering dusk. They had been on the trail since a little after six this morning and it was getting colder, the air so raw and sharp that it tasted almost metallic.

Kinstrey pulled his head lower into the collar of his sheeplined mackinaw so that only his strong aquiline nose now jutted out from its folds like a fierce beak. Compressed within the collar his flat cheeks drew tautly into a frown. They weren't going to make it to Berry's tonight; he knew that now. And if he was any judge this wind kicking up had a feel of snow in it.

Behind Kinstrey the wagons had just cleared a defile flanked by slate cliffs and patches of scrub growth. He lined his eyes somberly on the forward parallel ruts of the trail. Some distance ahead, and down, he could dimly make out the outline of a sheltered valley, where with luck water might be found, and graze for the oxen. He felt relief but it was relief mixed with a presentiment of trouble which had been graveling him ever since this morning, when they had left Tipton's.

He glanced suddenly backward across his shoulder. One of the Espenshieds had developed a hot axle and was starting to screech. Kinstrey gritted his teeth. There was no time now to stop, pull a linch pin, and then grease the axle from the tar bucket that hung from the rear reach pole of each wagon. Let the damned thing scream. They'd be making camp soon.

Still turned backward, Kinstrey's glance caught on the cape-wrapped figure of Effie Mannerheim. She looked small, riding Matt Calbraith's big-barreled trigueno, her slim, slightly pointed face buried in the cape's thick fur collar. He remembered her hair, brushed severely back to the nape of her neck, but there knotted by a thin ribbon, leaving a swatch of vivid yellow to flow down over her shoulders like melted butter. The blond hair had contrasted oddly with her sun-bronzed face and eyes of a deep and extraordinarily lucent brown.

Kinstrey's mouth pinched, observing her escort. Cass Calbraith was holding his lively grulla to a walk to keep beside her, and gesturing animatedly as he rode.

Really having a time for himself, Kinstrey thought, and recalling his trouble with Big Matt's son last night, angrily jerked his glance forward again. So Cass had finally found him a girl. All right; maybe if she was the right kind, she'd gentle him down. Only she hadn't struck him as the kind who'd stand for any nonsense, somehow.

Something wet and feathery slapped him in the face and his voice exploded softly, "Damn!" It was starting to snow, big, sopping, floppy flakes that came swirling out of the increasing darkness like spinning white pinwheels.

Kinstrey reined in his dun and waited for Pat Manogue, wagoner of the lead six-yoke ox team, to draw even with him.

"Snow!" He yelled it up disgustedly at Manogue, then jerked his head forward. "Valley yonderly." He was finding he had to shout above a rising wind to make himself heard. "Any notions about a camp site?"

Manogue cupped his mittened hands. "Scrivvy's Pass!" he yelled back, "Know it like the back of me hand. 'Tis a good place." And he nodded vigorously as if to bulwark the statement.

In twenty minutes the hills had drawn closer around them and they were in a protected swale where a brawling brook came rushing down from a wooded ridge to split one end of the clearing with mountain water.

With the cold intensifying and the snow still fluttering down Kinstrey would have been satisfied with almost any sheltered camp site at this late hour. But the one here beside this stream, where there was both good water and grass for the cattle, seemed like the answer to a prayer.

Kinstrey gave the signal and the wagons swung in a crude circle which presently was widened into a makeshift corral by stretching heavy log chains from vehicle to vehicle. Within was now a small but useful yard in which to hold the cattle and which also furnished some protection from the stormy night that was threatening.

Kinstrey now was satisfied to leave in Manogue's hands the routine of seeing the oxen driven to water, returned to the corral and then unyoked beside their wagons, where the equipment would be laid out in orderly arrangement in preparation for hitching up the next morning.

Each teamster had his own chores to handle, and now as water for the cooking pots was carried in and mess fires were started Kinstrey dropped down from his dun and stared gloomily upward. The whole dark dome of the sky seemed to have exploded in a welter of frothy whiteness. The snow hissed softly as it twinkled down, slanted by a slapping wind which blew it against the tilts of the Espenshieds in spumy gusts.

Kinstrey tied his horse to the lead vehicle, then started toward Matt Calbraith's wagon, moving through a smutch of chill darkness checkered by blinking lanterns and the pallidly spreading light from the campfires.

He called, "Marna!" from the foot of the wagon and almost immediately Marna Calbraith appeared at the front draw curtain, holding a lighted lantern out in front of her.

"Oh, it's you, Boise. I was wishing you'd come right over."

"How is he, Marna?"

"I didn't like his breathing a while ago. But he's asleep right now, thank Heaven." She stared out at the snow, the lantern beams enhancing bluish lights in her crow-black hair and giving an accent to a faint petulance on her full, ripe mouth. "All these men working for us," she said, "and Dad still has to try to do everything himself. What a mess he's gotten us into now!"

"He couldn't help getting sick."

"He could help it! He didn't have to stay out in the rain that day and help with that broken axle."

"No," Kinstrey admitted. "But Cass might have stayed and given a hand."

"You know Dad wouldn't have let him! He thinks Cass only gets in the way."

Kinstrey chewed on his underlip. "I know," he agreed reluctantly. "And I'm going to try to change his mind about that. But you'll have to help me."

There was a certain coolness in the clarity of her deep-dark blue eyes, but now her oval face softened as she looked down at him and said, "I will help, Boise. I know you think I pamper him too much. But that's only because Dad's always gone to the other extreme."

"We can change him," Kinstrey said, "if you'll both help."

The wind brought an oniony fragrance toward him and he sniffed. "Pat must be cooking tonight," he told her then. "Like me to bring you a dish of Irish stew?"

"Oh, will you, Boise? Bring yourself a bowl too. We'll sit here on the seat and dine royally together."

"I suppose I'd better wait, with Matt. Let him get all the sleep he can."

"We'll have a little party; just the two of us. I've still got half of a plum cake I've been saving." Her voice subtly altered. "I've missed seeing you, Boise."

Kinstrey felt warmth pile up in his cheeks. He hesitated, then with awkward dismissal said, "Cass tell you that we took on a passenger back at Tipton's?"

"Yes, and I was glad to hear it. I've felt lost without another woman to talk to."

"I'll introduce you later." Kinstrey turned. "But first I'd better see if that grub's ready."

They ate on the wagon seat, here sheltered from the snow somewhat, but made increasingly aware of the storm by the fat flakes twirling all around them and the rasping breath of the wind.

When they had finished eating, Marna turned toward Kinstrey and shivered.

"What a night!"

Kinstrey said, "You'd better get back in the wagon. I'll get some stew for Matt. He's got to eat."

"Please, Boise; not yet. Let's just sit and talk for a minute."

He looked at her and was stirred by her closeness, but also a little annoyed that she should delay him when there was so much to be done.

"Talk?" he asked gruffly. "What about?"

"You."

"I'm nobody to talk about."

"That's one of your troubles, Boise. You think you're nobody." He felt her hand slide into his, hold, and a warm quiver touched him alert. She said in a low but deliberate voice, "You've always underestimated yourself. You shouldn't."

"Pfah!" He realized he had used one of Matt Calbraith's expressions and had a vaguely uneasy feeling that the link of loyalty binding him to Big Matt might have become too strong for his own good. But in what coin other than loyalty could he ever have repaid all that Matt had done for him? He put this thought in words, with the gruff demand, "Where would I be today except for your father?"

Marna Calbraith shrugged. "Whatever you owe Dad you've already paid back in full. Now think of yourself," she said.

"What makes you think I don't?"

She sighed, laying her head against his shoulder. "We haven't been alone together much recently. Have you forgotten the last time, Boise—back in Placerville?"

He had to clear roughness out of his throat. "Marna, I tried to tell you then——"

She drew closer against him. "What, Boise? That you've got to prove you can be your own man?"

Kinstrey's voice was tight, harried. "Well, yes; in a way. How do I know how I'd be without Matt's hand guiding my arm?"

"Nonsense! Dad lets you have a free rein. He doesn't try to hobble you the way he does Cass."

Kinstrey looked down at her and felt his heart thud hollowly as she pressed against him. "It's different," he muttered, "with Cass. He's Matt's own flesh and blood. But I'm just a——"

"I know; you've said that before, too. You're just that kid grease monkey he picked out of a loggers' cook shack."

"I don't deny it."

Marna's voice was tinged with rancor. "You don't have to deny it! But you could at least forget it!"

"My father was a fiddle-foot, a drunkard," Kinstrey stated relentlessly. "And I can't even recall my mother. She never stayed around long enough for me to remember her."

"I'm not interested in your past, Boise; only in your future. But your bitterness and your exaggerated sense of loyalty to Dad has got you all mixed up inside. You're letting it tie you down. That, and the idea you could never have amounted to anything without Dad's help."

Kinstrey's voice was tight again. "You don't understand, Marna! It's the way I am. And I have to know. Before I think about settling down I've got to be sure. I've got to know I could amount to something in my own right instead of always walking in Big Matt's shadow."

"And how are you going to find that out?"

Kinstrey shook his head. "I don't know—yet."

"So *settling down* has to be deferred—whatever *that* means."

"You know what it means, Marna. You know how I feel about you."

"Do I?" asked Marna coolly. "Just when did you ever tell me, Boise?"

He gave her a goaded look, blurted, "Well, maybe I never spoke the words. But you're the only woman I ever looked twice at. You know that."

"Really, Boise?" She laughed lightly, carelessly; then her face was tilted up, smiling, and suddenly he gripped both her arms and pulled her urgently against him.

He felt a quick tightness run through her, but as quickly forgot it as she relaxed and flattened herself to his chest, her mouth rising to meet his, willing and unrestrained.

He had a warm, giddy sensation before she drew back from him; then there was only a feeling of emptiness and frustration as she gasped, "Mercy!" and with the incomparable absurdity of the female put up a hand to tidy the chaos of her loosened hair.

He watched with dumb fascination until she had made the necessary repairs, then stood and after a strained pause muttered, "I'd better get that grub for Matt."

She looked at him, her eyes wise, perceptive. "You better had. But do you know, Boise? We forgot our plum cake!"

He laughed heavily. "So we did." Then as he moved to back down from the wagon her hand reached out and caught the sleeve of his mackinaw; she pulled herself up to him and their mouths came together again. . . .

She murmured, "Boise, Boise," as he held her tight, and then there was a thud of muffled hoofbeats and a clear sound of voices. He lunged back from her with a guilty start, simultaneously, looking around and down, he vexedly became aware of two figures outlined in lantern light against the rippling dark slant of the snow.

Each was leading a saddled horse and in the next moment Kinstrey's identification was sure. Cass Calbraith held the lantern; and beside him, her blue cape looking ermine-trimmed with its thick embroidery of snow, stood Effie Mannerheim.

Cass now called out in an easy voice, "Hullo up there!" and if he had seen Kinstrey and his sister embrace he gave no outward sign of it. "Brought our horses over for a feed of oats," he explained. His glance touched Kinstrey, then went to Marna. "Sis, I thought you'd like to meet Miss Mannerheim," he said.

"Effie." Effie Mannerheim's unaffected smile, her random brushing at a snowflake that had pasted itself to the tip of her slimly tapered nose, brought Kinstrey an odd feeling of poignancy as he watched her. She continued to hold her gaze on Marna, saying, "I hope my coming along isn't going to be an inconvenience to you, Miss Calbraith."

"I'm afraid you'll be the one inconvenienced." Marna Calbraith's tone was neither detectably aloof nor totally cordial, continuing, "I was just telling Mr. Kinstrey, here, that I'm going to feel better having another woman in the party. I'm sorry, though, that our accommodations are so scanty."

"Oh, I'm used to roughing it. I'll make out."

"That's fine," Marna said perfunctorily, and looked down at Cass, who had led the two horses over to the wagon and now was tying them to a rear wheel. "Cass, rig up some kind of shelter for Miss Mannerheim under one of the wagons. We have plenty of tarps and blankets. Then I'll want you here for some things."

"Always something!" Cass turned, grumbled, "*Now* what is it?"

"You arrange a shelter for Miss Mannerheim first. Then come right back."

" 'Come right back, come right back!' " Cass mimicked in sullen falsetto. "I'm not your errand boy, Marna!"

"Cass!"

A faint pity stirred in Kinstrey as he saw Cass glance uncomfortably toward Effie Mannerheim, then, rankled, swerve molten dark eyes back on his sister.

"One of these days," he said with low-voiced vehemence, "you're going to quit talking to me like that in front of people!"

Marna's voice sounded a note of hurt surprise. "But you

know Dad is sick, Cass! I need your help. There are some things I can't—"

"Maybe I could help," Effie Mannerheim put in quietly. "I've done a little nursing."

Marna's tone had an edge of stiffness. "Thank you, but there's nothing you could do just now." Her glance went to Kinstrey, dismissing the girl standing below the wagon. "Boise? If you want to bring that stew now I'll wake him."

"Fetch it right away," Kinstrey said. He suddenly felt a need to get away from here, to shake the weight and irritation of increasing complexities off his shoulders, if only for a few short minutes.

He swung down from the wagon, and as he did saw something in Effie Mannerheim's eyes that oddly disturbed him.

"You can lash those tarps around the wheels of the Number One wagon," he tersely told Cass. "Miss Mannerheim can bunk there. She'll be out of the snow at least."

Effie Mannerheim said, "Please don't bother, I can do it myself. There's no need to——"

"No need to what? Who's that doxy?" demanded a bellowing voice from behind Marna Calbraith. As everyone, startled, swung about, the burly figure of Matt Calbraith appeared before the wagon's flung-back draw curtain, clad only in half-buttoned jeans and a red flannel undershirt.

"Father!" cried Marna. "Get back in the wagon!"

"Out of my way," roared Matt Calbraith, "you flibberty-gibbet!"

He was hauling on a big fur-collared mackinaw as he straddled the wagon seat and climbed over, teetering as he barely caught his balance on the driver's side.

"He's drunk!" Cass shouted in a suddenly alarmed voice. "Look out for him!"

"He's out of his head," Kinstrey said. "Let me talk to him."

Matt Calbraith had gripped the edge of the wagon seat and now was clumsily lowering himself over the side. His knees buckled as his booted feet touched the ground; then with a lumbering heave he was erect and backed against the wagon's right front wheel, breathing in pumping gasps.

Kinstrey's voice was flat, peremptory. "Matt, listen to me! Get back into bed."

Matt Calbraith's wild-staring eyes glittered; in the light

played on him by Cass's lantern his face looked alarmingly inflamed.

"You're in cahoots with her! Stand back!" he hoarsely commanded Kinstrey.

Effie Mannerheim stood tense but unflinching, watching him. He flung out his arm and leveled an accusing finger at her.

"You!" he barked. "You're a spy! Tell the truth now! Who sent you here to spy on us?"

Effie Mannerheim spoke with calming assurance. "You've made a mistake, Mr. Calbraith. I'm just a new member of the train." She swung her glance to Boise Kinstrey and in an even tone added, "You can ask Mr. Kinstrey, here."

Matt Calbraith seemed momentarily lulled. Then an angry purple congested his face. "That's a lie!" he exploded. "You're a bunch of dirty turncoats—the lot of you! Now stand back—I'm off to get help. And by the Holy Old Mackinaw I'll drill the first damned Judas among you that tries to lay a hand on me!"

A Root's Patent Model Colt swung up in his right hand and glittered as he heaved himself out from the wagon wheel. He lurched, steadied himself, then warily started backing toward the horses picketed out behind him.

"Matt!" Kinstrey called flatly. "For God's sake, Matt, come to your senses before somebody gets hurt!"

"You better button that lip, mister. I've had about enough jaw out of you." Matt Calbraith had a foot plugged in the stirrup of the grulla; with a dogged heave he made it into the saddle, the Root's Patent Colt still menacingly outthrust in his right hand.

"Nobody move," he warned. Leaning out to untie the horse he swayed and almost went over before a quick jerk backward saved him.

"He's crazy!" breathed Marna. "He'll kill one of us yet."

Cass said harshly, "He's drunk as a fiddler. He could never hit anything with that old parrot-bill anyway." He looked around as if to see whether or not Effie Mannerheim was watching him. Then he took a swaggering forward step with the lantern swinging in his left hand.

Kinstrey watched Matt Calbraith's hot, bright eyes pull toward the lamplit figure with crafty vigilance.

"Don't be a fool, Cass!" he warned sharply. "Keep back and let him ride. He won't get far."

Cass again looked back toward Effie Mannerheim. "Somebody has to get the old fool down off that horse," he said. His voice sounded unnaturally loud.

"Please!" Effie Mannerheim urged him. "You'd better do as Mr. Kinstrey says, Cass."

"Oh, sure!" Cass returned meagerly. "I've always been the trained poodle around here. Just call 'Cass,' and doggie'll sit up and beg!"

"Cass," cried Marna. "I want you to stop this foolishness!"

Cass sent a cold look at her, then returned his eyes to the thick, solid shape astride the grulla.

Matt Calbraith was forcing air in his lungs with long, pulling breaths. He seemed to be waiting for his heart to steady but there was no apparent lack of steadiness in the Colt anchored at his hip, like a sinister metallic extension of his right hand.

Cass hesitated. There was a pale compression at the corners of his mouth, a loud voice inwardly warning him; Do as they say, Do as they say! He knew that if he tried to speak at this moment he would have no voice of his own. But with the cold pressure rising in his throat he knew at last something that he did have—pride—and it started him into a step forward.

A great drum-wallop of sound roared shockingly with a blast of white smoke and the lantern rocked on its wire bail and with a tinkling crash winked out.

Marna screamed.

A wild shout resounded through the darkness. Then came a hard diminuendo of hoofbeats, fading, fading.

4

BOISE KINSTREY's big skewbald dun was blowing as he angled it down off the icy ridge and into the shelter of a draw. He halted it here briefly until he had made out the tracks again, then gently gigged it, worried now that he might have been forcing it too much.

He chewed fretfully on his underlip as he rode on. All the excitement and hullaballo back at camp had given him a late start and except for these hoofprints in the snow he still had nothing to show for the risks he'd taken with the dun on this chancy terrain. The prints were unmistakable horse tracks, however. And since they'd been the only fresh sign in sight when he'd left camp they had to be the tracks of Matt Calbraith's grulla.

Kinstrey let his horse make its own pace now, content for the moment to know that the storm was over. A couple of miles back the snow had started thinning and finally had stopped altogether. Now, however, a ripping wind was rising and he could feel the sting of icy snow particles against his face with each sweeping gust. He could feel the coldness seeping through the woolly barrier of his mackinaw and sinking into his bones.

I'll have to stop and light a fire, he thought, if I don't find him soon.

A numbness was beginning to settle through him. He stared ahead, aware that the unseasonableness of this snap only made it seem more bitter. A three-quarter moon had some time ago emerged from a black sky and now it coasted above him tinting the snow-crusted ground with an illusory radiance. But in all this white wilderness no horse was visible but his own. Ahead of him the tracks ran on. And that was all.

Kinstrey's worry increased. Maybe he was just following the tracks of a lost bronc. Maybe Matt had fallen off the horse and crawled away in the snow to find shelter. But what good was guesswork? There were the tracks. And after five, maybe six miles the tracks still were all that he had to go by.

If Matt Calbraith had got this far in his condition it would be a miracle. And it was going to take a second miracle to find him, if he was still alive, and get him back safely to the wagons.

Kinstrey thought now with sudden guilty remorse: I should have started out after him sooner. He remembered the scene back at camp after Big Matt had made his dramatic exit. Marna had fainted and for a time the only cool person in all the ensuing confusion had seemed to be Effie Mannerheim.

She had revived Marna and then there had been a furious clash between Marna and Cass. Cass had wanted to go with him after Big Matt; Marna hadn't wanted him to.

"Suppose you got separated from Boise?" she'd suggested querulously. "You wouldn't know how to take care of yourself in this Godforsaken wilderness."

"Then Boise could teach me," Cass had replied thinly.

She had walked up to him angrily. "Cass, you are not to go! Is that plain?"

"No!" Cass's voice lifted to a shout. "But one thing's plain! I'm through having you tell me what I can do or can't do! I'm through being your little monkey on a string!"

The corners of Marna Calbraith's mouth compressed into chalky whiteness. "Cass, lower your voice! Don't you talk to me like this, do you understand?"

"I understand," Cass said. "I understand too damned well!"

"You've got the dauncy over this girl—that's your trouble!"

"Damn you, you shut up!"

Shock sponged all the color from Marna's face. She looked bitterly toward Effie Mannerheim, then as her glance fell back on Cass her voice hardened deliberately with malice.

"So that *is* it! To impress a girl you met only this morning you try to get your head blown off! To look like a man you act like a boy. Well," Marna's laugh was shaky despite the bitter ridicule in her voice, "if that's the way you intend to charm the ladies——"

Cass had spun around. "I don't have to listen to this!" He had looked from Marna to Effie Mannerheim, ashamed and furious; then with abrupt, angry steps he had stridden off in the direction of the camp fires.

When the sound of the shot had first aroused the camp Pat Manogue, Dave Ebaugh and the rest of the drivers had come

running but Kinstrey had curtly explained the situation and
then sent them back to their chores. He had told them that
he would have Matt Calbraith back at camp within half an
hour; and he had believed it—then. But too much time had
been wasted; too many precious minutes had been taken up
with arguments, explanations, gab. And now . . .

Now a good hour had passed and he still hadn't caught up.
What had happened? Big Matt was a hard boot; but could he
have made it this far, burning up with fever and out of his
head in the bargain?

Kinstrey had been carrying his head low to shield his face
from the wind. Now he looked up and suddenly saw the
creek bottom ahead of him. An icy blast of air drove at him
and he felt the breath sucked from his lungs. If only the trail
led along that creek bottom he'd have the protection of its
high banks and some trees for a windbreak. He hurried the
dun. . . .

At the creek bank the dun slipped on the icy footing and
almost went over. Kinstrey cursed with a soft violence and
then had the dun righted and reached the stream bottom.
There had been only a trickle of water and this was now frozen and cowled with little undulating drifts of snow.

Above him the wind sniffed and soughed through a tangle
of frozen brush but here he had protection and now briefly
halted the dun to savor his respite from it. He looked down
and saw that Big Matt evidently had had the same idea as
himself. The horse tracks here turned generally north, following the sheltered course of the creek.

Kinstrey thought with gloomy irony: Thanks, Matt—and
headed the dun upstream. He rode for two or three minutes
and the high banks gradually flattened out and the wind began catching him again. It came in short, sharp gusts that cut
like a knife. He felt his breath chopped off, and lowered his
head again. When he looked up he saw a low rocky promon-
tory where the creek broke in an abrupt turn leftward. He
made the swing and in the next moment reined in the dun
with a blurt of surprise.

He had come out suddenly upon low flats where the creek
banks graded down almost to water level and wagon wheels
had cracked muddy fissures in the ice of the shallow stream
bed. But it was not simply the sight of fresh wheel ruts that
now gripped his attention and alertly straightened him in the

saddle. A couple of hundred yards to the right of the crossing two big freighters stood in bleak solitude in the moon's icy light.

Kinstrey felt a stab of foreboding as he glanced down at the tracks he had been following. They veered here, ascending from the creek bottom and pointing toward the wagons.

For a full half-minute Kinstrey sat saddle with the immobility of a satatue, his gaze concentrated on the motionless vehicles. Remotely a lowing sound reached him; oxen, he surmised, bedded down, probably in the lee of the wagons. The wind's steady soft moaning added counterpoint to the farther away blatting; otherwise the stillness ran unbroken, its eeriness enhanced in a white wilderness reflecting oddly bluish tints from the frosty moonlight.

An indefinable disquiet bored through Kinstrey, a sense of wrongness about these deserted-looking wagons that he couldn't precisely analyze but only felt. With an effort he sloughed off the feeling and swung the dun to the right, up out of the creek bottom.

The tracks ran on ahead of him—clear, deep, and almost ruler-straight now in the direction of the Osnaburg-hooded freighters. As the vehicles loomed larger before him, however, his uneasiness increased. He could now see dimly the blurred shapes of oxen huddled in cramped misery in a chain corral connecting the two wagons. But where were the horses of the outfit, if any?

Kinstrey's hand reached down to the Sharps rifle encased in his saddle boot, then withdrew. The piece was loaded; he didn't need to check that. Besides, if this outfit had had guards posted they'd have heard him by now. But as he drew closer to the wagons no voice hailed him and the stillness over everything suddenly seemed heavier, almost uncanny.

A shiver nibbled down through Kinstrey's numbed body; then when he was less than thirty feet from the vehicles he pulled in the dun and called loudly, "Hullo there in the wagons! Anybody home?"

No answer came to his call; only the weird echoes of his own voice pulsed back at him and with renewed misgivings he started on again, holding the dun to a chary walk.

The hoof tracks led on right to the wagons, where they became merged with a hodgepodge of other prints and blurred out completely. Frowning, Kinstrey stared down at the disturbed ground, then put weight on his stirrup and dismounted.

Oxen stirred restlessly inside the chain corral but from where he stood he could see no horses. He made a cautious circuit of the wagons and behind one vehicle saw a gleam of horse droppings in the trampled snow.

His glance judged their freshness; in the next moment his eyes ran toward a blend of fresh prints, all headed away from the wagons in a general westerly direction. He walked close and studied these, unmistakably the hoof prints of two or more horses, possibly as many as four. There had been men here then, men and horses. But where had they gone?

Kinstrey felt a slugging weariness as he swung around and mounted to the seat of the first wagon. Pulling back the draw curtain he sucked in a startled breath. The interior of the wagon was crammed to the tilts with dressed lumber!

Quickly Kinstrey swung down from the seat and walked to the rear of the second wagon. Letting down the tailgate, he showed no visible surprise, now, staring at the butt ends of a full load of smoothly planed pine boards. And now there could no longer be any doubt. These were the Murphys he had examined back at Tipton's; the wagons that Frank Ganahl and his men must have stolen from the Gerritys.

Abstractedly Kinstrey lifted the tailgate and dropped the holding pins back in place. But where was Ganahl now? And what had happened to Matt Calbraith? The tracks of Big Matt's grulla that he had picked up back at camp had led directly here. He had followed Matt's trail with meticulous slowness to make certain that the tracks had not diverged at any point. But there was always the possibility that he could have missed sign or that Matt had fallen from his mount and only the horse had reached here, drawn by the prospect of shelter.

A heavy concern fogged the pale blueness of Boise Kinstrey's eyes as he wheeled and started moving with preoccupied slowness back toward his dun. Something glittered in front of him and, stooping, he reached out and picked up a small, crudely round object from a boot-packed mark in the snow.

His heart tapped like a finger on a drum as he stared down at it—a smooth-worn Chinese coin with a square-shaped hole notched out of its center. And now, instead of doubt, he felt a pounding alarm. Of course, there could be other curios like this. But the only one he had ever seen had been carried as a pocket luck piece—by Big Matt Calbraith.

5

SOMETHING was wrong, disturbingly, alarmingly wrong, and Boise Kinstrey had his first sinking awareness of it when he was less than a two-minute ride from the deserted wagons and entering a wooded draw bordered with stands of young cedar and fat clumps of juniper. Kinstrey rode now with every sense alert and it required no special perceptiveness on his part to notice a dark area to his right where a tiny cedar motte showed only as a blur of black in conspicuous contrast to the white uniformity of snow veiling every other bush and tree.

He headed the tiring dun toward the spot, observing now that the tracks of a single horse here diverged from the others, going in that direction.

Inside the motte he saw how the close-growing cedars had come to be divested of their veils of snow. An axman had been at work in here under a canopy of interlaced boughs. Fresh, pungent-smelling chips lay about on the trampled snow, and three small trees had been hacked down and their branches trimmed off. The shorn scantlings, however, were gone and once outside the motte again Kinstrey knew at a glance the use to which they had been put.

The tracks of a single horse bore right, followed by parallel narrow indentations in the snow, almost like the impressions left by sled runners. But these were not the grooves made by a sled, Kinstrey now knew, but deeper, more ragged furrows, such as a travois might make. Often he had seen Indians use the travois for toting gear. And sometimes they utilized it for transporting the weak or sick.

A cold fear nudged Kinstrey as he renewed his study of the tracks. Two sets of hoofprints ran on due west but the marks of the travois pointed northward toward a high, dark belt of firs. Was Big Matt lashed to that travois? If so, the rider dragging him off into that evergreen wilderness could have but one purpose: to kill him and throw him into some gulch or cavern where he wouldn't be found. Was it Raimo?

Kinstrey hesitated, confronted with a desperate choice. Unless he followed the travois tracks Big Matt might die. But if he did the train might be attacked and still more blood be shed.

Even as he briefly wavered, however, Kinstrey knew what his decision must be. He owed his first loyalty to Big Matt; then to Matt's family. It was the way he would always feel. It was a grim decision, but no other was possible. He swung his dun north. . . .

The temperature was sinking fast. Kinstrey could tell by the wind's increasing bite and the pistol-like crack of frozen branches in the woods' eerie solitude. His arms and legs felt like sticks when he tried to move them. He had been on the trail now for a couple of hours and it was becoming a question how much longer he and his horse could go on. The dun seemed to be slowly dying under him. It moved, but each step seemed more liquid, less steady, on played-out legs.

Kinstrey wondered sluggishly how far behind he was. One fact encouraged him. Those droppings back at Ganahl's camp had been so fresh they'd steamed, which meant that he must have ridden up only short moments after Ganahl and his men had pulled out. Then too, it must have taken time to cut down those cedars and put together a travois. And a travois sagging under Big Matt's two-hundred-pound frame would slow down any horse, especially on an uphill grade.

These thoughts gave a lift to Kinstrey. He might not be too far behind his quarry now.

The dun's plodding climb lulled him; he tried to keep alert but the marrow-piercing cold seemed to anesthetize his brain and he had a vague consciousness of his thoughts wandering.

Matt's horse . . . he hadn't seen that anywhere. But maybe Matt had fallen off at Ganahl's camp and the grulla had just strayed off.

The snow was unbroken except for the narrow tracks tapering on before him and he tried to concentrate on these. But his thoughts still straggled. Fatigue crept insidiously through him, combining with the intense cold to drug all his senses.

Thought of the two riders that had gone on hounded him. Would Ganahl and Moss wait for Raimo to follow them, then attack the camp? Somehow, now, he doubted that. Although Ganahl's crew had staged an open attack on the Gerritys, that had been a small outfit and Ganahl in all probability would think twice before taking such a risk against a more heavily manned expedition. Particularly if he thought he could attain his ends by some sort of trickery. . . .

Man, how good a fire would feel! Evergreen boughs gave off a fine juicy heat. You could see the wood curl and the pitch bubble out. And the smell was like the very essence of all outdoors.

Kinstrey would never forget that fragrance. He remembered the time he and Big Matt had been timber cruising in the Oregon woods and had become blizzard-bound. He'd been only seventeen then and Matt had saved his life. Both their horses had frozen to death but Big Matt had noticed a brush-choked gap in a nest of boulders. He had burrowed through it and found a cave. And here they had lived for two weeks, precariously subsisting on a few rabbits and squirrels snared by Matt.

He had been no help whatever to the older man. On the second day he had come down with a chest congestion and fever and for more than a week Matt had fed him, kept him warm and nursed him through to the time when at last he could stand and weakly walk a bit. In the end it had taken them three hellish, almost unendurable days to get back to their camp, afoot, and on the last day he had collapsed and Big Matt, practically on the verge of dropping himself, had toted him in piggyback for the last ten miles.

And so he remembered, and would always remember, the pungency of burning evergreen. Big Matt had built a windbreak of rocks and tree branches in front of the cave and this had served to reflect the heat of the fire. And he had not let it go out as long as they had been holed up there. . . .

Kinstrey's thoughts idled, far away now. There was one other thing besides Big Matt's rough-tender devotion to him that he remembered and would always remember. Matt Calbraith had a philosophy for living that was as blunt and rough-hewn as he was, and many times and in many different ways he had impressed it upon Boise Kinstrey.

"Remember this," Matt often would tell him. "The world's no damned green footstool for a man to sit on and wait for a silver spoon to be shoved in his mouth. The world bends its knee to just one kind of people—those who demand it."

Or he would say, another time, "You've got to be a hard

boot to get along in this world, Boise, and you have to let people know you're hard or they'll walk all over you. Never be scared to walk heavy and make a big noise. It's the squeaky wheel gets the grease—remember that."

Kinstrey was hearing these words now as the dun topped a rise and emerged on what appeared to be an old wood road, flanked on either side by snow-capped stands of Jeffrey pine and a drear expanse of ancient rotted stumps. It was advice he had never forgotten; a rule of thumb that for better or worse he had come to live by himself.

His eyes became blank, focused absently forward. He had his own quick temper and stubborn streak and he had never been scared to walk heavy or, when it had seemed necessary, to talk up for his rights. A man could get to be a little high-handed maybe, sure; but people respected you only if you respected yourself. Maybe, though, he did go off the handle a little too easy. Like that morning with Effie Mannerheim. No call for him to have done that. But some females just got a man's back up. No special reason. Just some special kind of orneriness they all had, one way or another. . . .

Kinstrey's feet were icy. He put a gloved hand up to his face and pressed. There was no feeling in his face and he was conscious now of a queer light-headed sensation in the top of his skull. He had to keep reminding himself that he was the hunter and that somewhere out there ahead of him was the hunted. He had to force himself to remember that now even a split-second lapse of vigilance could be fatal.

The dun was skirting the snow-bent branches of a big incense cedar when a slip put it into a lurching skid. A limb raked Kinstrey's face and as he fought to control the animal a huge clod of snow dropped and almost heaved him out of the saddle.

Blinded and half-stunned, he was scooping snow from his eyes and face when he felt the dun shy again, then dance skittishly. He pulled it up short, and in the next moment felt his stomach lunge sickeningly as he looked downward to his left. The horse stood close to the rim of a high canyon, and but for its instinctive alertness might have gone over.

Kinstrey looked around him. The trail appeared to have ended abruptly. Hoof marks led off to the right, but the tracks of the travois seemed to vanish right here. Kinstrey felt his heart start to pound. With a dry swallow, he dismounted and peered downward from the edge of the cliff.

Shock shriveled his stomach. Halfway down a precipitous long slope some dark object was obscurely visible, wedged against the snowy shank of a massive deadfall.

Kinstrey breathed shallowly. Could it be a man? Charily he took a step and leaned farther over the brink.

The shot's abrupt crack hammered metallic reverberations between the hills. Kinstrey was spun; then his balance on the icy lip of the shelf was gone.

He had a sensation of dropping giddily off into space; he hit violently against something solid yet yielding. For a thin breath space the moon was a pearly eye goggling down at him; then it winked out in blackness.

6

THE CRASH of the shot in the frosty stillness sent a flutter of panic through Cass Calbraith. He reined in his trigueno and sat tensely forward in the saddle, listening. But now the only sound was the whine of the wind stirring through the pines and the occasional dry creak of a snow-laden branch. Cass shivered.

Hell of a night to be out, he thought bitterly. But he'd warned Marna he was through being bossed around by her. Bad enough he'd let it go as long as he had. But when she'd let loose on him in front of Effie Mannerheim it had been the last straw. A man could stand for almost any kind of embarrassment except being made to look small in front of a woman he was trying to impress. And, damn her, Marna knew that.

Cass ground his teeth, starting the trigueno on again. So now what do I do? he asked himself meagerly. Get myself killed just because I hate my own sister? Ride out here into this Godforsaken wilderness to cut a shine for a girl and maybe wind up as coyote bait?

The trigueno was climbing, was almost to the belt of trees Cass had seen limned darkly against the skyline from the cedar motte below. Still ahead of him were those peculiar narrow tracks that had started down at the motte, then pointed northward up this hill. And hoofprints of a following horse were still distinct. Were those the tracks of Boise Kinstrey's dun?

Cass thought grimly: They'd better be—and gigged the trigueno. It had been easy, picking up Boise's trail from the camp. But after leading him to the Murphys, it had got tricky. A lot of hoofprints had gone out from there, although the prints of one horse had remained noticeably apart.

These he had pursued as far as the cedar motte, where he had decided to follow the direction of the runner marks that had seemed to indicate some bulky object being dragged along in the snow.

What kind of an object? And what about that shot? It hadn't sounded too far from here. Maybe the old man had fired it; maybe he was lost. Or maybe Boise had finally caught up with him—and for being so damned loyal had wound up with a bullet in his belly.

A scowl indented Cass Calbraith's slimly youthful face. You blasted fool, he told himself. What's so special about this Effie Mannerheim that you have to be out here on a night like this trying to look like something that you're not?

Cass stared fiercely ahead. The girl wasn't exactly pretty; couldn't hold a candle to Marna, for looks. But for some reason she'd made him suddenly and more sharply conscious of his worst failings: never to take the initiative in anything, never to buckle down to a job, whatever it was.

So, what had impressed him about Effie Mannerheim was perhaps an opposite quiet strength and self-reliance. And maybe it was a feeling of shame that had led him to kick over the traces tonight. . . .

Preoccupied, Cass brought the trigueno up over a brushy ridge and in the next moment had plunged into the dark wood he had seen from the bottom of the hill. Lofty spars of white fir and Jeffrey pine hemmed him in. The coldness reached out with icy fingers, holding a vast stillness. Then, abruptly, the hush was shattered by the whicker of a horse.

Cass jerked taut and looked wildly around him. To his right two gigantic deadfalls lay interlocked in front of a shelf of high, wind-cleaned rock. He reached shelter in back of the boulder just in time.

A rider was coming downtrail. Cass was able now to hear a muffled thud of hoofbeats and presently a jingle of riding gear. He sat saddle rigid, waiting. Maybe it was Boise. Or maybe the old man. Crazy as a loon. Still crazy enough to shoot if anybody crossed him.

The hoofbeats grew louder, came opposite the barricade. Cass peered out, and as he did felt his heart give a lurch. The horse, a wiry buckskin, he had never seen before, but the flat, ugly face of the man forking it was unmistakable, even in the thin trickle of moonlight in which it was briefly visible. The mysterious night rider was Jack Raimo—one of the three men with whom he had played cards back at Tiny Tipton's, just one night ago.

Raimo, who'd tried to start a fuss with Boise in Sportsman's Hall. And the one Boise later on had gun-whipped, out past the corrals. Cass slowly let out a shaky breath. What was Raimo doing out here alone at this hour of the night? Was he on the wrong track here, after all?

The last audible footfalls of the buckskin died away down-trail but Cass still made no motion toward moving his own horse. He wondered what he should do now. Maybe he should follow Raimo. He remembered the other set of hoof-prints he had seen down at the motte—tracks bearing west, toward his father's wagons. It might have been horses of Frank Ganahl and Al Moss that had made those prints. . . .

A ball of fear clogged Cass's throat as he booted the trigueno, sending it back to the trail at a startled trot. There he reluctantly headed it north again. The tracks of some kind of runners still showed plain before him in the snow but he found his thoughts returning apprehensively to Raimo. Suppose those three were planning some kind of a coup? Maybe he ought to turn back, warn Pat Manogue. . . .

No, no! It was too late for that. He had to find Boise the first thing. Boise probably had the old man; apparently was hauling him on some kind of a sled. But why north? Why hadn't he swung west toward the camp?

Cass's attention lapsed briefly as the trigueno swung wide around the low branches of a big Incense cedar; at the same instant brush startlingly crashed to his left and he jerked alert.

His breath went out in a shocked gust as he pulled in his horse and then saw the other horse, plowing out of a stand of dwarf aspen less than a dozen yards from where he sat saddle.

Recognition came to him almost instantaneously; there was no mistaking Boise Kinstrey's big skewbald dun, saddled but riderless. Stirrup straps and stirrups flapped against the animal's glistening hide. The horse obviously had been ridden not too long ago.

A sick fear lurched through Cass as he dismounted and walked over and took the dun's bridle reins. He led it to a sapling and tied it, next tying the trigueno. Then he examined the Sharps snugged in the dun's saddle boot. It was loaded. No shot had been fired from it.

He thrust the piece back into its scabbard and turned, cupping his hands.

"Boise! Boise Kinstrey! Boise, where are you?"

Where are you? Where are you? echoed back weirdly to him. It was his only answer. The wind had subsided and the silence now was breathless.

An icy prickle needled Cass's scalp and he was conscious of a quaking in his legs as he gingerly started on afoot in the wake of the runner marks. Suddenly they ended. Then he saw why. He was close to the rim of a ledge that went down, down. He peered over.

His heart seemed slowly to lift, then hit with a shuddering slam against his chest. What appeared to be two motionless figures lay jammed against a snow-whitened deadfall, halfway down the rocky shank of the bluff.

Cass called in panic, "Boise!" but his paralyzed throat muscles forced only a weak squawk. He lurched upright, fear thudding in him like great thumping blows. Then he remembered the rope he had seen looped over the saddle horn of the dun. He started at a reckless, skidding run back toward the horses.

7

Boise Kinstrey opened his eyes and then for a long moment lay utterly still, staring up in a half-stupor at the low roof of crisscrossed evergreen boughs interlaced above his head. Behind him the smooth shank of a gray boulder made a solid wall. Blankets hung from the roof's side poles, weighted on the ground with small rocks. The front of the shelter was open; there a small fire of pine branches crackled and smoked aromatically.

Weakly Kinstrey raised a hand to his forehead. It felt hot and pain pulsed in a solid streak of fire across the top of his scalp. His left leg felt oddly heavy and when he tried to shift it pain jounced upward all the way to his thigh. He groaned and tried to think, but couldn't. A lethargic heaviness stole over him; at last he slept, fitfully.

Sounds from outside woke him, finally. He was listlessly indifferent to them. He felt completely limp. The sounds—flat, snapping noises, as though someone was breaking up limbs for firewood—continued sporadically. Then suddenly the fire blazed up and there was a dark blur in front of the shelter's narrow entranceway. A stooped figure came inside, sank down beside Kinstrey on one knee.

Kinstrey recognized the slim youth's face of Cass Calbraith but was too desperately sick to want to talk.

Cass said, "I snared a rabbit—one trick of the old man's that stayed with me. Think you could hold down a little food? You haven't eaten in a couple days."

The word food was all that remotely registered with Kinstrey. He made weak beckoning motions with one hand.

Cass fed him, slowly, carefully, a morsel at a time.

Kinstrey ate with a dogged effort, instinctively knowing that he must take nourishment or die.

At the end of a minute, he vomited. . . .

Stretched out in his dinky shelter on a bed of pine needles Kinstrey hovered for two more days between life and death.

He existed in a world of shadow and dream, in which he imagined Big Matt Calbraith always at his side, watching over him with the tenderness of a father for a son.

Fever raged in him. He called Big Matt "father," and was seventeen years old again and blizzard-bound with Matt in a cave in the Oregon woods. He could smell the pungency of burning evergreen and once had a vivid impression of tasting some rabbit stew. He knew he was in delirium even as everything seemed insidiously real. Where reality dissolved into vagary he never knew.

He awoke on the fifth day startlingly clear-headed, but limp with exhaustion. During the night his fever had broken and now there was a kind of light ringing in his ears and the glare of morning sunlight shafting into the lean-to made his eyes ache.

He heard footfalls outside; then a shadow darkened the opening of the lean-to and Cass Calbraith stooped and entered.

There was a static moment of stupefaction in which neither man spoke; in which each could only stare at the other with a kind of paralyzed wonder. Then Cass awkwardly broke the silence.

"Hi!" he said. "You look better."

Kinstrey rolled over on his side and tried to lift himself with his arms. He felt a stab of pain in his left leg and crawling needles of pain at the top of his head. His arms refused to support him and he sank back exhausted on his pallet of pine boughs.

"What the devil!" He sounded a little dazed. He went over onto his back again and stared up at Cass. "I'm weak as a damned dishrag," he muttered.

"You need some grub," Cass said. "I can fix that."

He stepped closer and Kinstrey felt a shocked dismay. Cass's eyes had a dulled, sunken appearance and his cheekbones jutted starkly out of a scrub of bluish-black whiskers. He looked like the wrath of God.

"Where's Matt?" Kinstrey asked abruptly. Memory was rushing back on him like a tide at full flood. "Now I can remember some things," he muttered. "Somebody shot at me. I'd been trailing this travois; figured maybe Matt was on it. Then I spotted something; down in a gorge. Right then was when——"

"It'll keep," interrupted Cass. He turned quickly. His voice sounded oddly hollow adding across his shoulder, "I found a stew pan and a little coffee in one of the saddlebags. Let's eat; then talk."

"No!" Kinstrey shouted, but Cass was gone. He could see him outside the shelter, hunkered over the still glowing embers of a camp fire.

"Cass!" Kinstrey tried to make it a yell but his voice wouldn't project. He stared down at his legs. The boot was gone from his left foot and the ankle taped with strips of sacking. Fear cut deep in him, brought a momentary surge of strength. His hands were like clubs but he hoisted himself and got his back to the wall of rock behind him. He sat panting then, watching Cass, while the fear pummeled him and built a fearsome roaring in his ears.

In five minutes Cass came in with a tin cup of hissing black coffee and a stew pan holding a half dozen strips of sizzling hot rabbit meat. He placed the stew pan and coffee cup beside Kinstrey. "Now, damn it, eat that," he said.

"I want to know about Matt," Kinstrey said flatly.

"He's probably all right," replied Cass in a stiff voice. "Eat your stew."

"Then you haven't seen him? He wasn't down at that deadfall where I fell?"

"I got you out of there. If he'd been there I'd have gotten him too, wouldn't I?"

Kinstrey's voice held a dull despair. "But what's happened to him then? Those runner tracks led right up to that bluff. I can't see——"

"Your stew'll get cold." Cass's tone was brittle. Kinstrey gave him a close look; then with a kind of desperate resignation he started to eat.

The rabbit tasted good, and the hot coffee stirred a tinge of color into the pallor of his cheeks.

He sat back finally, feeling refreshed and almost animated from the food and coffee.

"Platter licked clean," he said. "Now let's have it, Cass. From the beginning."

Cass shrugged. "It don't take long to tell. You remember the spat I had with Marna back at the wagons. Well, she got my back up. So I started out to trail you. Figured you might need some help."

"I needed it all right." Kinstrey's voice was grim. "Go ahead, Cass."

"Well, there's not much else. I heard a shot. Then I followed those runner tracks. They led to that bluff where you went over; I went down on a rope and got you tied. Then I climbed back up on it and had the dun drag you up out of there."

"Sounds simple—hearing you tell it." Irony in Kinstrey's words was modified by an undernote of surprised respect. "How bad was I hurt, Cass?"

"Pretty bad. You were shot at; guess you know that. The bullet put a gash in your scalp—pretty deep. Then when you fell you must've twisted your ankle."

Kinstrey was staring at Cass's hands. The knuckles were skinned, the flesh at the fingertips raw and inflamed. "And that's all?" he asked. "You didn't cut sign on Matt anywhere?"

Cass's gaze forced itself on Kinstrey, quickly withrew. "I never said I didn't cut sign."

Abruptly Kinstrey straightened, tensed. "What do you mean?" he barked. "Cass, don't beat around the bush with me!"

"I won't," Cass said, "now that you've got a little something on your stomach." His voice fell. "The old man *was* down there at the deadfall, Boise. He—he was hurt pretty bad."

"Pretty bad! How bad? Where is he now?" With a panicked heave Kinstrey was on his feet. Pain jumped in his swollen ankle almost beyond bearing. He sank weight on his right foot, gasping, staring with mounting alarm at the dulled look of stupor on Cass Calbraith's face. "Cass! Answer me!" he demanded tensely.

Cass's mouth opened. He seemed about to speak. Then it clicked shut.

"No!" Kinstrey shouted. He took a hopping step on his good right leg, dug his fingers fiercely into Cass's spindly shoulders. "He can't be! Why, all the good years were still ahead of him. He wasn't old yet! He never would have been——"

Cass interrupted tonelessly, "I'm sorry, Boise. He was shot twice through the back of the head. Probably while he was unconscious. He never had a chance."

Berserk anger and overpowering grief simultaneously shook Kinstrey. He smote his hands together in terrible dumb agony; a big tear started down his cheek and rolled unheeded onto his coat collar.

"Cass?" He had slumped back against the rock wall behind him, his eyes now staring, vacant. "Cass, I'll find the man. He won't get away. I'll find out who did it. He'll give himself away. Then——"

"He has given himself away," Cass said.

Kinstrey stood stock-still. "What did you say?" he asked in a softly absent voice.

"I think I know who did it," Cass said. "I saw him riding downtrail from here. Just a few minutes after I heard the shot he fired at you."

"You couldn't be mistaken?" demanded Kinstrey. "You're dead sure?"

"I'm sure. It was a face you don't forget. It was Jack Raimo," Cass Calbraith answered deliberately.

8

NATHAN BERRY was a rawboned, lumpish-looking man, often mistaken for a backwoods lout by imperceptive travelers who saw only a heavy-appearing face masked by a scrabble of dun beard bristle, and bland blue eyes in which a shrewd intelligence lay deceptively latent.

This morning Berry was standing outside of his well-built road station, watching a bull train start out from one of two huge corrals adjoining the station to the west, when his attention was diverted by two horsemen coming down the trace to his right.

Although the riders were still a good hundred yards from him his quick mind had already jumped to two conclusions about them. Both of them were exhausted, coming in on nerve, and they had in all likelihood been in some kind of trouble.

Berry noted the slogging gait of the horses and thought: Haven't been grained in days or I'm a Dutchman. The men, too, showed signs of wear; they sat stooped and slack-shouldered in their saddles, and one man had his left foot dangling away from the stirrup in a peculiar stiff way.

Hurt, surmised Berry; and dollars to doughgods they'll ask for a handout. He frowned. In this business you never knew from one day to the next. Always a to-do about something. Like four, five nights ago, when that train with the two women had pulled in. Remembered the outfit especially because you didn't see too many women of that class heading for the mines. And remembered the women—the pretty one at least—because of the tantrum she was having all over the place. A real beauty, though. He'd never seen——

"You the owner here?"

Nathan Berry's head jerked up. The two riders sat saddle less than a dozen feet away, staring curiously at him. Berry stared back sheepishly, almost as if they could know how he'd been dreaming about that particular dark-haired one. He said belatedly, "I run the shebang—Nate Berry," and at a

47

quick second look revised the opinion he'd had of these men from a distance. They'd had a time of it, all right. But they were no trail riffraff.

"We're looking for an outfit that might have gone through here within the last few days. Two women in it," said Boise Kinstrey.

"One light-haired and the other dark," Cass Calbraith said. "The light-haired one wore a blue cape."

"Four, five days ago," Berry said. "I don't rightly recollect which, but such an outfit did go through. Stopped for supper, then went on. Seemed in an all-fired hurry."

Kinstrey's left leg had gone to sleep. He moved it gingerly. "Man name of Ganahl in charge?" he inquired. "Blond hair, cleft chin—wore a gray wampus shirt?"

"He didn't give any name. Fitted that description, though. Had a train of seven wagons."

Kinstrey looked at Cass. "Women in the party act upset?" he asked the road rancher.

"One did. Dark-haired girl, mighty pretty." Berry ruminatively scratched his dun whiskers. "Other one didn't have much to say; just kept telling the dark one not to worry, that everything'd be all right."

"Recall a big Irishman did a lot of talking?"

"That I do. Sure was a talkative cuss. Had a brogue you could cut with a knife."

"How about a short skinny little jasper with a flat nose?" put in Kinstrey.

"No." Berry shook his head. "Can't say I place him."

"You're certain of that?"

"Mister, a slew of people go through this station in a day. I can't remember all of them."

Kinstrey frowned. "Maybe you noticed a kind of heavy-set jigadee—flabby face, scrawny neck. Looked like somebody'd pulled on it till it stretched."

"You sure can freshen up a man's memory, mister. Yep; I remember that one all right."

"But nobody asked for us? Kinstrey, Calbraith?"

Nathan Berry stiffened; then his right arm swung abruptly and he testily snapped his fingers. "Jupiter!" he exclaimed. "Now I know! All the time I been thinking about this dark-haired girl, but it was the other one left the note. Now how in nation did I forget that?"

Cass blurted eagerly, "A note! For me?"

The road rancher gave him a cool look, then with no further notice of the question began an abstracted exploration of the contents of his pockets.

"Here it is!" Suddenly, with a triumphant gesture, he held up a rumpled slip of paper. He ignored Cass's outreaching hand. "Which one of you is Kinstrey?" he said.

Over Cass's objections they were on their way again within the hour. Kinstrey was irritated. Cass's manner toward him had recently shown a real if grudging friendliness. But now it was reverting again to the old sullen hostility. And all because of that girl. Kinstrey frowned bitterly. If only the kid realized how much she galled him!

His annoyance evoked fresh recollection of the note she had left, addressed to him. It had been short—barely more than a notification that Marna knew, through Frank Ganahl, that her father was dead. According to the note, Ganahl and Al Moss had come upon a party of traders who had just buried a man they had found alongside the trail, frozen to death. Description of the dead man had fitted Matt Calbraith. Ganahl and Moss had then broken the news to Marna, who from their description had agreed that the victim unquestionably was her father.

Fishy as hell! Kinstrey scowled as his angry gaze bore forward. Still, there was just a chance that Ganahl could have made an honest mistake. Maybe he had run into some traders who had found a frozen corpse. And maybe the victim had been a man answering Big Matt's description.

Somberly Kinstrey's thoughts etched the closing lines of the note:

We waited over an extra day at the camp while Mr. Ganahl led an unsuccessful search for you and young Mr. Calbraith. Then Miss Calbraith said we would have to go on; that some kind of important business contract was involved.

I hope that by some miracle this may reach you and find both of you safe and in good hands.

Sincerely,
(Signed) E. Mannerheim.

Kinstrey's eyes probed forward, pools of blue vacancy. So

Frank Ganahl had led a search, had he? No doubt with the help of his friends, Gooseneck and Flatnose. Only, if Nathan Berry's recollection had been right Jack Raimo had not been with the train when it had reached the road ranch. *Why* was it Raimo hadn't been with the train?

With sudden apprehension Kinstrey thought of the date. Today was the twenty-ninth. Or was it the thirtieth? Anyway, it was lucky Marna had moved on with the wagons after dallying only a day. That contract with Ophir could be a gold mine in itself. Big Matt had known that and had gambled everything he had on being able to fulfill it. But now, with only Pat Manogue to assist her, would Marna be able to reach Washoe in time and get set up with the mill?

Manogue would help her a lot. He was rough-grained and tough and could lay his hand to almost anything. But he'd be no match for Ganahl in a game of wits. And suppose Ganahl worked his way into Marna's confidence? He wasn't with her just for the ride, that was sure. With sudden impatience Kinstrey glanced at Cass, riding beside him slump-shouldered, morose.

"Let's speed it up a little," he suggested.

Cass gave him a churlish look. "Speed up? With these wring-tails? Look; I told you before we should have put up at Berry's for tonight."

Kinstrey knew he was right, but said only, "We'll keep shoving. Every day counts now. Maybe every hour."

"All right," Cass said meagerly. "Kill the nags; wear yourself out. Who cares about that?"

Kinstrey's left leg felt numbed and the unhealed wound in his scalp suddenly started to throb. He snapped, "I'm all right. Just take care of yourself. That's all I ask."

"I took care of both of us for four days; remember?"

The shaft shot home. Kinstrey flushed. "Damn my rotten temper!" he said. He forced Cass's glance back to him, added with sober vehemence, "What you did for me I could never pay back."

"Hogwash! I wasn't asking for any applause."

"I know that."

"Then think about yourself a little. It's what Marna does."

"Marna? She thinks of you. Maybe too much; but you're her brother. She just wants you to——"

"All she ever wanted of me was to jump when she snaps

her fingers. You don't know my sister, Boise. She waited back at camp for us a day—*one* day."

Kinstrey chewed his lip. "That Ophir contract's too good to lose, Cass. Even the wood's going to be cut and ready for us. All we have to do is saw and deliver."

Cass looked at him oddly. "Marna knows all that. She's an ambitious woman. Haven't you caught on to that yet?"

"She wants those profits for you, too, you know."

Cass laughed sourly. "Marna never wanted anything for anybody except Marna!"

"You're wrong, Cass."

"And you're blind. You must be really gone on her. You know something, Boise? You're not a bad fellow. Sometimes I could almost feel sorry for you!"

Kinstrey felt a hot gush of anger, then abruptly suppressed it. Cass was still just a kid; he had a lot to learn yet. But he had Big Matt's guts. He'd proved that. . . .

A feeling of cold deadness sank through Kinstrey. He remembered the mound of raw earth under the big Jeffrey pine which Cass had shown him. Here, with no tool but a piece of flat rock, the kid had scrounged out a shallow grave for Big Matt after the first day of thaw. Again, now, he was remembering the look of Cass's hands on that morning when Cass had first told him about Big Matt. Fingers torn and caked with dried blood from digging his own father's grave. . . .

The irony of it caught him now; hit hard against the still fresh grief weighted at the pit of his stomach. Big Matt would never know, now, that he had reared a son worthy of himself. He hadn't realized that sometimes youth had to be tried by fire; that adversity brought out true temper. And Matt had never given Cass the opportunity to be so tested.

Kinstrey's eyes cruised forward. If they were lucky they should be across the Divide in a few hours and by nightfall make Woodford's on the other side of the mountain. In two miles they crossed a bridge and struck for the summit. Pack trains had broken through a few remaining patches of crusted snow, leaving traps of slimy black muck that had to be constantly avoided. In spots the trail was honeycombed with holes and the horses proceeded warily, instinctively alert to the danger.

Kinstrey gave attention to the dun. The Divide never

seemed to come. But that was always the way, crossing mountains. There would be a series of elevations; then with barely noticeable change the descent would begin.

Woodford's would be six miles distant, on the eastern slope. Eighteen more and they'd be in Genoa. Then on to Carson City, another fifteen miles. From there they would be in sight of Washoe. Washoe! The Promised Land and the land of promise. Eldorado on a mountain peak. Bonanza!

Kinstrey dreamed. They crossed the Divide. He never knew it. . . .

At Woodford's they had dinners of beans fried in grease, hot saleratus bread, and coffee strong enough to float an ax. Every one of the double-shotted bunks upstairs was filled, so they took "lay-outs" in a small downstairs room and slept the sleep of the just for ten solid hours.

The next night they made it to Genoa. And now, their fourth day on the trail together, they were at last moving toward Carson City, over a route strewn with the wreckage of vehicles of every imaginable size and variety.

Broken wagon tongues stuck up starkly out of sloughs of quicksand. Here and there a smashed stage or freight wagon lay over on its side, its stilled wheels fringed with stunted sage. Cases of store goods, broken furniture and heaped up whiskey barrels stood amid blasted earth and a charnal rot of putrified hide and scattered bones.

Despite the day's crispness the air stank heavily, but Boise Kinstrey was hardly more aware of this than he was of the vast tide of foot-sore, groin-sore humans struggling on ahead of him, around him and behind him. His gaze was eager, fixed forward intently. In the hazy far distance streamers of sooty smoke inked a turquoise-tinted sky. Sun Mountain, gleaming in snow-capped splendor, beckoned from the clouds like a bejeweled Jezebel.

Kinstrey felt a shiver of excitement stroke up his back. They had made a mistake calling the peak Sun Mountain. They should have called it Jezebel Mountain, after the dazzling wanton of the Bible who painted her face and adorned her head and then stood at her window, rosy as dawn, drawing the eyes of all men to her with lust and cupidity.

Kinstrey glanced at Cass, riding beside him lackadaisically.

"... hat smoke?" he said, pointing. "That's it! That dark blot up there is Sun Mountain."

"Solid gold and silver." Cass shrugged. "But what good's it going to do us?"

Kinstrey's voice rasped. "It's where Ganahl's headed."

"We've got no proof Ganahl had anything to do with what happened back there at the canyon."

Kinstrey was startled. "No proof!"

"Think about it," Cass said. "Remember what Berry told us? He didn't remember Raimo with the party. We've got no real proof that he was ever tied in with Ganahl."

Kinstrey thought with shock: He's right—but at the next moment recalled his encounter with Raimo at the wagons and demurred, "I suppose those pot shots Raimo took at me were just for sport?"

Cass again shrugged. "Oh, Raimo was with Ganahl all right. But the joker'd be to prove it." He paused, murmured, "Those three sure had opportunity laid right at their doorstep the night the old man went haywire and cut his picket string."

Kinstrey spoke absently. "You saw Raimo in the woods that night."

"Sure I saw him. But I didn't see him pull a trigger. I never saw him pulling any travois either."

Cass's objectiveness stung Kinstrey. "Raimo shot Big Matt and that's that! You found the travois later; even got those blankets off it you used on the shelter. They weren't ours."

"I'm talking about proof, Boise."

"To hell with proof! Maybe you'd like to see your father's murderer go free."

"You know that's not so."

"Then it'll make no difference what you saw, will it?"

Cass's look at Kinstrey's smoldering eyes was apprehensive, his silence a question.

"I'm going to kill Raimo, Cass." Kinstrey's voice shook with emotion. "I'm going to kill the back-shooting son of a bitch on sight."

9

THEY nooned next day at Dutch Nick's, a road saloon and rude barracks some distance beyond Carson. They were lucky to find seats at one of a half dozen long tables running parallel to a plank bar in the saloon's big common room, and Kinstrey didn't immediately notice the man with the scrawny neck and incongruously heavy shoulders who stood in the noisy press around the drink counter, wedged in beside the taller rawboned figure of Pat Manogue.

Manogue had just set down his whiskey glass and now was brusquely waving down the offer of his jowl-faced companion to refill it.

"I'll wait till I c'n kiss me lips to a bottle av good Irish potstill," he told Moss.

Al Moss grinned. "We'll get to Virginia City and line up the extra help Ganahl needs back at camp. Then you're a free man."

A keen speculativeness pinched Manogue's blue eyes with his rejoinder, "I'm thinkin' Ganahl would do better to be huntin' up Boise Kinstrey than lookin' to town for help. If him an' the lad c'n still be alive. What's Ganahl know of sawmills?"

"He's worked on engines and boilers. And you know saws. Marna Calbraith ought to be delivering to Ophir inside a week."

"Sure," Manogue gave back thinly. "And a pretty penny Ganahl will be makin' from the deal, now won't he?"

Moss's tone chilled. "I don't know about that end of it. I do know the girl got out of this whole mess lucky. First getting Ophir to give her more time on the contract; then getting Ganahl to run things for her."

"A very accommodatin' gent," observed Manogue dryly. "But was not his firin' of this man Raimo a bit short and suddenlike?"

"I explained that." Moss sounded irked, continuing, "Raimo was just somebody we picked up outside of Placerville—wanted to be with an outfit as far as Virginia City. Ganahl never cottoned to him much and after that night at Tipton's he told him he'd better go it alone. Nobody's seen hide or hair of him since."

"A fey thing," murmured Manogue.

"What's that?"

"Nothin', bucko." Manogue stared sourly at the mob pressing in around them, elbowing for room at the jammed bar. He nudged Moss. "Come on," he said. "Let's be makin' a start through this rag-tag or I'll be needin' me shillelagh to comb a head av hair or two."

"Sure; all right."

Manogue stepped out disdainfully against the forward surging crowd; at the same moment, as Al Moss fell in behind him, Boise Kinstrey glanced up from taking a last swallow of coffee and saw them both. A choking paroxysm seized him as he abruptly stood, rivulets of brown brew dribbling from the corners of his mouth.

"What's the matter?" Cass Calbraith asked him. "Drink go down the wrong way?"

Kinstrey's eyes were watering from the cramp in his throat muscles. He shook his head, gasping, "Look over there— coming away from the bar."

Cass turned. He stared, then softly whistled. "Holy Joe! Pat and Al Moss!"

Kinstrey said, "Stay right here, Cass. I'll be back."

A half dozen long strides carried him to within a few steps of the bar just as Manogue lunged through a knot of red-shirted bullwhackers at the outer fringes of the crowd.

At sight of Kinstrey he stopped dead in his tracks, then let out a mighty yawp.

"Boise! Boise Kinstrey, or I'm an Orangeman's uncle!"

His arms swept out; Kinstrey tried to duck, but was caught in a prodigious hug.

"Let go me, you big ox!"

"Let go ye! I'll fetch ye a clout in the whiskers, ye don't stand still! Man, man, where have ye——"

With a savage wrench Kinstrey tore himself free, the violence of his heave hurtling him back against a bearded behemoth in miner's homespun who towered even over Kinstrey's head.

The giant grabbed him. "Not so fast, bucko! Stay in place and you'll get your drink."

Kinstrey raged, "To hell with a drink!" and glared irately across the man's shoulder to where a squirming figure had just broken through a conflux at the far end of the bar and was now making a break for the doorway.

"Stop that man!" shouted Kinstrey. "Stop him, somebody!"

A dead stillness dropped over the room's clamor, and Kinstrey took instant advantage of the lull. In surprise, the giant's grip on him had slackened; he jerked loose from the man, spun, and then amid a suddenly renewed buzzing of voices he was butting and flailing a path through the mob, still shouting, with helpless desperation, "Stop him! Stop him!"

He saw Moss duck through the doorway; then as he reached it himself he was caught in a jam of teamsters just entering. He lunged and felt himself rudely buffeted as the thirsty, perspiring bullwhackers resentfully fought past him. Arms, elbows, flayed at him amid muffled curses; then with a last frantic thrust he was outside, and for a moment tracked, gulping fresh air in his lungs.

He looked around him but there was no sign of Moss anywhere. To his left several big bull trains were lined up in parallel parade. To his right corrals and a scattering of flimsy outbuildings extended for a distance of a couple of hundred yards or more. Kinstrey thought glumly: A needle in a haystack. Then he saw two men in the homespun dress of miners emerge from a stablelike shed a few yards distant. He swung to the right and reached them.

"Either of you see a man run this way?" he asked. "Had on a blue-and-black shirt; about five foot nine or ten."

"Feller just run to that shed yonder." The man who nodded was tall, shaggy, unkempt. "Come out on a buckskin; really larrupin' it. Rode like he was goin' to a claim-jumpin'."

"Which direction?"

"Toward Devil's Gate. Jasper steal your bronc, friend?"

"Nothing like that." Kinstrey's tone was flat, disgusted. He said, "Well, much obliged, boys," and wheeled around.

In the dining room a crowd stood curiously at the single front window staring out at him. He ignored a few brusque questions growled at him as he re-entered the front door, then saw Cass and Pat Manogue motioning to him from an empty corner. He walked over to them.

Manogue glanced at him with heavy self-reproach. "Cass has been fillin' me in on things," he said. "And to think I had the slippery spalpeen right in me hands."

"He's gone now. No use to cry over spilt milk," Kinstrey said.

"Faith, an' ye're bein' a merciful man to a blunderin' baboon! But there was no gettin' out av here after ye'd left. The door was jammed like th' gate to a Killarney fair."

"I found out one thing," Kinstrey said. "He rode toward Devil's Gate."

"Then he still must be headed for Virginia City," offered Cass.

"Still?" Kinstrey shifted an inquiring look toward Manogue.

"Our outfit's settin' up over on Washoe Creek," explained the wagon boss. "Moss an' meself was on our way to Virginia City to hunt up an extra hand or two." He scratched his chin, scowling ruminatively. "But why would th' dirrty buzzard-head high-tail it for th' City now? Ganahl thinks ye're dead. Why wouldn't Moss run to him first, t' warn him ye've not yet traded your gun fer a harp?"

"Just one reason." Kinstrey was terse. "There was someone else he wanted to warn first."

"But who c'd that be? There's no wan——" Suddenly Manogue's mouth fell open. "Holy McFoley! Raimo, be God!"

Grimly, Kinstrey nodded. "You saw how Moss acted when he spotted me; like he'd just seen a ghost. Raimo must have told him I was dead."

Cass broke in. "All right; suppose Raimo *is* in the City? I still don't see why Moss would break his neck getting to him ahead of Ganahl."

"I do." Kinstrey's voice was flat. "Suppose I'd gotten to Raimo first and forced him to talk? *That's* what scared Moss."

Manogue's blue eyes kindled. "Swith! Then him an' Ganahl was mixed up in Big Matt's murder. The minute he recognized Boise he went bustin' out av here. You'd have thought he'd just stole th' cross off an ass's back."

Cass frowned. "That's still guesswork."

"To you, maybe." Kinstrey gave him a curt look, then turned to Manogue. "Ganahl at camp when you left there?" he asked.

"He was that." Manogue frowned. "But he's a hard man to hold onto. Talked av goin' to th' City himself to see a man about sellin' his lumber; Jackson, Johnston, Jordan—some such a name."

"Ganahl hired any men outside our own, Pat?"

"A couple. Av th' kind that're one minute lookin' for wurrk, an' th' next prayin' they won't find it." Dourly, Manogue shook his head. "It was no skin off me, but I told Marna what I thought av Ganahl th' day she hired th' four-flushin' Beau Broomell. Ye'd have thought I was a ruddy Orangeman, be God, th' look she handed me!"

Kinstrey stiffened. "Marna's all right, isn't she?"

"She's let nothin' trouble *her*."

Kinstrey flushed. "At least she's had spunk enough to set things rolling!" He caught a covert exchange of glances between Cass and Manogue and felt his irritation mount. "How much have you done back at camp?" he curtly asked Manogue.

"B'iler's ready for a head o' steam. Saw riggin's mostly still in th' wagons." Manogue was terse. "But don't lookit me like that. The lady didn't hire *me* for th' boss."

"There's no blame on you, Pat."

"I'd bate the puss off anybody who'd say so!"

"I don't doubt it." Kinstrey grinned. "But right now I want you to ride back to camp and keep an eye on Ganahl."

"I'll do it. But suppose he ain't there?"

"You can send Cass to notify me, in that case. I'll be in Virginia City."

"So will I," said Cass. "So he'd better send somebody else."

Kinstrey swung around. "I'd like you to go with Pat, Cass."

"And I'd like to start making my own decisions for a change." Sullen belligerence compressed Cass's mouth. "I'm going with you," he stated flatly.

Kinstrey could feel the heat rushing to his face. Then, uncheckable, his choler exploded into wrath. "All right," he blurted, "let's lay it on the line then! It's that pesty girl, isn't it? She's got you so addled in the head you think she's more important than the Ophir contract!"

Cass tensed. "Maybe I do at that!" he flared back, stung. "It's no business of yours, is it?"

Manogue answered. "None, bucko," he said softly, and slanted a look toward Kinstrey. "A gurrl like her could make a man ferget to lift his hat passin' a chapel."

Kinstrey glared at him. "You've said enough! Now pack up your blarney stone and roll your freight."

"Touchy's th' man who wears a hair shirrt." Standing, the wagon boss removed a stub-stemmed pipe from his pants and noisily blew dottle from it. "A hair shirrt often will itch a man where his galluses cross."

"You'll itch where I touch a boot to your fat behind if you don't start moving!"

"Order yerself a cloud an' a harp before you try that, bucko." He half-leered at Kinstrey, wheeling; then he was strutting from the room, his shoulders squared in an impudent swagger.

"That damned arrogant mick!" Kinstrey swore under his breath. He swung around distractedly, no longer even aware of Cass standing there watching him.

Footsteps sounded behind him as he started for the door, limping from his still tender ankle. He looked back.

Cass was doggedly following him out of the room.

10

BOISE KINSTREY rode with a fierce impatience. But behind him Cass's trigueno was moving at a bare snail's pace, pulled down by a cut fetlock, and his own horse seemed little better off.

Anger still smoldering in him flared anew each time he thought of Al Moss. The damned slippery buzzard-neck! But at least he now had the certainty of one thing. Even if Moss was not directly involved in Big Matt's murder he must have guilty knowledge of it.

Moss had run like a spooked jack at just the sight of him. And now Moss was on his way to Raimo; was running to warn the ratty little gunjack who had casually snuffed out the life of Big Matt Calbraith. Big Matt gone; murdered. It was still hard to believe. Sudden wetness glistened in Kinstrey's eyes as he tossed a look back over his shoulder.

Cass's dark eyes still were sultry under knit brows; since they had passed through Devil's Gate, a mile or so back, Cass had barely grunted at him.

Kinstrey swung his gaze forward again, a feeling of tolerance now leavening his earlier annoyance with the younger man. Cass *was* young; and he'd probably never done any serious womaning before. Let the kid cut his rusty. What right did he have to interfere?

Kinstrey was suddenly aware that traffic along the trail was increasing. Silver City lay behind them now and they were approaching the outskirts of Gold Hill, which seemed little more than an assemblage of ramshackle shanties, wind-torn tents of canvas or old blankets, and a scatteration of smoky hovels dug out of the mountain's flank, with potato sacks and discarded shirts for door coverings and empty whiskey kegs for chimneys.

Men were afoot, ahorse, on wagons, pulling handcarts. A few of the travelers were dapperly attired and sat hand-tooled saddles on blooded horses. But mostly it was men just trudging: adventurers, hobos, fugitives from the law, whiskey drummers, organ grinders, peddlers bent under huge packs, and red-shirted miners, picks and shovels slung across hunched shoulders as they yanked on the ropes of heavy-laden burros or great clumsy Percherons.

Once Kinstrey noticed a woman wearing man's clothes, and another time he was hailed raucously from a tossel-topped rig, where a harlot with painted cheeks and simpering face sat enthroned, dangling a fancy sunshade.

The scene had almost a carnival atmosphere, and Kinstrey thought: Big Matt would have loved this. And he felt his still fresh grief rubbed raw again.

To his rear three mountainous loads of logs swayed behind a sixteen-mule team hauling a freighter with two back-actions coupled behind it. A bow of bells suspended above the bear-skin housings of each mule's collar jingled melodically as the animals toiled up a continuing grade flanked by quartz mills, tunnels, dumps, sluices and a conglomeration of frame and adobe huts. Hoisting shacks dotted every rise; stamp mills stood beside every trickling rivulet.

Kinstrey's eyes cruised, rapt with interest. The earth thundered with movement. Dull explosions reverberated from murky caverns. The air was filled with flying cinders and powdery alkali dust. Kinstrey touched his saddle horn; his fingers came away gritty. This was Sun Mountain. But the sun was hidden. Man's violation of the mountain's metal heart hung a perpetual dark pall over the desecration,

Kinstrey stared away through the swirling murk. Below him stretched a vast panorama hemmed in by overwhelming mountains. Hills undulated in endless procession; a quick-silver curve twisting among them was the Carson River.

Kinstrey straighted, stretching the cramp from his muscle-bound shoulders. It won't be long now, he thought. And at last they came to the grimy gates of Eldorado. . . .

As Boise Kinstrey and Cass Calbraith rode into Virginia City's C Street Al Moss was beginning his search of the town's dives and honkytonks for Jack Raimo, and a distance of two blocks upstreet, where the false-fronted mercantile of Jules Mannerheim stood at the corner of Glory Climb, Marna Calbraith held station at the store's front window marveling at how a town as raw and new as this one could attract her so powerfully.

Virginia City was barely started yet, but already its busy main drag bore a cosmopolitan aspect. A never-changing pageant moved past Marna's window: shambling Piutes, clad in picturesque rags; pigtailed Chinese coolies balancing baskets of wash from wooden shoulder yokes; Mexican vaqueros parading on silver-mounted saddles; miners in blue jeans; Frenchmen in tight pants; pudgy Germans puffing on fat curved pipes. Another block upstreet there was a tent-and-counter saloon called grandly, *Café de Paris,* and a bit beyond that a dark and smoky *bier-keller,* where noisy Teutons roistered and sang.

Marna's eyes grew thoughtful. Yes, some day this booming town hugging a mountainside would be a big and splendid city. Then those who had been the first comers and who had shown themselves alert to opportunity would be the City's future nabobs and first citizens.

She felt her thoughts lift watching the unending stream of traffic that was moving kaleidoscopically past her window. She had a mind capable of holding care just so long, and then a capacity for jettisoning it like so much unwanted cargo. What had happened to her father had been terrible and a great pity, but it would be useless to pretend that they had ever been very close to one another.

Perhaps it didn't pay to commit the emotions too deeply, without reservations of any kind. Take Cass. She had tried, honestly tried, to be a good sister to Cass, and what had it gained her? Abuse and estrangement, nothing else. And now both Cass and Boise were missing and might be dead. Facts had to be faced. Trails were unsafe; bandits and road agents roamed everywhere.

A faint look of petulance budded Marna Calbraith's softly full mouth. With her help Boise might have become a big man here in this Utah Territory. But now . . .

Beside the doorway a cracked wall mirror hung askew. Marna caught a reflection of her slimly oval face in it, and smiled. She was young, intelligent and attractive, and all that had been her father's would now be hers. Why should she look back then—why should anyone ever look back? Only the old or the sick in mind did that.

Behind her she could hear Jules Mannerheim shuffling about; in a moment he appeared with a taper and lighted a tin-shaded coal-oil lamp hung from chains in the center of the ceiling.

Marna glanced around in wry distaste as the light nakedly revealed the store's jungle of dim arteries threading mysterious stacks of boxes and barrels and coils of thick, tarry rope.

To her right strong smells of paint, fresh yard goods, spices, saddle soap and "Dog-leg" tobacco wafted from a littered counter. Above it wires stretched in parallel lines offered a display of blue cotton overalls, denim jeans, corduroy breeches and red wampus shirts. Cowhide boots with "pullers" and "Nigger" shoes dangled beside a row of flatcrowned hats, all black, and a showing of vari-colored braces and leather belts studded with brass nailheads. Across the room, sides of bacon, called "Jew's Abomination," hung from a row of steel ceiling hooks.

Jules Mannerheim's amber-dark eyes were melancholy but kind; an aquiline nose protruded from a craggy, bearded face, relieved of outright ugliness only by a gentle, mobile mouth.

He glanced toward Marna and asked, "Effie is not back yet?"

"No, not yet."

Mannerheim's accent was slightly guttural. "I will start supper. She will come soon, *nein?*"

He was starting toward the back of the room, when a small bell jangled and the front door swung open.

With her casual turning, sudden shock bleached Marna's face.

Behind Effie Mannerheim in the doorway stood Boise Kinstrey and Cass Calbraith. "I—I met them outside—on the street." Effie explained a little breathlessly.

Marna Calbraith stood rigid. Then she took a dazed step. "Boise!" she whispered, and her voice sounded drained of all belief.

It took a little time for Marna to recover from her shock. Effie Mannerheim introduced Kinstrey and Cass to her uncle and then Jules Mannerheim brought Marna a glass of sherry. She sipped the wine and gradually color filtered back into her cheeks. Then Kinstrey told her his story and heard hers.

He learned that Ganahl had separated the two wagon outfits back at Carson, sending the Calbraith wagons, with Moss

in temporary charge, on to Washoe Creek, while he had proceeded with his own two vehicles to Virginia City, escorting
Marna and Effie Mannerheim safely to their destination.

Then, accompanied by Ganahl, Marna had gone to see
Philip Deidesheimer, superintendent at the Ophir, and pre-
vailed on him to extend the contract made with her father,
although at that date the instrument already was technically
in default. Deidesheimer had told her to set up the mill machinery and get started as quickly as possible, and Ganahl,
after selling both his wagons and lumber to a speculator
named Johnson, had headed back for Washoe Creek to rejoin
Moss and take charge of the operation for her.

Marna finished her wine, silently held out the empty glass
for Jules Mannerheim to take and said, "Boise, you can't really believe Frank Ganahl had anything to do with my father's death?"

Kinstrey's voice was flat. "Can you still believe his story
about those traders?"

"There could have been a man found who looked like
Dad. Oh, I don't know! This whole thing is such a mess!"
Marna pressed hands to her temples, staring up at him.
"*Please*, Boise, sit down. You look exhausted. So does Cass.
We'll have supper; *then* talk."

Kinstrey shook his head. "I've wasted too much time already. I've got to find out whether Raimo's in town and, if he
is, whether Moss has gotten to him yet."

Marna paled slightly. "Boise? You really think Ganahl
might seize our wagons? You know the investment father had
in all that machinery."

Cass said, "Sure, Boise knows. To hell with the men, Boise.
Just be sure you save that investment."

Marna turned on him, white with fury. "Why don't you go
back to Sacramento? Maybe you could get a job selling rib-
bons. You'll never be good for much else!"

Cass sneered, "And leave you here to lap up all the gravy?
Oh no!"

"Then what *do* you intend to do?"

"Stick with Boise." Cass's tone was curt. "And make sure
you don't smart me out of my share of things."

"Your share!" Marna's voice was caustic. She darted a virulent glance toward Effie Mannerheim, then added with soft

derision, "You need a guardian more than you do a share of anything, doesn't he, Boise?"

Kinstrey said, "He needs to be let alone, Marna."

"So now *you're* going to coddle him! I tried that, and all it ever got me was abuse."

"Maybe you should try treating him like a man." Kinstrey regretted his words at the instant of speaking them. He saw Marna stiffen and was suddenly reminded of all she had been through recently. He turned, guiltily, and asked Jules Mannerheim, "Is there a livery near by, Mr. Mannerheim?"

The store owner nodded. "*Ja,* sure—Gardiner's. A good place."

Kinstrey's glance sought Cass. "Cass, one of us has got to get a fresh horse and ride back to Pat. Tonight."

Sullenly Cass's eyes shifted from Effie Mannerheim. "Why? What can happen out there tonight?"

"Maybe nothing," Kinstrey said honestly. "On the other hand, Moss might get back to Ganahl. Then you'd be one more man—in case of trouble."

"Sure," Cass said. "You hang around town and be the big gun with Raimo. I'm good enough to be your errand boy."

"This is no errand boy's job. But don't go if you're scared."

Cass bridled. "Who says I'm scared?"

"Nobody. But I'll have to go if you don't."

Effie Mannerheim tossed a knowing glance to Kinstrey, looked back quickly at Cass. "I can show you where the livery is," she offered. "I'll walk you there if you like."

"That should be an inducement," Marna contributed silkily.

Cass jerked around. "By God, that's enough from you! I'll go just to get shut of your jawbone!" With a defiant gesture he took Effie's arm. "I need some clean air. Let's get out of here," he blurted out harshly.

Effie looked back across her shoulder. "I won't be long, Uncles Jules."

"I trust you, *liebchen.* Just do not loiter on the street; is dark already."

"I'll be all right, don't worry."

Jules Mannerheim's eyes swerved to Kinstrey when she was gone. "She is a little one to be so spunky," he said.

"It's not the size." Kinstrey smiled.

"*Ach, nein!* Well, I go back; work to do."

They waited until his footsteps faded out; until a door slammed remotely. Then Marna turned.

"Thank God you are safe, Boise!"

"I'm tough to kill. But Marna, go easy on Cass. He's going to do all right."

"With that girl throwing herself at him? I hope so. Anyway, I've done all I can. Now I wash my hands."

She was wearing an olive-green dress with short puffy sleeves and a tight bodice. Lamplight glistened on her crow-black hair and red mouth. The dark blue of her eyes seemed to contain a deep and serious stillness as she placed a hand on his arm.

"Aren't you going to kiss me, Boise?"

She wore a little silk packet of sachet between her breasts and the scent wafted excitingly to Kinstrey as he drew her against him. He had been hinting to himself lately of some doubts that he now forgot as she sank yieldingly against him. An eager quivering spread through him. He bent his head to her open mouth. . . .

11

Boise Kinstrey's dun stood hipshot at the rail outside Jules Mannerheim's mercantile. The weary animal barely lifted his head as he was untied. Played out, thought Kinstrey; he'll have to be grained and rested. He didn't mount, but took the bridle reins and started downstreet afoot, leading him.

It was about six-thirty. The night air held a nip but the temperature was above freezing and Kinstrey left his mackinaw unbuttoned as he trudged along. Almost every other shack or falsefront was a saloon; gushes of yellow light sprang from doorways, and raucous sounds of laughter and revelry beat at the night. Kinstrey marveled that this new, still raw town could already have such lustiness and vitality.

His thoughts went back to Marna Calbraith and a renewal of desire surged through him. She had kissed him with passion; she had Big Matt's forthrightness at least. But certain things disturbed him. Sometimes when he was with her he had a balked feeling that he was being led, that not all of her purposes with him were straightforwardly intentioned. But then, no man ever fully understood a woman. He wasn't meant to; and if a woman ever thought he did she'd probably not want him.

Kinstrey's mouth split in an absent-minded grin and at that moment a voice with laughter in it said, "Look out or we might bump!" and he jerked up his head and saw Effie Mannerheim.

He felt sheepish over the grin and wondered if she had seen it. He stopped and was conscious of an annoyance he couldn't define. "Cass should have walked you back to the store," he said, and noticed that her slim, rather tapering nose had a light dusting of freckles across it. She had on the blue cape; but underneath, he now noticed for the first time, she was wearing jeans in which she looked casual and leggy and somehow innocently winsome.

She dismissed his remark with a smile. "I'm no child, Mr. Kinstrey."

Kinstrey's eyes took new note of her. "I know," he said. "That's what I mean."

"I'm used to being alone," she told him. "I can take care of myself."

A warming sympathy stirred in Kinstrey. He, too, had known the feeling of loneliness. It was like a dark well inside you, bottomless—and empty.

He said, "You've got an admirer now. Cass has taken quite a shine to you."

"I'd rather he hadn't. I do feel sorry for him, though."

"What do you mean, you'd rather he hadn't?"

"I may not look it but I'm twenty-two years old. Cass can't be more than eighteen."

"Nineteen," Kinstrey said.

"All right, nineteen. I'm still a little old for him, don't you think?"

Kinstrey felt oddly irritated. He said, "Where's Gardiner's? I'm going to see you home."

"You don't need to."

"Never mind! Come on; show me Gardiner's."

He walked beside her in stiff-lipped silence. The livery had a night swamper who was a Piute and who barely grunted at him before taking his dun and leading it away down a lane of dark stalls.

Walking out, Effie Mannerheim told him, "That was Soldier Charley. Did you notice his army hat and the row of medals across his shirt?"

"They mean anything?"

"Not a thing. Charley's a town character; peddles pine nuts and does odd jobs around. Sometimes he runs errands for Uncle Jules. Hardly talks, most of the time. It's hard to tell whether he likes you or not."

"He cottons to you, all right. I could see that."

"I try to treat him as if he's human. Not many do."

"Well, maybe I'm in the lodge. He saw me with you."

They walked on through a run of silence. Then Effie Mannerheim asked, "Why did you stay in town tonight? I know you're worried about the wagons."

"I wanted to check around. I know who killed Matt Calbraith."

"So?"

"If he's in town I'll kill him."

Effie Mannerheim looked up at him studyingly. "Yes. You would, wouldn't you?" There was neither approval nor disapproval in her voice.

"You don't think I should?"

"There is no law here. Who can say?"

They were nearing Mannerheim's store when an unusually tall man wearing a white sombrero, choker scarf and buckskin waistcoat appeared in front of it and, apparently recognizing Effie through the spill of light from the window, stopped. "Is that you, Miss Mannerheim?"

Effie went on. "Yes, and this is Mr. Kinstrey." She nodded to Kinstrey, said, "Mr. Kinstrey, this is Mr. Johnson."

"Lank Johnson." The tall man held out a hand on which an immense diamond glittered. A Colt's pistol protruded from a beaded holster at his right hip. "Glad to know you, Kinstrey."

"The same," said Kinstrey.

Lank Johnson looked back at Effie Mannerheim. "Miss Calbraith in?"

"She was."

"I guess she's expecting me; I'll go in." Johnson turned. "Pleasure to meet you, Kinstrey." Then he was gone through the doorway.

Kinstrey's tone was querulous as he peered down at Effie Mannerheim's faintly disturbed face.

"Who is that dude?"

"He's a promoter who owns a big tract of timber over near Ophir City; he's got sawmills there too. They say he's already made a fortune, just selling lumber to the mines."

"He trying to make a deal of some kind with Miss Calbraith?"

Effie Mannerheim hesitated, and something in her manner puzzled Kinstrey until she finally replied, "I guess he'd like to buy her out. He's always on the go over something."

"Hmph! Well, thanks for helping out with Cass."

"He just needed a little push."

"And you supplied it."

"Then I'm glad, for your sake." A strand of flaxen hair had become recalcitrant and she was tucking it back under her knitted sock cap.

The gesture touched Kinstrey. Her slim, rather pointed face had lost much of its trail tan and in the light beaming out through the store window it seemed ineffably pale and brushed with a faint sadness.

"Why," asked Kinstrey gruffly, "for my sake?"

Her smile for the first time was just a little arch. "Maybe," she told him, "I did it because we have something in common. We both know what it means to be lonely."

"So, Marna's been babbling about me, has she?"

"A woman must talk to someone, Mr. Kinstrey."

"Boise," Kinstrey said. There was a peculiar roughness in his throat. What triggered his erratic impulse he didn't know, but without questioning it he suddenly leaned down and kissed her on the cheek. She stared up at him in blank astonishment. Then, before she could utter a sound, he had turned and was moving away with long, free-swinging strides, downstreet.

The Indication Hotel was a gimcrack wooden structure with a broad falsefront, behind which a barrackslike framework contained a dozen small private rooms, virtually never obtainable at any price, and three barren dormitories where bunks and layouts were available at a dollar a night.

Kinstrey stopped there first, but with no result. The owner, a man named Cahoon, didn't know Moss and said he had seen no one answering Jack Raimo's description around town. Kinstrey thanked him and left.

He began a tour of the saloons. He found that about every fourth door led to a bar, some little more than roofs of canvas with an assortment of random-length pine slabs for siding.

He shouldered his way through throngs of roughs, loafers, sagebrushers, prostitutes, gamblers and plain miners. Men in gaudy colored shirts offered him alleged bargains in "The Rogers," "Lady Bryant," "Woolly Horse" and other supposedly valuable leads at prices ranging from ten to seventy-five dollars a foot. But no one seemed to have heard of Frank Ganahl or Al Moss, and Kinstrey's description of Jack Raimo was met with blank looks or dismissive shrugs.

After an hour of futile tramping around Kinstrey was again feeling the soreness in his sprained ankle; his shoulders slumped, and he began to limp heavily. He had now covered almost one whole side of the street and had worked his way back to within half a block of the livery. A couple of men to

whom he had talked thought they had seen a man answering
Al Moss's description but weren't sure. And neither one could
recall having seen or heard of Raimo.

Kinstrey debated whether to go on to the livery and head
out of town or stay and continue a probably futile search.
Three doors ahead a lighted window bore the legend, *Orndoff
& McGee*, and from within came the unmistakable glass-
clinking hubbub and clatter of another oasis of refreshment.
Should he try one more place?

As he hesitated a woman sidled up to him and he caught a
reek of cheap perfume and a glimpse of a hard, laquered
face.

"How about it, mister?"

Kinstrey stared at her in cold disgust and she shrugged. A
man in miner's garb was just coming out of the saloon, rock-
ing tipsily. The woman started toward him, swinging her hips.

"Just a minute!" Kinstrey called sharply after her.

She turned. "Change your mind, mister?"

Kinstrey walked over to her, limping. "No," he said; "but
you might have some information I'd pay for."

"What kind of information?"

Kinstrey described Al Moss and Jack Raimo.

"Why, sure!"—The streetwalker's husky voice took on a
gusto suddenly—"I seen them boys just a couple of minutes
ago. Come out of Blue Chip Billy's, across the way there.
One went upstreet; other one headed toward Gardiner's Livery."

"The livery?" Kinstrey's tone was flat, urgent. "Which one
was that?"

"Little jasper, I think. That's right; it *was* the little one.
He—"

"Thanks, thanks!" Abruptly, Kinstrey pressed a silver dollar into her hand; then he had spun around and was bending
into a kind of loose hopscotching run to avoid strain on his
weak ankle.

He'd caught up with Raimo! The voice of violence roared
in his ears; an urge to kill swept him as he ran on at his
maladroit gallop and reached the broad front ramp of the
livery.

A lighted lantern hooked to a projecting steel arm hung
above the building's wide portal. Kinstrey didn't notice the
horse droppings at the foot of the incline. His boot sole skid-

ded on the excrement; pain flashed up in his sore ankle and he had a sickening awareness of his feet flying out from under him. The ramp's planks seemed to leap upward and he felt a jolting concussion against his chin.

Hoofs stomped in muffled tattoo and a horseman appeared suddenly in the livery's entryway. Dazed, Kinstrey had lurched up to one knee and was gulping for breath. Jack Raimo at that instant recognized him and with a quick movement slipped his gun as he started the horse down the ramp.

With frantic strength Kinstrey lunged erect. A savage gout of pain tore up his leg; he felt his knee sink under him. And at that moment Raimo had his gun slanted. He fired.

The deflexing of Kinstrey's leg saved him. A bullet fanned past his ear; at the same instant he took weight on his good leg and flung himself toward the horse, wildly lunging for Raimo's arm and finding it.

A grim exultation leaped in him as he heard Raimo cry out in alarm; then, holding a dragging weight on the hand still gripping the gun, he stripped Raimo out of the saddle with a single powerful heave.

The very violence of the maneuver was Kinstrey's undoing. Raimo's weight wasn't great, but the suddenness of its bearing upon Kinstrey forced pressure on his bad ankle. A crucifying pain spurted and as his leg crumpled and he toppled backward Raimo rode him to the ramp like a cowhand viciously bulldozing a steer.

The pain knifing up through his leg and even into his groin nearly blinded Kinstrey with its intensity; he saw Raimo's big Navy Colt as just a blur above him and barely rolled in time. Raimo's blow struck glancingly across the side of his head, but still half-stunned him. He clawed groggily for the gun but Raimo jerked back and he got only the gunslinger's wrist.

Kinstrey was hurt. Sweat budded the taut lines of his jaw as he sawed in a breath and strove desperately to deflect the gun's muzzle that Raimo was slowly but inexorably forcing toward him.

He didn't hear the padded footfall from the top of the ramp; Raimo did, and was as alert as a cat. The gunman's head jerked around but not in time to dodge the dark streak of rawhide whistling at him. The whip's wire tip laid open his hand, and with dull surprise Kinstrey heard him blurt out in agony, heard the gun drop and go clattering down the ramp.

But Raimo's reflexes were incredibly fast. With almost an acrobatic agility he sprang erect, whirled. His buckskin still stood on the ramp, hipshot. He vaulted to the saddle and kicked back with his spurs, jolting the horse into a frantic run. Hoofbeats exploded thunderously on the ramp, then became a muffled drum roll out in the street, fading rapidly.

Kinstrey groaned, heaving up to a sitting posture. He leaned forward and tenderly drew his boot from his puffing foot.

A voice above him said with no inflection, "You stop one more clout on head and Soldier Charley no ketch um money."

Kinstrey's eyes fluttered upward. He stared at an army campaign hat, crusted with pine sap and streaked with stable sweepings, seated low on a head of coarse black hair and shielding fierce black eyes. The face underneath the hat was gaunt, copper-dark and completely enigmatic. Kinstrey looked wonderingly at the yellow piping on a pair of faded blue cavalry trousers, then up at a ragged gray shirt fringed with a row of jingling medals. He grinned.

"Miss Mannerheim told me about you," he said. "Thanks for helping me out."

Soldier Charley's hawklike visage remained stolidly expressionless. "No want um thanks." The lanky Piute gestured with the buggy whip still in his hand. "Me help you *mucho* big lot—cost um four bits."

"You get me a stick so I can hobble in to my horse," said Kinstrey, "and I'll make it eight bits and a new shirt."

"No want two shirt. One shirt heap plenty, fix up nice."

Kinstrey nodded, his face sober. "You're really spraddled out, Soldier. All right; double the money."

"You bust leg all to smash?"

"No. It's just a bad sprain."

"You wait; me fix um."

Soldier Charley was gone quite a long time. When he returned, finally, he was leading Kinstrey's dun and carrying a bottle, a handful of gaudy rags and a crude crutch fashioned out of a couple of pieces of mesquite.

Kinstrey was surprised at the soothing effect when the Piute presently began gently massaging his ankle with a greasy liquid poured from the bottle.

"What's that junk?" he grumbled.

Soldier Charley had finished working in the oil and now with remarkable deftness was strapping the ankle firmly with strips of colored cloth.

"Piute make um stuff. Heap good, ketch um sprain." He finished his bandaging, stood. "Take um pay now."

Kinstrey's mouth gaped. This Indian had more gall than a horse thief. But there was a kind of sour dignity mixed with his audacity and Kinstrey managed a wry grin digging into his jeans' pocket.

"Here," he said, and held out three silver dollars.

Soldier Charley didn't even blink, accepting them. Impassively he stowed the coins in the top of his boot. Then he helped Kinstrey mount and handed him up the crutch.

Kinstrey peered down at the inscrutable dark face under the bedraggled hat. "If you ever want another job come and see me," he said.

Soldier Charley grunted. "Why you give um?"

"I might have been killed here tonight. What made you horn in?"

"You friend girl," Soldier Charley said.

"What girl?"

"*Muy buena—muy bonita.* She buy basket pine nuts every day. Two bits."

"I see." Kinstrey had trouble keeping a straight face.

"Me go now," announced Soldier Charley. He seemed to stiffen abruptly; then before Kinstrey had quite grasped his intention his right hand whipped smartly to his forehead in a held salute.

Kinstrey was puzzled only for a second. Then he realized what was expected of him. When he returned the salute Soldier Charley's hand dropped. "Well, thanks again," Kinstrey told him.

Soldier Charley said nothing. He emitted a taciturn grunt, wheeled, and then was striding majestically back into the livery.

Kinstrey started the dun, unsure whether to laugh or feel peeved. Reaching the street, he swung his horse toward Gold Hill, thinking: Why, I could have tossed the rascal a whole hatful of dollars and he'd never have blinked an eye!

The dun felt stronger under him after its rest and feed of oats. The pain in his ankle was subsiding now that his weight was off it but it still throbbed dully to remind him of his encounter with Jack Raimo. Suddenly Kinstrey leaned out from the saddle and spat, as if to rid his mouth of a foul taste.

He might wait a long time before getting another chance at Raimo; at least, as good a chance as he'd had tonight. The cold-eyed, runty, cat-footed killer of Big Matt Calbraith would now be doubly on his guard. And now knowing that Kinstrey was still alive, doubly dangerous. . . .

Kinstrey's eyes pinched somberly, reaching to the darkness at the head of the street. And all at once the night seemed blacker and colder than it had before.

12

It was sunrise when Boise Kinstrey heard hammering and a ringing of voices, but sound carried such a distance in this thin mountain air that a full ten minutes elapsed before he finally rode into a glenlike clearing in the hills and so reached the mill site on Washoe Creek.

He found Pat Manogue and Geehaw Jenkins setting rafters above a sizable frame structure that was to house the saw frame and the main shaft, or arbor, on which the mill's drive pulley and saw would later be mounted. Dave Ebaugh was coming up from the creek carrying water, while the two other members of the crew, Wilmer Browne and Mike Cloona, were busy back at the wagons, evidently clearing up breakfast gear.

Kinstrey was greeted effusively by Manogue and Geehaw, then learned from the wagon boss that Cass had ridden in safely more than two hours ago and now was asleep in one of the wagons. When Manogue himself had reached camp, the evening before, Ganahl had already left—bound for Virginia City, Geehaw Jenkins had thought. A guard had been posted in case of his unexpected return but the only unscheduled visitor had been Cass, who was bushed and had gone to bed within short minutes of his arrival.

Kinstrey sat his dun in a tired slump, looking up bleary-eyed to where Manogue stood with his right arm hung over a ladder at the peak of the still roofless mill building.

"What about those two men Ganahl hired?" he asked.

Manogue leaned from the ladder away from Kinstrey and spat. "They're no longer wurrkin' here. And good riddance to th' rubbidge!"

Kinstrey nodded to the right of the mill structure, where a smaller building stood completed except for a paneless window and a doorless doorway.

"I see you put up the boiler shack first. Engine ready for a head of steam yet?"

"Ready as a County Mayo man f'r a muss with th' constable." Manogue gestured expansively. "We'll have a roof on this shebang by noon; then we c'n unload th' frame an' main shaft and be after startin' to tie things together."

"You've done all right, Pat." Kinstrey's glance shifted to Geehaw, who stood on a ladder opposite Manogue's, waiting for the wagon boss to peg in his rafter. "How're you, Geehaw?"

Geehaw scratched at a lock of sparse gray hair, his grizzled face crinkling in a grin as he nodded toward Manogue.

"As good as you could expect of a man who has to work with the feeble-minded."

Manogue glared at him across ladders. "G'wan, y'ould cock! It's a mercy o' God I didn't fire yerself, while I was in th' mood av th' thing."

Kinstrey said, "Think I'll crawl into a wagon and get a little shut-eye. If I'm not up by noon, wake me, Pat."

"By noon!" Manogue looked outraged. "Man, have ye got a slate off? Ye look hardly able to hould yer ruddy head up off'n yer shoulders this minute!"

Kinstrey grinned a little forcedly. "Six hours will do me; noon—don't forget," and swung the dun around.

Behind him, as he rode back toward the wagons, he could hear Manogue bawling at Geehaw and Geehaw yipping back. He smiled. Everything about Manogue was big—including his mouth.

Dave Ebaugh had left to join Manogue and Geehaw, and Wilmer Browne and Mike Cloona were preparing to leave as he came up to them on the dun and greeted them briefly.

Cass's livery horse was tied to a rear wheel of the last Espenshied in the line; Browne and Cloona were moving away as he started the dun toward it. On a belated impulse he reined the horse around and pulled in, letting his eyes cruise over the layout of the camp.

He liked it. Ophir had chosen well, picking this site close upon timberlands and with plenty of water available to make steam. Immediately to the left of the main building there was a gentle rise, ideal for rolling logs down onto the saw carriage, and at the top of this grade a level area held a huge quantity of piled-up logs, already bucked into proper lengths and ready for the saw.

Kinstrey's gaze continued to cruise approvingly around the camp. To the right of the mill lay another flat stretch of ground where the squared timbers which would be the mill's principal product could be handily yarded. A fork of Washoe Creek skirted this area, a section of the swift flowing water glimmering now as the lifting sun dazzlingly caught on it.

There was, Kinstrey pondered, just one drawback to the location. The mill site was halfway up a mountain and there was no trail of any kind up its eastern slope, which would have been the shortest route for anyone coming from Virginia City. In order to get here he had been obliged to skirt halfway around the base of the mountain and then come in from the south, following a twisting, tortuous trail that must have taken him ten or twelve miles out of his way.

Kinstrey had a sudden desire to see what lay beyond the stream, to the right of the mill. By now his eyes felt woolly with sleeplessness and his fatigue was like a great paining weight pressing upon him. He gigged the dun anyway, forded the creek and finally reached a spot where the level ground sheered off into a long downgrade.

He gazed down. Logging operations had denuded almost the whole easterly flank of the mountain, leaving terrain virtually barren except for stumps, heaps of slash and tangled meshes of second-growth. He could see, though, why no road had ever been built up this side of the mountain. There were too many chasms and rocky gullies, for one thing. And the pitch was much sharper than on the longer southerly flank. Still . . .

Abstractedly Kinstrey wheeled the dun and started it back toward the wagons. It couldn't be much more than a mile from here straight down to the main road below. Hauling timbers down the south end road would add at least ten and maybe twelve miles to the trip to Virginia City. He wondered if the contract with Ophir called for the mill to deliver directly to the mine.

Riding on past the mill he reached the wagons and charily dismounted. Then, hobbling on the crutch Soldier Charley had made for him, he led the dun to a wagon wheel and tied it. He'd have to have a talk with Marna about the contract, he decided; there probably was a copy stowed away somewhere among Big Matt's effects. There must be some kind of a will, too, come to think of it. . . .

At this moment Kinstrey oddly was reminded of Lank Johnson. Johnson, according to Effie Mannerheim, had been seeing Marna in hope of buying her out. Naturally Marna wouldn't listen to any proposition like that; not now, with Cass and himself back. Still, he ought to see her and talk over the contract; then maybe they could go over to Ophir and have a talk with Phil Deidesheimer, the superintendent.

Staring vacantly away Kinstrey felt his eyes droop and suddenly was aware of nodding. He jerked up his head with a start. The first thing he had to do was get some sleep. Get it and be done with it.

Steady sounds of hammering came from his right. A fierce impatience battered against his tiredness. Reluctantly he turned to climb into the wagon to which he had just tied his horse.

For three days the weather remained moderate—temperatures averaging above freezing—and work on the mill progressed rapidly, with fewer interruptions and setbacks than Boise Kinstrey had believed possible. He had been satisfied to have a roof on the mill and leave other structural refinements to a later time. What he wanted was to see sawdust spurt and watch timbers for square-sets start accumulating out there in the yarding lot. He was impatient to start moving lumber. But he couldn't shake off a feeling that things were too quiet; much too quiet to make him easy in his mind about Ganahl.

Ganahl had not come back. There had been no word of any kind from him. Kinstrey, therefore, had been forced to conclude that he must know about himself and Cass. Ganahl probably had picked up again with Moss and Raimo, and who could guess what he would do now? It was highly unlikely that he would just disappear. And even if he did there was still Raimo. Raimo intended to kill him. Killing was Raimo's trade.

Kinstrey's years of mill experience with Big Matt Calbraith now stood him in good stead. Of all the men who had come here with the wagons only Manogue and Dave Ebaugh and Cass had ever seen the inside of a sawmill, although Geehaw Jenkins had a natural aptitude for "tinkering," and Mike Cloona was an exceptionally able carpenter. But the important thing was that he knew and could trust these men.

Under Kinstrey's knowing direction they worked diligently and by nightfall of the second day they had the heart of the mill—the frame or "husk"— mounted on its steel wheels and light steel track. The drive pulley and saw also were mounted, and the drive connected to the power unit housed in the adjoining boiler shack.

By dark of the third day headblocks for holding the log and setworks for adjusting it successively to proper sawing position were in place, and Kinstrey estimated that a day of final checking and tests would put the mill in readiness to operate.

That night after grubpile he told Cass and Manogue, "I'll saw, tomorrow. You can help Pat set the headblocks, Cass."

Cass sat hunkered at the edge of the dwindling cook fire, moodily shaping a cigarette. "Sure," he said, "I'll be a big help, won't I? All the old man ever taught me about machinery."

Kinstrey dug teeth into his lower lip. Lately it seemed as if the kid hardly ever opened his mouth without rubbing him the wrong way. What Cass needed most, maybe, was to have a little of the slack taken out of him, and if he kept on this way someone would be bound to oblige him sooner or later.

Kinstrey forced restraint into his voice to say, "At least you'll be taught now," and then spoke to Manogue. "We'll have Wilmer Browne tend the firebox," he said. "Mike Cloona and Dave Ebaugh can handle the hooks and feed the carriage."

"I'll have to be brushin' up on me hand signals," muttered Manogue. "It's been a devil of a time since I've watched a sawyer and set a headblock."

"You won't need signals," Kinstrey replied. "I'm pretty sure Big Matt said the posts would all be twelve inches square. We'll make our lines twelve inches to start, anyhow. Then I'll have to get to the City and have a talk with Deidesheimer."

Cass said, "The timbers can be anywhere from twelve to fourteen inches square."

Kinstrey jerked around. "How do you know that?"

Cass looked smugly pleased by the startled glance Kinstrey shot at him. "It's in the contract," he replied. "I found a copy on the old man. He always carried anything like that around with him."

"We could have gone off half-cocked!" Kinstrey snapped. "Why didn't you mention this before?"

"Why didn't you ask me? Maybe I know a little something

once in a while." Sullenly, Cass twisted around from Kinstrey's accusing gaze, adding in a pettish voice, "I'll show you the contract if you like."

"Thanks!" Blood congested in Kinstrey's face as he lunged erect, trying to imagine what a stiff cuff across the mouth would do for that perpetually sullen expression Cass wore. He suppressed an impulse to find out, and wheeled. "I'm going to turn in," he stated abruptly; "good night."

Manogue scrambled to his feet. "Aw, man, what's yer hurry now? Show a tither av understandin' f'r th' lad, can't ye?"

Kinstrey didn't answer. He was already striding angrily away from the firelight and in another moment was lost in the darkness.

Tension mingled with a repressed excitement in Boise Kinstrey the next morning as he watched Mike Cloona and Dave Ebaugh cant a big log down onto the saw carriage while Pat Manogue then dogged it and set the headblocks. Cass stood in the runway behind the carriage and, to Kinstrey's pleased surprise, seemed to be observing the operation with a studying care.

Kinstrey stood with his hand at the carriage control lever, aware of a nervous impatience now as Manogue ran up the center movable block and dogged it to take any possible spring out the log. Looking back through the open rear of the mill, Kinstrey could see Wilmer Browne standing in the doorway of the boiler room. Browne waved to him, indicating steam was up, and now Kinstrey was aware of the familiar throbbing hum of smoothly oiled machinery and could feel the mill's timbers quivering with its vibration. Manogue had finished setting the end blocks and cranking them tight, and now as he signaled readiness Kinstrey levered the idle pulley to power pulley and the carriage glided forward.

A thudding bump was followed by a steady high whining as the huge circular saws ripped into the green pine and made their line, flinging a spray of sawdust high into the air. Elation swept Kinstrey. They were in business—at last! The freshly sawed board dropped to the board roll; then as Kinstrey gigged the carriage back to its starting position Manogue, aided by Cass, moved the log forward for the sawing of another line.

By the end of an hour operations appeared to have become routine, and with the separate drive belts of carriage and saws both working smoothly and the lofty black stack of the boiler shack unraveling a ribbon of thick blue smoke against the sky, a feeling of nervousness and anxiety that had been nagging at Kinstrey ever since his flare-up with Cass last night gradually began to ebb.

Cass was not only working out well with Manogue, he seemed to be taking an intelligent interest in what he was doing, and by noon, when the feed was shut down and the men knocked off for grubpile, Kinstrey estimated that the morning's operation had netted close to five thousand board feet of finished posts.

That, he knew, wasn't the kind of production Big Matt Calbraith would have shouted about but it was a start and in a couple of days he'd have the rust worked out of his system and be sawing his lines both faster and smoother.

He knew now, however, that he would very shortly be needing an augmented crew. A camp cook was an essential, for one thing; and for another some extra bullwhackers for hauling the timbers into town and a man or two handy with tools who could help Mike Cloona throw up a bunk house of sorts. Any day now this moderation in the weather could be expected to end and then either deep snow or intense cold could be a severe handicap in hauling their posts to Virginia City, even by ox team.

Finished with his meal of fried bacon and hot beans laced with blackstrap, Kinstrey finally found Cass sitting alone near one of the wagons and strode over to him.

"You're doing a good job on the headrig," he told him forthrightly. "Keep it up."

Cass looked both pleased and faintly embarrassed. "Thanks. I never had a chance to learn anything, before. I aim to, now."

"Cass, you said this morning that the contract called for delivery of sixty thousand feet a week to Ophir. When's that supposed to start?"

"Well, Marna wangled an extra week out of Deidesheimer. That gives us till the fifteenth."

"Six days from now." Kinstrey spoke with relief. "We'll make that, with a little hustle."

"Sure," Cass said.

From the direction of the mill a shout drew Kinstrey's attention. Wheeling, he saw Pat Manogue standing on a knoll a little forward of the boiler shack, pointing downward excitedly and then urgently beckoning him over.

"Now what?" Kinstrey sounded merely irritated but as he started toward the knoll a sense of foreboding curiously renewed itself in him. There were still so many things that could go wrong here, so many issues and problems that still were vague and unresolved in his mind. He heard Cass walking behind him but didn't stop until he reached the rise and Manogue said, nodding downward to the trail up the mountain, "We're havin' company—and rale fancy, from the look av that rig."

Looking down the slope, Kinstrey saw a surrey drawn by a team of light-stepping blood bays. Two minutes passed, and then as the surrey topped a last rise and came into the mill yard Kinstrey recognized its occupants. The drive was Lank Johnson and behind him in the rear seat sat Marna Calbraith and Effie Mannerheim.

Cass muttered at Kinstrey's back, "Something's up!" and then Kinstrey started toward the carriage. He saw Marna delicately flutter a lace handkerchief to him in greeting but before he could reach her Lank Johnson was on the ground and had his hands up to her. She laughed as he swung her lightly down, then said, looking around, "Why, Boise—I never expected you'd have this much done!"

Kinstrey said, "No? Why not?" and was about to step around her, seeing Effie Mannerheim still alone and unassisted on the rear seat, when Cass abruptly lunged in ahead of him.

"Let me help you," Cass said. "And welcome to Sawmill City."

Kinstrey threw a curt look past him at Effie Mannerheim; she said. "Why, thank you, Cass!" and then, oddly rankled, he pivoted at the sound of Marna's voice murmuring, "I believe you've met Mr. Johnson, haven't you, Boise?"

Lank Johnson stood with an affably extended hand on which a diamond the size of a large pea glittered.

"Glad to see you again, Kinstrey."

Today the promoter was wearing a lamb's wool jacket over his buckskin waistcoat. His gray broadcloth breeches held a sharp crease and now, in daylight, Kinstrey noticed that the beaded holster slung from his hip held a gun that was pearl-handled.

Kinstrey responded to the handshake grudgingly. "What brings you out this way, Johnson?"

"Business," replied Johnson evenly. "I told Miss Calbraith, here, that I'd like to have a look at your plant. I own a couple of mills myself, you know. It just might be I could make you a good offer on this one."

Kinstrey stiffened, snapped, "No deal, Johnson! This mill's not on the market."

"No?" The polite skepticism in Johnson's voice angered Kinstrey. "That's not just the way I understood it from Miss Calbraith," Johnson murmured.

Kinstrey spun, faced Marna. A fez-shaped red hat sat her head at a jaunty angle and made a vivid contrast with the gleaming black of her hair, but a look of petulant concern now marred her mouth as she reluctantly met Kinstrey's glance.

"I have been thinking of selling, Boise," she told him. "But mainly on your account."

Kinstrey gaped at her. "On *my* account!"

Marna said, pouting, "Does that surprise you? Ganahl's in town, Boise. And he's been heard making threats against you."

"Threats?" Kinstrey said. "Where'd you hear this?"

"I've seen Ganahl and Moss together myself. And Mr. Johnson, here, overheard some remarks Ganahl made one night in a saloon."

Kinstrey looked at Johnson. "What kind of remarks?"

"Unpleasant," Johnson said. "He was a little drunk but he made sense. Felt he'd had a pretty good thing of it out here, I guess. You upset his applecart. He made some threats." The promoter shrugged. "Of course, it could have been the whiskey talking. I'm just telling you what I heard."

"Oh, sure," Kinstrey said. He looked back at Marna; the deep blue of her eyes held a worried intensity, he thought.

"You don't need to worry about us," he told her; "we can take care of Ganahl." He paused, then added, with meager emphasis, "Just let him start anything."

"But Boise!"—Marna sounded querulous—"I am worried! You're more important to me than the mill. And Mr. Johnson has made me a very good offer. He—"

Cass strode forward from beside Effie Mannerheim. "I'll bet he has," he said.

Marna whirled around. "What do you mean by that?"

Cass said, "When were you ever interested in anything but yourself? Besides, how do you know *I'd* want to sell? Maybe you'd ought to ask me."

Marna's voice rose with scorn. "Ask *you!* Why should I? You're not even twenty-one yet. You've nothing to say about this!"

"Maybe this time I've got as much to say as you have!" Belligerently, Cass stepped up before his sister, his eyes riveted on her in cold fury. "You never did have to eat humble pie before, did you? All right. We'll see how you like the taste of it, for a change!"

Marna met his virulent gaze with soft contempt. "I wonder if you have the faintest notion what you are ranting about?" she retorted evenly. "If not, I suggest you leave us. Mr. Johnson is too busy a man to have time for nincompoops."

"Mr. Johnson will have time or me," Cass said flatly. "And if his time's so valuable maybe he won't want to waste it trying to buy something you can't sell him and I wouldn't if I could."

Kinstrey, watching Marna, now saw her tense, heard her voice flare.

"You haven't a thing to say about this!"

"You're right," agreed Cass. "But neither have you. Nobody can sell this plant without Boise Kinstrey's say-so."

Marna spun, her eyes wide, shocked, on Kinstrey. "Boise! Is this true?"

Kinstrey stood rigid, staring at Cass. "If it is, it's news to me, Marna."

"News or no news," Cass said, "it's true. The old man left a will. And I just happen to have a copy in my pocket. Like to see it?"

Marna blanched, gasped. "A will! I don't believe you!"

"You better had."

"But—I don't understand. You said Boise—"

Cass gloated. "I said Boise has the say-so here now, and he does. He's executor of the estate. That means you'll get yours when Boise says you can have it—and not before!"

13

Two MORNINGS LATER Kinstrey saddled his dun, which now was thoroughly rested and skittish, and prepared to leave camp for Virginia City. He had expected Cass to get his back up when he announced his intention of going alone, but Big Matt's son reacted with surprising equanimity.

"Go ahead," Cass told him, with no discernible rancor. "You don't have to worry about me."

They were standing at the edge of the camp clearing, a few yards from a temporary pen where the oxen were corralled. The morning was frosty, and the crisp mountain air carried a resinous pungency of freshly sawed pine.

"I'm not worried about you," Kinstrey said. "I just want you to understand I'd have had you along if you could be spared here. As it is, I'll need you to set for Pat. He'll saw today."

"I'll do my best."

"You've been doing fine. Keep it up and we'll make a double date of the trip next time."

With that Kinstrey stepped up into the saddle and took the reins of the dun. Cass didn't move. Kinstrey looked down at him and saw on his face that peculiar, irresolute look of a man trying to bring out words that are painful to speak.

"What's the matter?" he asked.

"Give my regards to Effie," Cass blurted.

"Why, sure," Kinstrey said. "Sure, I'll be glad to." He hesitated, then said gently, "Just don't let it throw you, though, if things shouldn't work out."

"They'll work out."

"Maybe; I hope so."

Cass abruptly changed. "What's that mean?" he demanded sharply.

"Well, there's a difference in ages. You're only nineteen. Effie's twenty-two."

"How the hell do you know how old she is?"

Kinstrey bit his lip. "Marna told me," he lied quickly.

86

Cass's dark eyes kindled, probing up at him with sudden suspicion. "Marna'd better mind her own business! You can tell her I said so."

"All right, *all* right," Kinstrey said softly. "Just keep your shirt on. I'm on your side—remember?"

Cass stared at him, his mouth rigid. "Are you?" he said. He gave Kinstrey a brittle last look, wheeled abruptly, then without a further word was striding away.

Kinstrey opened his mouth to call after him, then clicked it shut. What was the use? Sooner or later the kid would have to get his come-uppance. He'd only tried to prepare him— and got a snub for his pains. Now, in all likelihood, the kid would be getting himself all worked up again. And just when things had seemed to be smoothing out, for a change.

Kinstrey started the dun, his mouth clamped bleakly. Smoothing out? At the moment things weren't exactly smooth between him and Marna. But he'd fix that today. Then he'd hunt around and hire the extra hands he was now sure they were going to need here at camp. He especially wanted to find a cook; meals were too haphazard, and in time the men would be bound to start grumbling.

Kinstrey rode slowly down the pine-bordered trail, his eyes vacant with reflection. Cass had sure put the hair in the butter yesterday, with his sudden disclosure about the will. Evidently he'd had the will in his possession ever since Big Matt had died but had been saving his knowledge of it as a weapon to use against Marna, when and if he might need one. And yesterday had seemed the opportune time to him; he had been unable to resist pulling Marna down from her high horse.

A frown budded Kinstrey's mouth as he let the dun make its own careful pace down the twisting trail. When Marna had arrived at camp with Lank Johnson, she had seemed dead set on selling out to him. But only because she was worried; because she was afraid of what Frank Ganahl might do, Worried, she had said, for him. . . .

Kinstrey's eyes darkened. There was a willful streak in Marna just as there was in Cass, and later, when he had flatly refused to authorize sale of the mill, she had made no bones over her displeasure with him. She had become withdrawn, and her leave-taking, which had come shortly afterward, had been distinctly on the chilly side.

Anger surged in Kinstrey with his thought: Damn these people with chips on their shoulders! Then, suddenly, he was recalling the words he had spoken to Marna the night Big Matt had decamped; *I've got to know I could amount to something in my own right, instead of always walking in Big Matt's shadow.* But now, with Cass's revelation of the will, what had been changed? The will bound him anew. Big Matt's shadow still stalked him, even from the grave.

The frown frozen on Kinstrey's face deepened. Then he was remembering the night at Jules Mannerheim's, when for a few giddy moments he had held Marna and kissed her, and she had responded passionately to his embrace. But that day at camp she had been aloof and almost hostile, as if that moment at the store, and others like it, had never really happened. How could women be so changeable?

You damned fool! Kinstrey berated himself. That's how they hold a man; being fire one time and frost the next. He felt jarred, resentful, and at the same time heavily sick with some kind of vague longing that he could not quite analyze. Women! An image of Effie Mannerheim's alert, expressive face drifted into his mind and he felt exasperated anew.

He took the dun around a bend where the trail leveled briefly before it dipped again into another long downgrade. He thought now of the news Pat Manogue had given him this morning. He hadn't been unduly concerned about it—then. But now he had time to think about it and he no longer felt sure.

He had never seen the two men Ganahl had hired for work at the mill—men Manogue had, upon arriving in camp and finding Ganahl gone, immediately fired. But this morning one of the pair—a man named Ben Raymers—had driven in with a haul of logs from the Ophir Company. The teamster with him Manogue had never seen before, but he had been positive in his identification of Raymers.

"It was him all right," Manogue had affirmed with vehemence. "Gazebo with a pimply nose an' a hatch av black whiskers across his ugly pan!"

"Well," Kinstrey had said, "I guess we can't stop a man from earning an honest living. He didn't hang around camp, did he?"

"He knew better!"

"All right. Then just keep an eye on him the next time he brings in a load."

"There's no nade t'be tellin' me that! Not after th' way th' stupid cod beslobbered his damned logs all over our skid ramp back there."

"He's probably just new at the job," Kinstrey had discounted. But later, walking across to the mill, he had wondered. Raymers and his crew had dumped their load, helter-skelter, on the short grade leading down to the saw carriage, instead of in the regular storage area, above it.

All the logs previously delivered to the mill site had been unloaded and made ready in neat piles above the incline. These, however, would have to be wrestled and jacked around and probably used before other, better-seasoned sticks could be skidded down to the carriage. No real harm had been done, this once. But if the error should be repeated enough times . . .

A troubled look fogged the mild blueness of Boise Kinstrey's eyes. Had Raymers made an honest mistake or had someone paid him to scatter the load in such a way that extra handling and loss of time would be unavoidable? It was just possible that Ganahl had finally begun to strike back.

Kinstrey's eyes thinned, roving ahead. It did seem strange that, since his encounter with Raimo in Virginia City and Ganahl's disappearance from camp, things had been so quiet. Too quiet, now that he had time to think about it. Kinstrey's jaw locked. Was the truce over—at last?

He slowed down the dun. Maybe he ought to delay his visit to town for a day or two. Maybe it wasn't just accidental, Raymers showing up this way as boss of one of Ophir's hauling crews. Maybe, if he *didn't* go back—

A sound of hoofbeats was suddenly loud and strong behind Kinstrey. Abruptly alert, he swung the dun off the road and twisted around in the saddle. A rider hammering down the long grade immediately behind him was pressing his horse to a full gallop.

Kinstrey was reaching forward to slip his Sharps from its saddle boot when the rider saw him and slowed, and in that moment he recognized Cass Calbraith and came back straight in the saddle with a sudden catch of breath.

Cass was hatless, his face soot-blackened and his clothes disheveled. Froth flew from the mouth of his horse as he pulled it in so abruptly that it reared, almost throwing him out of the saddle.

Foreboding made a sickening lunge through Kinstrey with his sharp demand. "What's wrong?" and then, for the first time sniffing the acrid stink of smoke in the air, he knew.

Cass's eyes were bloodshot. He had his horse quieted now, and spoke in hoarse, jerky gasps.

"Fire!" he blurted. "Somebody—set—they—they—Dave—"

Kinstrey cut in tersely, "What about Dave?" and wheeled the dun with a cranky rein jerk.

Suddenly he was aware of Cass's face, white as bone dust behind the oily smudges smearing his cheeks.

"Dave's dead. Shot! They—"

Kinstrey swore as he gut-hooked the dun. The startled animal took two great leaps before stretching out. Kinstrey continued cutting it with his spurs as he raced back up the mountain.

A sight of blackened desolation greeted Boise Kinstrey's eyes as he finally rode his hard-blowing dun into the center of camp and paused to take stock of things. In a semi-sheltered clearing that graded to a lower level, some thirty yards to his left, the charred skeletons of two Espenshieds still winked with sparks through a dense pall of smoke, while a third, with only its tilts burned off, stood otherwise intact. The two remaining wagons appeared to have escaped damage entirely.

Kinstrey let out his breath in a slow gust of relief as his gaze explored forward. Allowing fear to overpower his imagination, he had visualized the entire camp as a gutted ruin. It was not. Ahead of him some fifty yards the mill and boiler shed stood open to view and neither building seemed to have been marred. He swung in the saddle to look back. A short distance to his rear the camp's oxen stood stolidly in their pen, staring out at him with the stoic indifference of their kind. They too apparently had been unmolested.

Slowly, it began to dawn on Kinstrey that actual physical damage had been small. Loss of two Espenshieds was relatively unimportant; the principal costly and tragic loss in all this was the death of Dave Ebaugh.

Boise Kinstrey's eyes held a somber vacancy as he now gigged the dun and swung it left, starting downward toward the wagon clearing. Here, on lower ground, the wagons had been almost out of sight of the sawmill, beyond. And here the raiders had struck—apparently with impunity.

Kinstrey rode on slowly and presently came upon Mike Cloona and Geehaw who, armed with water-soaked blankets, were beating at a heap of still smoldering rags in the bed of the Espenshied with the incinerated hood.

At the sound of the dun's hoofbeats both fire fighters wheeled tiredly, peering up at their mounted visitor out of bloodshot eyes.

"Cass rode down after me," Kinstrey said in response to their slightly befuddled stares at him. "What's happened to the others?"

Geehaw Jenkins took a soggy bandanna from his jeans' pocket and swiped it across his char-streaked forehead.

"Pat's with Wilmer Browne," he said. "They're diggin' a grave. You heard about Dave?"

"I heard. How did that happen, Geehaw?"

"Nobody rightly knows. He was the only man outside—messin' around with that last load of logs that was dropped all to hell an' gone down by the saw carriage. Reckon he seen the smoke and ran. Nobody heard the shot—machinery makin' too much noise, I guess. Anyway, Pat wanted Dave and when Dave didn't answer his call he went out to see what was wrong."

Mike Cloona was a small, dark, wiry man, inclined to taciturnity and a sometimes mordant humor.

"There was quite a bit wrong," he said now with dry understatement.

Hoofbeats sounded behind Kinstrey. He pulled around in the saddle and saw Cass. Cass rode up beside him, looking sweaty and ill-humored.

"What're we going to do now?" he asked.

A plaintive irritability in his voice rubbed Kinstrey the wrong way.

"What do you think?" he said. "Saw wood—naturally."

Cass nodded to the two gutted wagons. "You'll freight a lot of posts in them."

Kinstrey bit down on the angry retort he felt tugging at his tongue and shuttled a glance between Geehaw and Cloona.

"Anybody see any of the raiders?" he asked now.

"Nobody," Cloona said, then added grimly, "Except Dave."

"Dave must've surprised 'em though," amplified Geehaw. "They only had time to throw oil on two of the wagons. That third there—" He nodded to the Espenshied with the burned tilts—"just caught from the others."

Kinstrey sniffed and could detect a strong taint of coal oil still in the air. He frowned, asking, "How many were in the raid? There must have been tracks."

"There was," said Geehaw. "Tracks of three horses. They went north, but that don't mean nothin'. There's a slew of old wood roads up in these backwoods. They probably split up soon's they were out of camp."

"Probably," Kinstrey murmured. He turned in the saddle, putting his attention back on Cass. "Cass, find Pat, will you? Tell him to have these good wagons hauled up nearer the mill. He'd better move the oxen, too; the men can knock a new pen together."

Cass scowled. "Where're you gonna be?"

"In the City," Kinstrey said. "Tell Pat I want guards kept posted day and night. The mill can be shut down till I get back."

Cass gaped. "The City?" he said. "You're going to the City—*now?*"

Kinstrey swung the dun. "I'll be back in the morning, tell Pat."

"*Morning!* But Boise—"

Kinstrey looked back. "Damn it, I'm not going to argue with you! We've got to have more men here. I'm going to find some." He gigged his horse. And suddenly he felt sore and bitter and lonely, and filled with a smoldering rage that made him almost fear what he might do, today, to anyone who crossed him.

14

IT WAS HIGH NOON when Boise Kinstrey rode up Virginia City's C Street. In front of Jules Mannerheim's mercantile he pulled in, swung down from the saddle, and then tied the dun to an iron hitching post in front of the store's wood-awninged front.

Both street and sidewalks were, as usual, in colorful flux. Conestoga bells jangled as heavy freighters drawn by oxen and mules plowed sluggishly upstreet and down. Traffic snarls were continuous, and apparently could be untangled only by a flow of sulphurous oaths and an exchange of abusive invective between drivers.

A motley crowd also jammed the board walks. Everyone seemed in a hurry, with little time for talk and none whatever for civility. All of them money-mad, Kinstrey thought darkly, and started across the walk.

He pushed his way through a crowd of scuffling miners to reach the store's front door, and as he did it came open suddenly and Effie Mannerheim stepped outside. She was dressed for the street, wearing her blue cape and a little black turban hat ornamented with a sprig of gold braid. Seeing him, she stopped and uttered a surprised cry.

"Why, Boise!" she said. "We didn't expect you in town today."

Her use of his first name startled him faintly, although he now remembered having told her to call him by it. It was like her, he reflected, to remember—and to have taken his invitation at face value.

"We've had some trouble out at the camp," he admitted reluctantly. "I came in to see Phil Deidesheimer. And to hire some extra men if I can."

The way she cocked her head up at him made him think of an alert chipmunk. "I hope it wasn't bad trouble, Boise."

"It was. We had a man killed. And two wagons burned."

"That's awful! How did it happen?"

"Don't know much about it. I was on my way to town, and the men were in the mill. All except Dave Ebaugh. He's the one they shot."

"What a terrible thing!" Effie Mannerheim's mouth compressed; then she murmured, "I wish there was some way I could help you, Boise. I haven't forgotten how kind you were to let me join your train at Tipton's."

Kinstrey stared at her with a look of blank surprise. "Why, I wasn't even civil to you that day!"

She smiled at him. "You had a lot on your mind. You still have."

"That's the truth. Is Marna in?"

Effie Mannerheim seemed to give a little start at the question. "No," she said. "Mr. Johnson—no, she's out."

Kinstrey stiffened. "What's this about Johnson?"

"Oh, it's nothing. Except that Marna's been wanting to go through one of the mines, and Mr. Johnson has a connection with the Gould and Curry. So today he arranged to have her taken down in one of the hoists."

"Fine." Kinstrey's tone was bitter. "She picked just the day for it." He turned. "Well, I'll mosey on, I guess. Ophir office upstreet?"

"Yes. I'm going that way; maybe you'd like me to show you."

Kinstrey said, "I could use a guide," and they started down from the store porch together.

"What kind of extra help do you need?" she asked, as they made slow progress along the crowded board walk.

"Two or three men who can be generally useful," he told her. "And a camp cook. I guess that'll be the hardest to find."

"Yes; I imagine it will. A lot of people come to Uncle Jules, though, to ask about jobs. Did you plan to drop back to the store later?"

"Well, I did want to see Marna. What time do you think she'll be back?"

Effie Mannerheim's voice cooled faintly. "I really couldn't say. She's not talkative about her plans to me."

Kinstrey grunted, said, "Well, I'll drop by anyway," and then Effie halted, and he realized they were in front of a hardware store.

"I have an errand in here for Uncle Jules," she told him.

"The Ophir Office is on the next corner. That gray-painted building."

"Well, I'll see you later then—in case you do hear of somebody I could get for a grub-wrangler."

She looked disturbed for a second, then asked, "You think it was Frank Ganahl who was behind your trouble at camp this morning?"

"Not much doubt of that." He told her then about Ben Raymers, and Pat Manogue's identification of him as one of the two new men Ganahl had hired to supplement the camp crew before Kinstrey and Cass had shown up to upset his plans.

"It's a shame," she murmured, when he had finished. "I mean all this trouble happening just when the market for lumber is the highest it's ever been."

Kinstrey stared at her. "How do you know that?"

She reacted with surprise to the sharpness in his voice. "Why, simply enough. I heard at the store just yesterday that Ophir is paying up to two hundred dollars a thousand feet now. Gould and Curry likewise."

"Two hundred!" Kinstrey sounded incredulous. "Are you sure?"

"I heard it from Ezra Ball, one of the shift bosses at the Gould and Curry. The mines are simply devouring lumber. They can't get—"

"Excuse me," Kinstrey cut in abruptly. "I'm late. I'll have to scoot along."

He was aware of her staring after him as if he had suddenly taken leave of his senses but he was in too much of a hurry to linger for explanations. The Ophir office was a story-and-a-half frame building painted a dull slate gray, and by the time he reached it and entered the front waiting room he could feel his heart pounding with a thin, irregularly angry beat.

To his surprise he had no trouble getting in to see the Ophir's superintendent. A front office clerk simply went to a rear door after he had stated his business, knocked on it, and in another moment came back, telling him, "Go ahead through. Nobody's with Mr. Deidesheimer right now."

He found Philip Deidesheimer, a square-visaged man with a dark spade beard and broadly heavy shoulders, seated at a flat-topped desk piled mountainously with a disorderly array of maps and rolled blueprints.

"Mr. Kinstrey?" Deidesheimer said, and nodded courteously toward a chair. "Sit down. Glad you dropped by; I've been wanting to have a talk with you."

There was anger and nervous tension in Kinstrey and for an irresolute moment he ignored the chair and stood tracked, remembering words, and a man now dead, and the responsibility he had taken to be that man's living voice, now. *Be a hard boot! Walk heavy and make a big noise. It's the squeaky wheel gets the grease.*

big Matt Calbraith's rule of thumb. And, when Big Matt had been alive, his. But now . . .?

Boise Kinstrey looked down at the gray, shrewd, quietly scrutinizing eyes of the man behind the desk and suddenly knew, by some intuitiveness beyond reason, that Big Matt's formula would fail if tried here.

He sat down in the chair Philip Deidesheimer had pointed out to him. "Maybe you've been wanting a talk with me," he said, "but all I've wanted is to avoid one with you."

The Ophir superintendent's chuckle sounded deep in his throat and it was like a plug suddenly pulled out of Kinstrey, draining away the pent-up fury and frustration that had been fermenting in him.

"You know something?" Philip Deidesheimer said. "The second you walked in here I could see you had a chip on your shoulder. And I was hoping you wouldn't ask me to knock it off."

Kinstrey's grin was a little forced. "Why?"

Deidesheimer chuckled again. "Because I'd have obliged you. And that's never the way to get anything settled."

"Maybe you're right."

"I know I am. You've got troubles—I can see that. What's on your mind, my friend?"

Kinstrey hesitated, then under the older man's disarming frankness abruptly unbent. "You asked for this, remember!" He told then of all that had happened in town and subsequently at the mill site, concluding with a lugubrious shrug, "And now we're going to have to furnish you with posts for just half the price you'll be paying other suppliers."

"You think so?" murmured the superintendent.

"I don't think. I know what the contract calls for."

With casual unhurriedness Philip Deidesheimer took two cigars from a box on his desk, tossed one to Kinstrey and placed the other between his teeth, biting off its sealed tip.

"Light up," he said.

Kinstrey struck a match, held out the flame to Deidesheimer's cigar, then applied it to his own, puffing.

"Now," Deidesheimer said, tilting back in his leather-upholstered swivel chair, "let's forget about the contract for a minute."

"Forget about it!"

"On my invitation." The mine official smiled, waved cigar dismissively. "Right now contracts don't mean much in the Utah Territory. Suppose you decided to sell your lumber somewhere else. Do you think I could stop you?"

"If you couldn't the courts could."

Philip Deidesheimer shook his head. "This is dog-eat-dog country, my friend. We haven't got any courts yet. And when we do have, the dockets are going to be too jammed with boundary-line disputes to leave much room for any little two-bit lumber contracts."

Kinstrey gaped at the strong, quiet face of the man behind the littered desk. "Are you inviting me to tear up our contract and sell lumber wherever we please?"

Deidesheimer ignored the question to ask, "You know about my square-sets for supporting the walls of a mine?"

Kinstrey nodded. "Yes. They're like the cells of a honeycomb. You keep on building new cells as you prospect a vein."

"We build a pyramid of cribs, that rise constantly," amplified Deidesheimer. "Then we have to lay floors of strong plank upon each set. On top of that we have to build steps that lead to trap doors from floor to floor. You can imagine the amount of wood it takes to shore up just one drift."

"Yes."

"Now about this two hundred dollar price. So far we've only gone that high once—a time when we'd almost run out of timbers and had to outbid Gould and Curry on a shipment. I understand, though, they've paid as high as that since."

"So I heard."

"Well, anyway, the average price we've been paying is a

hundred and fifty dollars a thousand. In time that will un-
doubtedly go higher. If it does you'll get the extra money."

Kinstrey was thunderstruck. "You mean you'll pay us a
hundred and fifty now, in spite of the contract?"

The mine superintendent's mouth curved a faint smile
around the cigar clamped in it. "Oh, but I expect a lot in return."

"What's that?"

"Wood," answered Philip Deidesheimer succinctly. "And I
need it fast—faster all the time. I'd pay almost any kind of
bonus you'd ask for speeding up deliveries."

"You haven't had even one yet."

"I know that. And I'm making allowances. But you'll take
care of Ganahl."

Kinstrey's teeth bit down on his lower lip, slid away.
"What makes you so sure of that?"

"Sizing up a man is part of my job. I don't often make
mistakes."

"Thanks for the compliment."

"Call it an estimate." The mine superintendent smiled.
"One that I'll expect dividends from—later."

Kinstrey remembered his first morning at camp. He'd
crossed the creek, looked down that denuded east slope of the
mountain. And had then been seized with the idea that had
remained pocketed at the back of his mind ever since. . . .

His eyes probed at Philip Deidesheimer across the desk.
"Mr. Deidesheimer, maybe you could start collecting some of
those dividends right now."

"Yes? How?"

"We're supposed to haul to you here at Ophir; I know
that. But our main business should be milling lumber, not delivering it."

"Go ahead."

"All right! Suppose I could show you a way to cut freighting time way down—save ten, maybe twelve miles of travel
each way. Would Ophir be willing to help out with the
hauling if we—"

"Help with it! Man, we might do all of it!" Sparks flew
from Philip Deidesheimer's cigar with the suddenness of his
heave forward in the swivel chair. He leaned tensely across
the desk. "What have you got in mind?"

"A flume," Kinstrey said.

"Flume? What d'you mean—where?"

"Down the east slope of the mountain out there," elaborated Kinstrey. "We could divert water from the creek. It would work; I'm sure of it. And at the foot of the slope there's a little rill of spring water that runs into a natural basin where there's a pond. That would take care of our run-off."

"By George, I believe you're right!" Philip Deidesheimer drew on his cigar with short, excited puffs. "You've studied the ground?"

"All I need to. There's a small ravine or two—a few other sink spots. But I can bridge those."

"How soon can you start? What will you need?"

"With some extra men I could start first thing in the morning."

"I'll furnish the men. How about money?"

"My men will wait till I sell our first shipment of posts. But I don't know about—"

"I'll have a dozen men out at your camp by nine tomorrow morning. Their wages will be paid at this end. What else do you need?"

"Nothing," Kinstrey said.

Philip Deidesheimer drew a pad toward him, scribbled briefly, then tore off the sheet and handed it across the desk to Kinstrey.

"Use this any way you like," he said. "I'll deduct the amount from whatever we owe you for your first shipment of posts."

Kinstrey stared down at the small slip of paper clutched in his hand. "Five hundred dollars," he muttered. "But I don't need—"

Philip Deidesheimer had stood and was now holding out his hand. "Good-by," he said. "Just hand the slip in to the cashier on your way out. You'll need a little ready cash."

Kinstrey heaved up from his chair and fumblingly shook hands. "All right, Mr. Deidesheimer. Thanks. I just hope you won't have any regrets about this."

"Let me worry about that." Philip Deidesheimer sat down. He picked up a rolled blueprint from the pile on his desk and spreading it murmured, "You're a man of ideas, Mr. Kinstrey. I predict you'll do well with your mill." And then he seemed to forget Kinstrey entirely.

Kinstrey stood with awkward indecisiveness a moment, then turned. At the door he swung around and glanced back. Philip Deidesheimer had seemed almost carelessly indifferent to the threat posed to the mill by Frank Ganahl. Did he really understand the kind of man Ganahl was?

As he stood hesitating the Ophir's superintendent glanced up abruptly from his blueprint.

"Something else, Kinstrey?"

"This—Ganahl," Kinstrey began, then at the sudden look of impatience in Deidesheimer's eyes checked it. "No," he said. "No, there's nothing else, thanks." He wheeled around. He opened the door very softly and went out.

A feeling of buoyant optimism imbued Boise Kinstrey as he left the Ophir office and moved out again into the busy tide of traffic on the board walks. He now had not only cash in his pocket but the promise of strong support for the mill from no less a person than Philip Deidesheimer, one of the most important men in Virginia City. What more could he ask? What more, now, could Marna herself ask?

Kinstrey walked abstractedly, unconscious of the jam of people around him. At camp, provisions were running dangerously low. With this advance from Ophir he could replenish the camp's larder and in addition give each man a couple of weeks' wages. And tomorrow he'd get started on the flume. Deidesheimer had said—

He thought he heard his name called—at first only a vague impression above the street's boisterous and continuous hullabaloo. Then he heard it again, nearer— "Boise!"—and saw Marna Calbraith. She had just ducked under the hames of a team of lead mules halted at the curbside, and now as she stepped up to the board walk, her face prettily flushed from running, Kinstrey saw Lank Johnson behind her.

"We were on the other side of the street," she panted, halting in front of him. "I thought I'd never make you hear. We've been looking for you."

She was wearing the red hat shaped like a fez and had a gray fur thrown around her neck, giving her an addedly casual and jaunty look.

"Looking for me?" Kinstrey asked, a little aloofly. "What for?"

"We just saw Effie," Marna explained, "and she told us

about the trouble at camp." She placed a hand on his arm, looking up at him appealingly. "Oh, Boise! Now can't you see I was right the other day? Things can't go on this way—they just *can't*."

Kinstrey's jaw was rocky. "You're right," he said.

Marna's glance up at the thin, not unhandsome face of Lank Johnson, now standing beside her, was quickly, covertly triumphant.

"Then you *will* hear Mr. Johnson's offer?" she said to Kinstrey.

"No," Kinstrey said.

"But you just said—you agreed—" Marna was flustered, her voice angry with surprise.

"I agreed things couldn't go on this way." Kinstrey's own voice was flatly calm. "Well, they can't. And they won't."

Johnson said, "Marna? I told you. This isn't the time to talk about it." He looked sympathetically at Kinstrey, adding, "Kinstrey's just been through some tough trouble. Anyhow, if he doesn't want to sell, that's his business."

Angrily, Marna swung to face Kinstrey again. "Boise, I think you're just being a stubborn know-it-all! Father sank every penny he had in those wagons and the mill equipment—you know that! So what if Ganahl keeps you so busy you never *do* get to sawing any logs? How are you going to buy food—let alone pay *wages*?"

Kinstrey said levelly, "I'll saw logs. *And* take care of Ganahl."

"How? And what about your men? They won't work indefinitely for just a lick and a promise."

"They won't have to." Kinstrey took a packet of bills from his pocket and briefly displayed it. "The men will be paid tomorrow morning," he said, and then before Marna could ask, disclosed the source of the money.

"Well," Lank Johnson said, with conviction, "that ought to take care of *that*." He held out his hand. "Good luck, Kinstrey. And no hard feelings. I'll admit I'd have liked your plant. But something else will turn up. It always does."

The tall man's apparent sincerity won Kinstrey's grudging respect. He shook hands. "Thanks," he said, and ran a tentative glance back to Marna. "Now are you satisfied?" he said.

Marna said in a thinned voice, "I've only been thinking about you, Boise."

Johnson said, "We're heading back to Mannerheim's. Going that way, Kinstrey?"

"I haven't had lunch yet. I'll see you later."

Watching them push on into the busy street throng, Kinstrey didn't move for a long moment. Then he saw the sign, MACKWOOD'S DINING ROOM. OPEN ALL HOURS. He headed toward it.

15

IN MACKWOOD'S, which was dirty, crowded and filled with the smoke of greasy cooking, he paid two dollars for what purported to be a prime cut of Mexican beef, but after he had eaten and left the place it was with a dissatisfied feeling that his hunger had only been held at bay, not overcome.

On top of that he had heard disturbing talk in the eating house—of decreasing food supplies which later might develop into serious shortages if Sierra passes became snow-clogged and supply trains to Virginia City were cut off.

The rumors led to his return to Jules Mannerheim's store, where, on what he thought might be a far-sighted impulse, he ordered a wagonload of provisions to be sent out to the camp.

Jules Mannerheim brushed aside his attempt to pay on the spot, after he'd explained about the advance from Philip Deidesheimer. "*Ach!* Later," he mumbled with a flutter of hands, and then hurried to the front of the store to serve a customer who had just come in.

Effie Mannerheim, working behind the counter arranging displays, smiled at his discomfiture. "Uncle Jules probably thinks you should pay your men first," she told him.

"Maybe he should have grabbed while the grabbing was good," Kinstrey replied a little thinly.

"Nonsense! Will tomorrow morning be all right for the provisions? I can get Soldier Charley to drive out with them."

"That will be plenty of time. Lucky for us, the wagon we kept our food stores in wasn't burned."

"That was lucky. And it reminds me. Lank Johnson was here a while ago. He brought Marna back; she had a headache and has gone to bed."

"So?"

"He wants to see you."

"Me? What about—did he say?"

"Why, yes. He saw a man going into Blue Chip Billy's—

103

says it was a man he saw having a confab with Frank Ganahl the other night."

Kinstrey became alert. "The night Johnson heard Ganahl make those threats against me?"

Effie said, looking disturbed, "I don't know. Anyway, he wanted me to tell you that this man's left hand and forearm was bandaged up, but that part of the hand was exposed and looked as if it had been burned."

"Burned!" Kinstrey abruptly went rigid. "How long ago was this—when did he see this man?"

"Not long ago, I guess; he didn't say. He did say he'd be at Orndoff and McGee's for the next hour, if you wanted to drop in there."

"It's not Mr. Johnson I want to drop in on." Kinstrey's tone was grim. "Tell him I'm obliged, though, if you see him." He was starting to wheel when her voice caught and stopped him.

"Boise? Do you think you ought to go alone? Blue Chip Billy's has a bad name. It's a hangout for—"

She stopped at his terse interruption, "Don't worry. This might only be a coincidence; probably is."

"Then—be careful."

"I'm always careful." He turned impatiently.

"Boise . . . ? I'm sending a man out to you—Joe LeBeau. He's worked in sawmills. A little Frenchman. He—"

Kinstrey had started away. He jerked around irritatedly. "That's fine, Effie; thanks. We'll talk about it later."

"Boise, wait! I think I've found a cook, too." He was striding rapidly now and she threw her voice after him, lifting it almost angrily. "Boise, do you hear me? A cook. *Cook!*"

He had reached the door. He looked back across his shoulder at her and for an instant a fleeting grin relaxed the tautness of his jawline. He waved. Then he was gone.

Blue Chip Billy's was a dive. It was a low, flat-roofed building, bordered on one side by a trash-littered lot and on the other by a shabby frame structure to which it was united by a short enclosed passageway. The next-door establishment went under the name of Red Chip Rosie's, and was a honky-tonk.

Boise Kinstrey approached the cafe warily. His first excitement at Effie's news had had time to cool, and now caution tempered his eagerness. He reached the rubbish-strewn lot and halted.

The day was raw and bleak, with a hint of snow squalls in a steadily rising wind. Kinstrey's eyes thinned abstractedly. He had lost his feeling of sureness about this, and his uncertainty made him uneasy. Maybe the man with the bandaged arm really was one of the firebugs. But suppose he had the others with him?

A frown etched itself on Kinstrey's forehead. He hadn't thought of that possibility before. Maybe he *should* have dropped in to see Lank Johnson before coming on here, alone. Johnson had acted like a pretty good sport about the mill. Maybe Johnson would have come here with him. He could still turn around, go back. But should he?

Kinstrey's frown tucked in his lower lip as he made his decision. No! If the man was still in there he might leave. It was too late to turn back. He'd have to play this lone-handed; figure some way to toll the man outside, if there were others with him. Maybe he could finagle him out into this junk-cluttered lot. Then . . .

Abruptly, Kinstrey started across the lot, side-stepping heaps of splintered crates, broken crockery and miscellaneous rubbish. Behind the saloon he saw with relief the rear door he had hoped he might find there. The door was slightly ajar. He pulled it open fully and stepped into a shedlike unheated room.

A storeroom, evidently. A bundle of mops and brooms stood in a disorderly assortment amid a tangle of pails. Kinstrey strode past a pair of oil drums that rested on a plank trestle supported by sawhorses; he opened another door. Instantly a gush of warm air and a barrage of sound rushed at him. He walked out onto a sawdust-sprinkled floor, pausing, then, to look around.

He was in the barroom; adjoining it on the left was a broad alcove. A couple of dozen men stood at the bar drinking; two not far from where Kinstrey was standing gave him a sudden sharp look, then swung their glances with what seemed almost a deliberate effort at disinterestedness. Neither man had a bandaged arm. But why had they stared at him, then looked away so abruptly? Or had he only imagined that?

A sudden whooping and loud hand-clapping drew Kinstrey's gaze to the alcove. A crowd of rough-garbed men were swinging a thinly clad girl to the top of a battered-looking piano. Below her, a thin man with his shirtsleeves rolled up and a brown derby cocked back on his head ran a brief capriccio across the keyboard and the room stilled.

The girl's thickly roughed face took on a set, implastic smile as the piano player cued her; then as his fingers assaulted the keys she wriggled her hips in time to the beat and began to sing:

> Oh, he married her, he married her,
> How could he be so cruel?
> She was so poor, she had to use
> His wooden leg for fuel!

The lyrics became bawdy as the girl raucously sang on, but Kinstrey no longer was noticing her. A man had just stepped back from the crowd jammed in the alcove, a man with his left arm bandaged up to the elbow!

A sudden exultation swept Kinstrey. With but one thought in mind—to draw the man outside, where he could talk to him alone—he strode into the alcove and tapped him on the shoulder.

"Talk with you a minute, friend?"

The man, clodlike of frame, turned slowly, showing Kinstrey a stolid face and reddened, wet-looking eyes.

"Me, mister? Sure; go ahead," he responded without visible surprise.

"Rather talk out back if that's all right with you." Kinstrey nodded toward the door through which he had entered the barroom. "This involves a claim. There might be something in it for you."

"Yeah? You don't say." A narrowed look which gleamed in the man's eyes, then was gone, Kinstrey read for cupidity. The man said, "All right; come on!" and turned. Kinstrey swung to follow him, missing the covert glances that passed between this man and the two at the end of the bar who had drawn his notice earlier.

Kinstrey was forced to hurry to keep up with his man, who already was through the doorway and into the storeroom. Kinstrey went through and had taken two steps when it struck him belatedly that the man's acquiescence might have come a little too willingly.

The padded footfall in back of him was swift, barely audible, and he jerked around more from an instinctive feeling of danger than any actual awareness of it.

His breath caught as he saw the gun uplifted above his head and, startlingly near, heard a woman's clear, high scream. His arm shot out, but the gun barrel then was a tangential dark streak sweeping down and could not be deflected.

He felt the concussion and shock against the side of his head. He tried to grapple with his assailant but his legs were no longer steady. From the doorway a percentage girl was staring into the room, her face rigid with fright. A dark figure sprang past Kinstrey and slammed the door on her.

Through a remote buzzing in Kinstrey's ears he heard a click. *Key? Key twisted in a lock?* ...

He was trying to hold on but there was a great, thick fog swirling around him and it didn't seem to matter, really. When the man hit him again he slumped. A boot hovered, then ground down on his face. Rupturing of flesh and bone tore an agonized cry from him. The room sank away in blackness. ...

Boise Kinstrey was first vaguely conscious of a hum of voices, a blur of faces around him. Then someone said, "Here's Doc Secord; let him through," and Kinstrey heard stertorous breathing beside him and became aware of a pair of thick-wristed hands fumbling in a small black leather case.

Something had been jammed under his nose and a voice gruffly said, "Breathe!"

Kinstrey obeyed. The sharp reek of ammonium carbonate stung his nostrils and made his eyes water. He gasped and jerked upright.

"Whew!" He grinned weakly.

The doctor said, "Help him into a chair, somebody. I'm getting too damned fat to work on a man leaning over."

Kinstrey felt himself hoisted to his feet, half-carried. He slumped in a chair.

Secord took gauze, court plaster and a roll of bandage from his leather kit. He went very methodically to work and at the end of five minutes told Kinstrey, "You've got a busted nose and are just damned lucky you've got such a thick skull. That'll be eight bits."

Kinstrey was surprised at his own steadiness as he stood up. His broken nose throbbed painfully and his head felt tender and sore but those were minor ailments that would quickly pass. As Doc had said he'd just been lucky. He might have been killed, or at the least badly crippled.

He murmured, "I'm obliged to you, Doc," and reached to the pocket inside his mackinaw. He could feel his heart give a great, hollowing pound as his fingers touched emptiness. It was nothing that his own wallet, with some thirty-five or forty dollars in it, was gone. Gone, too, was the thick packet of bills that he had carried with him from the Ophir office. The five hundred dollars that had been his insurance against further delaying troubles out at camp.

In the wild hope that he might have transferred the money to another part of his clothes Kinstrey searched frantically through his other pockets. He found exactly what he had known he would find—nothing.

A dryness was filling his throat. He became aware of the doctor's keen blue eyes studying him shrewdly.

"Never mind if you're broke," Secord said.

Kinstrey stared at him with angry frustration. "I'm no bum! I had money—till those blacklegs jumped me. They—"

"Forget it! Come see me in a couple days and I'll have another look at that nose."

The medico was waddling away and Kinstrey stared after him with an incensed and mounting bitterness. A voice beside him said huskily, "Mister?" and pivoting around sharply he recognized the woman who had solicited him on the street the other night. "I'm Bessie Talbot," she said. "Remember me?"

Kinstrey nodded. "I remember."

"You were hunting a man named Moss. Another called Raimo?"

"That's right. What about it?"

"Those men who jumped you. I've seen them before."

Kinstrey came alert. "Yes? Where?"

"In here," replied Bessie Talbot. "They were with Moss and another man. A tall, blond fella with kind of a cleft in his chin."

Kinstrey tensed. "How many men came after me? You know their names?"

"I know one—Red Danahy. He used to be a swamper

here. I didn't know the fella with him. Or the one with the bandaged arm."

"So. There were three," murmured Kinstrey.

"I got suspicious when I seen Red and the fella with him follow you to the door. I went over but I was too late. Maybe you heard me scream."

"Yes." Kinstrey nodded absently. "Well, thanks, Bessie. When was it you saw them in here with Moss and the blond-haired man?"

"Oh, maybe two, three nights ago."

"I'll have some money in a few days. I won't forget you, Bessie."

"Ah, I didn't tell you this for money. I don't go for rough stuff, that's all."

"You *and* me," Kinstrey said. He turned. "Thanks again. Thanks a lot, Bessie."

He started for the front bat-wings. Some of the miners crowded along the bar eyed him curiously but none spoke. A man had been jumped, slugged, rolled. It happened all the time. Come day, go day. In Virginia City a man wasn't condoled with for being a sucker.

The piano was still clattering, the girl singer still blatting lustily to its accompaniment. Outside, Kinstrey took one short glance upstreet, then swung in the direction of Jules Mannerheim's. Mannerheim was out when he got there, Effie behind the counter, alone. She started at the sight of his battered face.

"Boise! What on earth happened?"

He told her, grudgingly, almost curtly, then said, "I'm heading back to camp—this afternoon. Tell Marna I asked for her."

For the first time he could remember, her voice held censure for him. "Boise, why weren't you careful? You could have taken Mr. Johnson with you. I told you that was a bad place."

"All right. You told me. Now let's forget it."

Her eyes shrank under his curtness. "Very well. But I can wake Marna if you like. She might want to—"

Kinstrey's laugh was bitter, interrupting her. "Know what a sucker I've been? I'll bet she would! She'd be all set for me then. I'd have to sell out just to get her off my back."

Effie Mannerheim said quietly, "You won't sell out."

"Won't I? How do you know?"

"I think I know you. You'll just fight harder because of this." She looked earnestly at him across the counter. "Boise, I sent a couple men out to your camp. This Joe LeBeau I told you about and one other, a man named Milt Mygatt."

He stared at her, puzzled and at the same time vaguely disturbed. Why did she take all this trouble for him? Surely she didn't think—

He stopped thinking himself and gruffly said, "I'd better be pushing my freight; thanks for sending those men." Then he turned.

She said softly, "Good-by, Boise. I'll see you get those provisions first thing in the morning," but in his deep preoccupation he barely heard her.

The dun stood hipshot out at the store hitching post. He untied it and swung up to the saddle, only at that instant aware of Lank Johnson hurrying toward him from the store front.

Johnson came up to him, flustered-looking and a little breathless. "I just heard the news," he panted. "Lord, Lord, man, why didn't you come to me first?"

Here we go again, thought Kinstrey wearily. Still, this man had only tried to help him—and against his own interests, too.

"I didn't want to bother you," Kinstrey said.

"But I *expected* you to see me first. When you didn't come I went over to Billy's myself. That's how I found out."

Kinstrey said, "At least now I know it's Ganahl. That should be worth something."

"I suppose so—if you can ever lay hands on him." Lank Johnson looked dubious, then said, "Look, I know I'd be working against myself, but I admire a man with your guts. I'd be glad to make you a loan if—"

"No!" Kinstrey was curt. He realized it and softly added, "I'm obliged, but no thanks."

Lank Johnson shrugged. "Just as you like. Well, good luck. And if you change your mind, let me know."

"I won't change my mind, about anything," Kinstrey said. He lifted a finger in negligent salute and swung the dun. The sky had turned a sullen lead color and a persecuting wind blew rawly up the street. Snow, though Kinstrey. That'll be just what I need. He urged the horse on. What more could happen to one man in one day?

Kinstrey didn't notice the spit of snow against his face until he had reached the south trail up the mountain and the dun had begun to climb. It was thin snow, almost a fine sleet, and didn't seem as if it would amount to much. At this stage of things, however, just the thought of snow depressed Kinstrey. Deidesheimer had promised to send out a dozen men tomorrow to start work on the flume. Any snow would be a handicap. And a heavy fall might make it necessary to postpone operations indefinitely.

Kinstrey's eyes cruised up the whitening trail, his mouth clamped grimly. They'd start tomorrow, somehow. Barring a blizzard, or some other act of God.

Effie Mannerheim's words came back to him. "You won't sell out. ... You'll just fight harder because of this," Kinstrey's jaw knotted. Sure; he'd fight. Fight, and then fail. He needed Big Matt; that was the truth of the matter. Walking into that rat-hole of a saloon with more than five hundred dollars in his pocket! Who but a numbskull would have done a thing like that? And now Philip Deidesheimer probably would lose all confidence in him, and quite justifiably. Getting that money had been a test of his responsibility and he had flunked the test. The fear that had always haunted him was no phantom, then. He had a right arm, but it had never been anything but a kind of projection of Big Matt's. And now, with Matt Calbraith dead, he was helpless. ...

With a dull pang his thoughts ran backward. He remembered the night on the wagon, when he and Marna had talked, quarreled, embraced. He remembered snatches of conversation. "I'm not interested in your past, Boise; only in your future." And: "You're the only woman I ever looked at twice; you know that."

That had been the night when he had told her of his feeling that he must prove himself before he could think of "settling down"; that he must prove his ability to be somebody without Big Matt's supporting hand always at his arm.

And now ... what had he proved? Only that he was no good alone; only that she probably was right in wanting to sell out. So why didn't he let her sell? He was a failure at bossing Big Matt's outfit; he'd shown that. What was staying his hand, then? Was it just a streak of stubborn willfulness that still made him want to run this mill himself—prove he could run it—just as Big Matt would have expected him to do?

Working his teeth absently into his underlip, Boise Kinstrey frowned. The truth was he couldn't shake off his sense of obligation to Big Matt Calbraith, even now. It was why he wanted to do things exactly as Big Matt would have wanted them done. *Was it also why he expected that some day he would marry Marna Calbraith?*

The question, to Kinstrey, had the effect of a needle jabbed suddenly and unexpectedly into his arm. He stiffened in the saddle and for a moment his face assumed a perplexed and oddly baffled look. There was a rift now between him and Marna and the gap could easily and quickly widen if he made no effort to bridge it. He remembered her anger toward him in town, her asking, "How are you going to buy food—let alone pay *wages?*"

Those, he was forced to admit, were sensible and practical questions. So how was he going to answer them? It was highly unlikely that he would recover any of the money that had been stolen from him. And now he would have to scrape by on what provisions he had. Who could have any confidence in him, now?

He thought of one, and felt a warm stir within him. Effie. Effie in her quiet, self-possessed way telling him, "You won't sell out."

The remembrance strangely stimulated him. What the devil! Manogue and the men were loyal; they'd wait for their wages. And there was still at least a week's supply of grub on hand. ...

Kinstrey's eyes lightened, searching ahead. It had almost stopped snowing and to the west there was a pale glow in the sky where the sun filtered opaquely through a layer of cumulus. Maybe that was a sign—an omen of better days to come. A few yards ahead, Kinstrey's glance alighted on a lightning-split Jeffrey pine which he now remembered as a landmark quite close to the approach to camp. A couple more turns, one short grade, and he'd be there.

Kinstrey relaxed, letting his thoughts idle. Would the men Effie had sent out now be at camp? he wondered. Joe Le-Beau. And a Milt somebody. He could certainly use a couple of good men; and LeBeau had mill experience, according to Effie. He wondered how she had found these men. Through the store, probably. Everybody came there. Still, she was a whiz, that girl. He had a vague recollection of her having mentioned something about a cook, too. But he might have misunderstood about that, because there seemed to be nothing specific he could remember.

A cook. That was the big, important thing now, with these extra hands who would have to be fed. And a bunk house where the men could have warm, secure shelter. So, tomorrow—

Kinstrey started. Across the snow-powdered stillness a gusty downwind passed on the high, driving whine of saws ripping into green wood. Kinstrey lightly spurred the dun, his first reaction one of angry disturbance. Then he remembered. LeBeau was an experienced mill man. And maybe the other new man, too. So Manogue could keep a couple of men on guard and still get a little work done. What harm was there in that? Angered now only by his own impetuosity, Kinstrey pulled down the dun.

He found himself on the last short upgrade. He topped a rise and the camp was in sight. He pulled rein.

The mill looked good; even *sounded* good. A flag of blue-white smoke rippled from the boiler shack's tall black stack. The saws bit, sang, brought their voices up in fierce crescendo.

Kinstrey sat hunched forward in the saddle, absorbed, the saws' clangor music to his ears. In his mind's eye he could see the huge spiked blades gashing their great kerf through a chunk of savory pine, flinging showers of sawdust. This was a thing he loved. The mill. Its sounds, smells, hurly-burly—everything.

A slab had dropped and now the carriage would be gliding toward the saws again. The skeletal building vibrated to the throb of machinery. The stack puffed its blue breath to the sky. Kinstrey heard the grinding bump of saws and log butt colliding, the tortured shriek as steel fangs struck, the high, increasing screech, mounting, mounting. . . .

It never attained climax. There was a rending crash, an abortive convulsion of steel twisted upon steel, a vast upheaval of flung wood and metal. Half the mill roof crumpled, vanished, as if at the blast of a mighty cannon. In the boiler room the engine clanked, coughed, then shuddered to a stop. Wild yells lifted suddenly.

For a breath-space, Kinstrey sat in the saddle transfixed, unable to draw his eyes from the jagged crater torn in the mill's roof. He pictured the havoc inside.

"Great God Almighty!" he breathed.

Then he gut-hooked the dun.

16

Boise Kinstrey's first glance at the mingle-mangle of buck-led saws and wrenched and twisted belting inside the mill brought him to a stunned halt, a single step in from the door-way. The big room was a shambles—pulleys ripped, belts thrown about in serpentine entanglement, the log that had been on the carriage heaved and pointed upward like a huge cannon barrel aimed at the yawning cavity in the roof.

A sick despair flooded Kinstrey as he stared at the wreck-age. Then his glance shifted. Pat Manogue and his men were working on the upended log, pulling it slowly and carefully down to the floor with the aid of a large grappling hook sunk in its butt.

Kinstrey silently watched, standing motionless. An accident of this sort always looked bad, but the damage was not irrep-arable. Big Matt Calbraith luckily had had the foresight to bring along extra saws and a spare drive pulley, as well as much miscellaneous equipment which he had foreseen might prove useful. This was stored in a small storage bin which had been built onto the boiler shack to protect it from the weather, and now would be not only useful, Kinstrey grimly reflected, but indispensable.

He strode across the littered floor and only then did Pat Manogue glance up and see him.

"So ye've come home f'r th' wake," Manogue said. His face was a dark beet color from straining on the log, but now the others had it lowered and a small, wiry man was bent down, minutely examining the butt. Suddenly the small man whipped around and Kinstrey stared at a swarthy lean face dramatically accented by black pits of eyes and a flam-boyantly downcurving black mustache.

"*Que voici!*" he exclaimed to Manogue. "*C'est un long clou—sans contredit!*"

A tall, big-eared man standing beside him told Manogue, "*Clou.* That's French for spike."

"I know what it manes!" roared Manogue. "Didn't we just

115

bust a hundred an' fifty dollars worth av saw steel to smithereens? Even a bloody Orangeman w'd have th' understandin' t' know it was no ball av cotton we hit!"

Kinstrey said, "I thought I was supposed to have the temper around here," and moved past Manogue. "You Joe Le-Beau?" he asked the little man with the big mustache.

"Oui, M'sieu! An' thees—" he nodded to the long-faced, big-eared figure beside him—"thees ees *mon partenaire,* Milt Mygatt."

Kinstrey said, "Boise Kinstrey," and gave a short handshake to each man. Then he bent over the ruptured log butt. The saws had driven into the thick spike, almost, but not quite, severing it. Kinstrey straightened. "I'll have another look at this later," he said, and faced LeBeau again.

"Understand you've had mill experience," he said.

A flash of white teeth came with the Frenchman's grin. *"Oui, M'sieu. Et mon partenaire, aussi."* He nodded toward Mygatt. "He ees experience' setter. I saw."

"You know how to hang a saw?"

"Mais out! Je lime aussi—am filer too. Do many theengs, thees Joe LeBeau!"

Kinstrey grinned, liking this cocky little man. He looked at Mygatt. "He as good as he claims to be, Mygatt?"

"Better," said Mygatt. "You got extry saws an' riggin', he'll have sawdust flyin' here again inside forty-eight hours."

"I need you two," Kinstrey said. "But I can't pay anybody till I can get out our first shipment of posts. That may be a week yet."

LeBeau shrugged. *"Ce n'est pas rien, M'sieu. Nous avons faim.* Feed us, we work lak hell!"

Kinstrey grinned. "It's a deal. You'll find all the extra stuff you need out in the boiler shack. Let's see what you can do."

Geehaw Jenkins and Mike Cloona were standing beside Pat Manogue, and now Kinstrey became aware of Cass and Wilmer Browne coming in through a rear door.

"Where've they been?" he asked Manogue, nodding toward them.

"Ye said to keep guards posted, didn't ye?" Manogue said. "Well, they've be'n out lockin' barn doors after th' horse was stole!"

Kinstrey said, "Let's start clearing away this mess. We ought to have an hour or two before dark yet."

Manogue stood tracked, glowering at him. "Who smacked ye in the puss?"

"Let's get busy here now. I'll tell you about that later," Kinstrey said.

Cass came up, his face bonedust-white, Wilmer Browne moving in silently to stand beside him. "My God!" Cass blurted it, staring around. "What happened?"

Kinstrey pivoted irritably. "Saws hit a spike. Where were you?"

"Where were we?" Cass puffed. "Why, up on the hill on guard. Didn't Pat tell you?"

"All right! Then get back there," Kinstrey snapped. He was instantly ashamed of his bullyragging tone, but then it was too late. Cass stepped up to him, flushing angrily.

"Don't talk to me like that, Boise!"

Kinstrey felt fatigue and tightness in him like a coiled spring, set to go at the touch of a feather. He bit his lip. "Sorry, kid; don't mind me today."

"And don't call me kid, damn you!"

"Mr. Calbraith, then." Kinstrey's tone was meager. Somewhere, behind Cass, one of the men laughed. Cass whirled, but now every man's face was studiedly innocent. Cass spoke with repressed fury. "Come on, Wilmer, let's get out of this madhouse!"

Kinstrey watched them go, aware of a pulse in his left temple suddenly throbbing erratically. He felt Pat Manogue's eyes on him, cold with rebuke.

He moved his shoulders in a tired shrug, then with an irritable twisting motion peeled off his mackinaw.

"All right, Pat; let's get this mess cleaned up," he said wearily.

The next day was one of the busiest in Kinstrey's memory. Breakfast was hardly over when two double-seated spring wagons reached camp, each carrying a half-dozen husky-looking men wearing striped mackinaws and gaudy wool caps. From the lead wagon stepped a strapping blond-haired giant who introduced himself to Kinstrey as Larsen Petersen, foreman of an Ophir gang sent here by Philip Deidesheimer to do a special construction job—some kind of a flume, was it?

With the mill still inoperative and no boards available until it was running again, Kinstrey took Peterson and his men down to the east slope, explained the project in view and indicated the proposed line of the conduit. When he left Petersen the Ophir men were already at work clearing underbrush and cutting small trees for trestle supports where ravines would have to be bridged over.

Back at the mill he found Manogue and Mike Cloona busily cleaning up what remained of yesterday's mess while Joe LeBeau and Milt Mygatt, helped by Geehaw Jenkins' tinkerer's hand, worked at rigging a new drive pulley preparatory to hanging the replacement saws, big, seventy-two-inch, twelve-gauge affairs that would cut kerfs of three-sixteenths of an inch. Cass and Wilmer Browne were again on guard, a waste of man power, as Kinstrey well knew, but a relinquishment for which at present he could see no alternative.

His mind was heavy with this thought as he walked to the back of the mill for a closer examination of the log which had caused yesterday's catastrophic upheaval. A painstaking inspection of the butt showed a spot where the bark appeared to have been cut out and then gummed over again with a kind of pitchy glue. Kinstrey picked up an ax from a wall bracket and finically began chopping around this gluey area. He was not surprised when at his eighth stroke sparks flew and black metal showed starkly against the flesh-colored wood. He replaced the ax in its bracket and, turning, saw Pat Manogue's eyes fixed on him in grim understanding.

"Another spike, hey, bucko?" Manogue said.

Kinstrey nodded bleakly. "Butt's probably loaded with 'em. All sunk and out of sight. Somebody did a mighty neat job of sealing over the bark after they were driven in."

"And who d'ye think that might be now?" Manogue's voice was thin with sarcasm.

"You know the answer to that as well as I do," answered Kinstrey.

"I'm not after needin' a crystal ball. 'Twas Raymers." Iciness gleamed in the black-deep blueness of Manogue's eyes. "He had block an' tackle that mornin'. He could've set those logs down on a gnat's eye."

"He sat 'em right where we'd be sure to pick up that spike in a hurry," Kinstrey appended grimly. He thought a moment, then murmured, "Raymers won't be back again, that's for sure. But we'll have to watch every unloading from here out."

"Until we c'n get to the sate av th' trouble, which is a man by th' name av Ganahl."

"Pat, those logs we get come from Ophir's own timber tracts, don't they?"

"That was me understandin'. Why?"

Vaguely, Kinstrey shook his head. "Just an idea. Maybe if I talked with the Ophir boss who hired Raymers we could find out something."

"I'm thinkin' that might be a foine idea. And ... Boise? Take it a little aisey on th' kid, hey? He's been strainin' his guts av late to act dry in back av th' ears."

Kinstrey murmured placatingly, "Sure, Pat, sure," then added, turning, "I did get a little frothy last night. Guess I was just tired."

He didn't wait for Manogue's comment on that, but walked to the door and went out. He felt at loose ends this morning. So much had to be done; so little had been accomplished. And Ganahl was the crux of it all. Until he could stop Ganahl he could never feel free, never breathe easy. And Raimo. He had neither seen nor had any word of Raimo since that night at the livery when he had almost had the will o' the wisp killer in his hands.

Kinstrey found himself walking toward the creek branch. He saw that Petersen's men already had built a crude bridge across the stream, fashioned out of small tree trunks. He crossed.

The Ophir foreman and his crew were about a quarter of the way down the mountainside, hacking away at a jungle of brush and creeper. To that point, Kinstrey observed with pleased surprise, a perfect cleared lane had already been slashed through the underbrush.

He swung around and started back. The work here was going well. Now if he could only get the mill running smoothly, get the flume built, then start making deliveries to Ophir—

He was daydreaming. The pretty bubble burst. It could be weeks—depending on the weather—before the flume was finished. Of course, they still had oxen and three usable wagons. But with thaws the trail down the south end of the mountain would be a quagmire. And maybe a death trap if Ganahl continued his harassing tactics. . . .

Kinstrey frowned, walking on. He walked abstractedly, with no sense of direction. What was Ganahl's stake in all this? He could understand Raimo. Raimo was a killer, a man who destroyed from some savage inner compulsion, horrible, but perhaps understandable, a mongrel dog who at some time had been kicked and hadn't forgotten. He was small, unimportant, inferior to other men. But he wanted to be superior. So he became superior—in the only way he knew how to be. With a gun. . . .

But Ganahl wasn't that kind. Neither was Moss. They were rogues. Rogues who might even kill. But only for profit. And what did Ganahl stand to gain if this mill didn't succeed? Could Ganahl have the crack-brained idea that Marna Calbraith might hire him back to run things for her, if experience could prove one Boise Kinstrey incapable of handling the job?

Kinstrey frowned, sauntering on. Somehow, this interpretation didn't quite satisfy him, left him with an uneasy feeling of doubt and distrust. But why should he disbelieve the evidence of his eyes? Twice, now, Ganahl's men had struck at the mill and both times successfully. What more proof did he need that Ganahl had ambitions to succeed him here?

Kinstrey found himself at the ridge where the rough trail down the south side of the mountain began. He suddenly felt very tired and irritably restless, and sank down on a flat rock beside the trail to build a cigarette.

He stared off moodily into space. A bunk house and a cook shack had to be built. No, that was wrong. A cook had to be hired first. And then additional supplies. Provisions at hand now wouldn't last more than another couple of weeks at most. They might only last a week. Then what happened? Of course, before that he might be able to make a small delivery of posts to Ophir and get paid for it. But suppose he couldn't, didn't? Suppose—

Abruptly, Kinstrey tensed. From downtrail, wagon wheels squeaked frostily on the still mountain air. Jumping up, Kinstrey threw down the cigarette he had just lighted. To his right stood a thick-boled pine. He ducked behind it just as a heavily loaded spring wagon hove into view, drawn by a team of matched roans.

Kinstrey let out a startled grunt as he recognized the occupants of the wagon. Soldier Charley was driving. And seated beside him, her thinly inclined face set in its usual expression of thoughtful composure, was Effie Mannerheim.

As Kinstrey stepped out into view he heard her quick ejaculation of surprise, then as Soldier Charley impassively pulled the team to a halt, she exclaimed, "Why, Boise! I didn't expect a welcoming committee at this hour!"

She was wearing the sock cap today, so that only a few incorrigible wisps of her yellow hair tufted out prettily from around her forehead. Her slim nose was tipped red from the cold, and she sat huddled in her blue cape, her hands, in coonfur and silk gloves, plunged part way into a gray-fox muff which sat on her lap.

Kinstrey realized that he was staring before he finally said, "If I'd been expecting you I would have had a committee here. I wasn't, though. This is quite a surprise."

"Surprise!" She stared at him blankly. "But you ordered these provisions yesterday—don't you remember?"

He gaped back at her. "*Provisions?* You've got provisions in that wagon?"

"Why, of course! I told you I'd have Charley drive out with them this morning, didn't I?"

"Well, yes. Yes, I guess you did. But you know that I'm broke right now. I can't—"

"Uncle Jules says pay when you can. Where shall we unload?"

Kinstrey stared up at her. Her eyes, so softly brown and large, gave her an ingenuous look, and something about the wide, sloping lines of her mouth bespoke both artlessness and a kind of basic honesty.

"Do you know something?" he said. "You're stubborn."

She smiled at him. "You still haven't answered my question."

"All right! Drive straight on. First wagon you come to."

He followed them afoot, and Soldier Charley was already busy unloading when he reached the end Espenshied. He pitched in to help, and in a few minutes the job was done. He swung and came down out of the spring wagon with a light leap. Soldier Charley was standing at attention beside the driver's seat, his right hand upraised in a rigid salute.

Kinstrey said, "Thanks; good work, Soldier," and now aware of what was expected of him, crisply saluted in return.

"No want thanks." Soldier Charley's hand had dropped back to his side, but he didn't move. "Unload stuff heap job. Cost um four bits."

"But Charlie!" Effie Mannerheim protested. "Mr. Kinstrey helped you."

Under his pitch-smeared campaign hat Soldier Charley's tar-black eyes remained unstirred, inscrutable.

"No ask um help."

"Oh, well . . . here then!" Effie fumbled in a purse she had drawn from her muff. She found the necessary coins and handed them over. Soldier Charley took the money and stuffed it carefully into the top of his right boot. Then he mounted to the seat of the spring wagon and gathered up the reins.

He was already tooling the wagon around, heading it out of camp, when Kinstrey's yell exploded after him.

"Charley! Charley—wait! *Your passenger!*"

His cry went unheeded. Without even a backward glance Soldier Charley leaned out from the spring wagon's seat and rein-slashed at the rumps of his horses. Dust spurted. "Yup!" he shouted.

"Why, that red-skinned devil!" blurted Kinstrey. He wheeled around, dazed. Effie Mannerheim was stooped down, lifting a heavy long carpetbag up off the ground. Kinstrey goggled.

"Where can I put this?" she asked him.

"Put—put it?" stammered Kinstrey. "Say, what in blue blazes is going on around here, anyhow?"

"You told me you needed a camp cook, didn't you?"

"Well . . . yes! But—"

"Then you must have a wagon where I can keep my things," returned Effie Mannerheim. She smiled at his dumbfounded look. "I'm your new cook, Boise," she announced simply.

17

STEADY, DAY-BY-DAY progress became increasingly evident at the mill, even to Boise Kinstrey's critical and sometimes incredulous eyes. Within the forty-eight hours promised, Joe LeBeau had the replacement saws hung and the drive pulley restored, and sawing began even before the roof had been mended. By the week end, the yard to the right of the mill held an impressive pile of posts for Ophir, and in addition a good quantity of boards for the flume, on which work also was well under way.

Beginning at the creek, where the water could easily be diverted from it, the flume, constructed of planks nailed together in the shape of a V, already extended about a fifth of the distance down the mountainside and Larsen Petersen's gang were tearing into the job as though their lives depended on it.

Kinstrey had never seen a V flume but he had heard Big Matt Calbraith tell about them and knew the general principle for laying one. Built of boards cut randomly in sixteen- and seventeen-inch widths and with ends butted together to insure a smooth channel, the sides were slanted so that when lumber lodged for any reason, accumulating water, raising it from the tapered flanks, would inevitably free it. Flumes with perpendicular sides lacked this advantage.

It was on a Saturday morning, exactly ten days from the day Larsen Petersen and his crew had started clearing operations, that Kinstrey, walking down the flume line to talk with Petersen, found Philip Deidesheimer there, interestedly inspecting construction of the newest link of the conduit.

Deidesheimer greeted Kinstrey warmly. "Congatulations," he said. "You're coming along fine. Just thought I'd ride over to see how things were going."

"Glad you did." Kinstrey nodded to Petersen. "But there's the man to congratulate. He's getting a dozen men to do the work of two dozen, if I'm any judge."

Petersen looked pleased, said, "Rats!" and moved away to

where his men had begun building a trestle across a narrow ravine.

Regarding Kinstrey, Philip Deidesheimer took off his hat and thoughtfully plowed fingers through a mane of bushy hair which was tinged with gray at the temples.

"I'd guess your width would be about four feet at the bottom and five at the top," he murmured.

Kinstrey nodded. "Exactly. And the depth's thirty-two inches."

"Fine, fine," said the superintendent. "Any curves anywhere?"

"We may hit one," replied Kinstrey. "Down near the bottom where we have to swing a bit to hit the pond down there."

"Put in a wedge-shaped piece where you curve," suggested Deidesheimer. "It'll make a smoother current and prevent a jump-over."

"Now that's an idea! I'll do that," Kinstrey said with enthusiasm.

Deidesheimer, smiling faintly, said, "Starting Monday, I'm going to put another half-dozen men out here. That way maybe we could start sluicing down posts in another week or two."

Kinstrey nodded. "With luck maybe we could. I've got a couple wagonloads ready right now. I'll try and deliver them with oxen, first of the week."

"You keep sawing wood," Deidesheimer said. "I'll send out some wagons tomorrow to pick up anything you've got ready."

Half an hour later, back at the mill, Kinstrey's feeling of increasing optimism gained fresh impetus when one of the new big circulars got too tight and began snaking and he observed the prompt and efficient stratagem Joe LeBeau employed to overcome the difficulty.

The little Frenchman simply filled a bag with sawdust, tied a few feet of rope to it, and then let it down between the saw and the husk. Watching the operation, Kinstrey now remembered Big Matt Calbraith having once told him about this trick. The bag of sawdust caused friction and heated the center of the saw, which opened it up and caused it to run straight. Then, if the saw got too "open," the bag was pulled up and the steel cooled off.

Fascinated, Kinstrey watched Milt Mygatt set blocks on a new log after the bag had been lowered, heard LeBeau shout, *"Voila!"* and then lever to power. The carriage swept forward, saws tore into the pine with an agonizing screech, sawdust flew. A true, clean line had been sawed, and Kinstrey turned away, heartened.

Outside, feeling almost a surfeit of relief from the decreasing tension about the camp, he watched Geehaw Jenkins and Mike Cloona roofing a new camp bunk house which stood next to a new and already completed cook shack, into which had been built a tiny bunk room for Effie Mannerheim. Cass and Pat Manogue were at the mill, working as loaders; with oxen and wagons drawn in toward the center of camp, Kinstrey no longer saw any necessity for keeping day guards posted.

Night, however, was a different matter. Petersen's men rode back and forth daily to their job at the flume, so at night Kinstrey and his men were obliged to stand two-hour guard shifts, which was wearing both upon himself and them. I've got to get to town, he thought; I could use a few more men, just for camp guards.

He took makings from his mackinaw pocket and built a cigarette, his brow knitted. There was another reason he had to go to town, and soon. Ganahl was too quiet, and along with Raimo and Moss seemed to have dropped from sight completely.

Lighting the cigarette, Kinstrey stared through the smoke toward the cook shack. Inside it he could see Effie Mannerheim bustling about, preparing for the noon-day meal. He felt a deep thankfulness, even though she had told him she would remain only until he could look around in town and find a permanent camp cook. Already she had more than repaid his favor of permitting her to join the Calbraith train at Sportsman's Hall. Sportsman's Hall. How far back, how remote in the swift passage of time, all that seemed now!

Kinstrey sucked deep on his cigarette, so engrossed in his thoughts that he scarcely noticed the dropping of a flake of hot ash on the back of his hand. He shok it off absently. Effie wasn't what you could rightly call pretty. Not like Marna, anyway. Marna had beauty that hit like a blow, that took a man's breath. Effie, on the other hand, was attractive only at a certain angle. Where Marna was cut all from one bolt, Effie was contrast. There were times when her face seemed too sharp, the flesh too firmly molded over basically good bone structure. But there were other times—in certain lights and at certain angles—when the clean tautness of her features did, indeed, seem to possess a kind of stark and vivid comeliness.

Kinstrey took another deep drag on the cigarette, his eyes squinting in disturbance. He didn't know why he was trying to compare the woman he planned to marry, Marna, with one who, until recently at least, had seemed to possess some kind of gadfly instinct for getting under his skin.

He thought, now, of Marna's unexpected visit to the camp yesterday. She had been driven in, as usual, by Lank Johnson, but he was beginning to see through that little stratagem. Effie seemed lacking in the usual craft of her sex, but Marna, all woman, certainly did not. And it was as plain as his busted nose what Marna was up to. With Lank Johnson as her leverage she was trying to make him jealous. Trying to force his hand on sale of the mill by pretending a sudden interest in a human beanpole who decked himself out in clothes nobody but a show-off would wear and flashing a ring that belonged on the slim finger of a woman, rather than a man's. Well, she'd get nowhere with that kind of female hanky-panky!

A ridge of muscle in Kinstrey's jaw tautened as he remembered Marna's rather frigid reaction to his suggestion that she take a look at the posts already sawed and yarded, and then cross over the creek and see the flume for which he was getting the backing of no less a person than Philip Deidesheimer, superintendent of the Ophir.

Lank Johnson had said, "I'd like to see that flume, Kinstrey," and had strolled away, leaving them alone where the promoter had drawn up his buckboard in the shadow of the camp's three big Espenshieds.

And then Marna had sniffed and said, "Deidesheimer! What can he do if Ganahl starts anything? He has a mine to look after. He can't be jumping around all over the territory to watch out for your piddling little business!"

"I'm not asking him to," said Kinstrey. "We're doing all right. If you'd just take a look around—"

"I didn't come here to look around. I came to see if you hadn't finally come to your senses."

Kinstrey's mouth locked. "Not in the way you mean," he told her, his voice flat. "And neither has Cass."

"Cass!" Marna threw her voice scornfully. "He never did have enough sense to think for himself. And I certainly don't expect him to have now with that little flibbertygibbet from the store out here to get her hooks in him!"

Kinstrey colored. "You're wrong about that, Marna. Effie just feels she owes me a return for letting her ride in from Sportsman's Hall with us. She's too old for Cass, and knows it."

"Cass doesn't know it! And I'm sure whether Effie Mannerheim knows it or not it will make no difference in her plans!"

"Why are you so dead set against Effie? If it wasn't for her and her uncle, you wouldn't even have a place to stay."

"Oh, wouldn't I! I imagine I could have found accommodations somewhere."

Kinstrey tried a new tack. "Marna, I wish I could make you see how foolish you'd be to sell out now. There'll be a fortune in this mill. More than enough for you and Cass both."

"What good is a fortune, if you and Cass never live to see it? We met Cass as we were driving in." She paused then, her voice rising to a gloating note as she continued, "He told us about that spike business. And Effie told me what had happened to you that day you were in town. Boise, how *can* you be so blind—so *stupid!*"

Kinstrey stared at her, flushed, dark, beautiful—her face lovelier, if anything, in anger. Anger put a snap in the dark blue of her eyes, a heightened color in her smoothly modeled cheekbones. And her fur-trimmed coat lay open against the comparative mildness of the day, revealing the frank, exciting contours of her bodice.

Suddenly all the half-submerged desires in Kinstrey surfaced. He took a step up to her, swung her into his arms.

"Marna ... let's not quarrel. Why can't it be the way it used to be between us?"

He was looking straight down at her, conscious of a scent of violet lotion, of the clean, natural smell of her coiled black hair. He put his mouth down to hers even as her hands flattened against his chest, petulantly pushing him back.

A step sounded in back of them. With a flustered grunt

Kinstrey dropped his hands and turned. Lank Johnson was coming around the front of one of the Espenshieds, stepping over its long tongue. He seemed not to notice Kinstrey's agitation.

"Well, I saw your flume," he announced easily. "You're quite an engineer, Kinstrey. In fact, you've given me an idea for my own two mills."

Kinstrey shrugged. "Take it. I've got no patent on it."

Lank Johnson smiled, a little quirk stiffening the sides of his mouth, and that was all. "If Phil Deidesheimer bought it you can bet your bottom dollar you had something." His voice changed. "Did Marna tell you we ran into Cass?" He shook his head. "I was sorry to hear about your damage from that spike—partly for selfish reasons, frankly. I don't like to see Ganahl undermining my own organization."

Kinstrey looked at him. "Your organization?"

"Why, yes. All the logs you get here come from timber tracts that I either own or lease. I also have the contract from Ophir for hauling. Didn't Deidesheimer tell you?"

Kinstrey was startled. "Why, no, he didn't."

Johnson was frowning. "Well, it's a fact. So now Ganahl's getting me involved in his shenanigans. This Raymers Cass mentioned came over hunting a job from my wagon boss just a few days ago. We needed an extra man so Judson—that's my foreman—gave him a try." The promoter's frown deepened into a scowl. He continued, "What gripes me is that Ganahl was able to plant one of his damned hoodlums in one of my outfits. That's getting too close to home for comfort."

Kinstrey shrugged. "How can he hurt you? I'm the one he's after."

Johnson's voice was pettishly resentful. "That may be. But none of my foremen knowingly hire trail trash. I've built up too good a reputation in this Territory to have it damaged by letting even one rotten apple slip into my organization."

"As long as you know the apple," suggested Kinstrey dryly, "it shouldn't be too much trouble to throw it away."

A grim tenseness flattened Johnson's mouth. "Don't worry, I'll take care of that." He seemed belatedly to become aware of Marna pulling at the sleeve of his flashy machinaw—and looking up at him, Kinstrey thought, with a feigned archness.

"I think we'd ought to be going, Lank. I feel chilly."

Johnson gave her a hand into the buckboard, then turned

and again faced Kinstrey. "You should have come to me that day in town," he said. "I'd have gone over to Blue Chip Billy's with you. Expected to, in fact."

"Thanks," Kinstrey said grudgingly. "But that's over the dam, now."

"I would have liked this mill, Kinstrey. I'm not going to deny that. But I happen to admire guts, too. You're going to do all right here. Shake hands on it?"

Kinstrey had glanced up at Marna to observe her reaction. She had been pouting, looking down in cold disapproval both at him and Johnson. And after he and the tall promoter had shaken hands, and Johnson was in the rig and tooling it out of the yard, her good-by to him had been only a cool nod and the flatly spoken prophecy, "You're going to be sorry about this, Boise!"

Now, as Kinstrey stood watching Effie Mannerheim tinkering around in the cook shack across from him, busy at some chore or other, he suddenly felt an irresistible impulse to go over there, to talk with a woman who would at least give him a smile and a friendly word, for a change. And maybe more?

He felt a swift pound in his throat as he threw down his smoked-out cigarette and strode long-gaitedly across the yard. Before he could reach the door of the cook shack Effie came out of it, bundled in her blue cape, and stooped over a pile of cut cordwood stacked alongside the door jamb.

Kinstrey came up behind her softly. "This is a man's job. I'll fill your woodbox," he said.

She jerked upright and spun, startled momentarily. "Oh!" She held a hand to her breast as her breath checked. "My goodness, but you gave me a turn!"

"Didn't mean to." Kinstrey stared at her and was surprised to feel his pulses race. There was a smudge of flour across the tip of her slightly tapered nose, and a homey-looking apron fastened around her narrow waist, under the opened cape. She looked glowingly youthful, Kinstrey suddenly thought, and, in a certain unself-conscious way that was distinctly her own, piquantly feminine. He sniffed, turned toward the doorway, then grinned at her. "Something smells mighty good."

She gave him her quiet smile. "You smell more than one

thing. The full menu will have corned beef and cabbage, boiled potatoes, bread, baked beans with blackstrap, cheese, dried apple pie, ginger cookies and tea." He seemed to be only half-listening, and she added, as if to draw his attention, "Come in, if you'd like a sample."

He was standing quite close to her, so close he could see the pale band of freckles speckling the bridge of her nose and catch from her clothes, or hair, the clean kitchen redolence of fresh-baked bread.

"How about this kind of sample?" he said. There was a queer dryness packed in his throat as he drew her against him. She tried to pull back, but then it was too late. He found her mouth.

She cried out tensely, "Boise, no! Please, Boise!" but the sound was muffled against his cheek as she sought to jerk back from him.

Her resistance nettled him. She was struggling fiercely against him, but now lodged stubbornly in his mind was the fear that he would look ridiculous if he failed to gain her compliance. With angry roughness he forced her lips back to his. Her resistance slowly slackened. Then with a little moaning sound her head dropped back and she seemed to go limp. A fierce exultancy swept him, but was short-lived. The voice came at him like a whip crack—seemingly out of nowhere.

"Let go of her, you sneaking bastard!"

Kinstrey spun, then let out his breath as he recognized the spindling figure of Cass Calbraith emerging from a pine motte to the right of the shack.

Cass's face was livid; he strode toward Kinstrey with short, kicking steps, his scuffing boots angrily flinging dirt.

Kinstrey had time to say, "Cass! Now wait—" and that was all. Cass hit him before he was fully turned, while he still had one hand falling away from the arm of Effie Mannerheim.

The punch slammed into his stomach, doubling him forward, and as his breath gushed with the shock Cass hooked with a vicious short right to his jaw.

The blow staggered Kinstrey. He felt it jounce from his right cheekbone and rake excruciatingly across the still tender ridge of his broken nose, dropping sudden nausea to the pit of his belly.

Cass's angry breath pelted his face: "That's just a taste, big man!" and then there was Effie Mannerheim's voice, crying in panicky appeal, "No, no! Stop it, both of you!"

He ignored both voices. In his guts was a cold, hard stone of anger, anger with himself for his philandering, anger with Effie for having affronted his male ego by resistance, anger with Cass for so callowly playing the role of the injured rival.

Cass was rushing him, trying to finish it in a barrage of wild blows as Kinstrey's backing kindled rashness in him. One clout of Cass's ran over his guard and tore a side of his mouth, but he only grunted, licking at the crimsoning crack. He was circling now, and his long left, outreaching Cass, was beginning to flick out with hard, jolting counter-punches.

These jabs began to harass Cass, brought reddening and then a painful bruising to his jaw, and finally goaded him into the infuriated charge for which Kinstrey had been waiting and now was ready.

A looping left was high across Kinstrey's shoulder; a scything right swished past his ear as he jerked his head. Then he had his opening and took cool and deliberate advantage of it. His own big right hand pistoned.

The blow slugged Cass in the mouth, rocked him back on limp, suddenly trembling legs. Cass was licking absently at a bead of blood strung on his torn underlip as Kinstrey stepped lithely after him.

"You've been asking for this a long time," Kinstrey said.

He didn't like to do it again. Cass seemed to be standing out of sheer nerve, stupefaction glazing his blank, staring eyes. But he struck again because Cass had to be taught something, had to learn that no man can expect the advantages always to go his way.

Kinstrey heard Effie Mannerheim's shocked cry as the punch crunched on Cass's nose and squirts of scarlet jetted. Cass's knees wobbled and for a short, pitying moment Kinstrey was sorry. Then it was too late for regret. Cass's face was a mask of sickly whiteness smeared with red. Kinstrey heard a dry sob, but never knew if it was from Effie or Cass. Cass's knees buckled, heaving him over. He fell with his face to the frozen earth.

18

BOISE KINSTREY came out of Blue Chip Billy's knowing now with certainty that he had been wise to waste no time in getting here to Virginia City to hunt for Cass. Cass was headed for trouble—maybe big trouble. He had to be stopped. He had to be found while there was still time to help him. If there was. . . .

Kinstrey found his thoughts swinging to Effie Mannerheim as he started walking away from the saloon. He remembered her coldly advising him, before he had left, "Maybe you'd better start looking for another cook while you're in town, Boise." His jaw hardened at the recollection. Then a grim smile slightly relaxed it. Little lady, he thought, there's going to be a big surprise for *you* when I get back.

He strode on, his head lowered against a wind that tore savagely around corners, rattled doors and signs, and swept up grit which it hurled against windows like an angry discharge of buckshot. The famous "Washoe Zephyr."

Kinstrey's mouth quirked at the irony of the name, but now his thoughts again shifted as he pulled up the collar of his mackinaw and scrounged his head deeper in its woolly shelter. He'd had a lucky hunch making Billy's his first stop. The saloon's regular entertainer had been ill and Bessie Talbot had been taking her place. And once again the crossing of his path with Bessie Talbot's had brought him needed information.

Cass, Bessie had told him, had been in the saloon only half an hour earlier, and so had Red Danahy, one of the three men involved in the theft of Kinstrey's five hundred dollar money roll. Cass had had several drinks at the bar, according to Bessie, and later he and Danahy had left together.

The news had jolted Kinstrey. "Danahy, eh? And you're sure it was Cass with him?"

"From your description, positive," Bessie Talbot had stated unequivocally.

"I don't suppose you noticed which way they were headed," Kinstrey suggested.

"No ... but your friend had on a pretty good load. Danahy likely figured either to roll him or steer him into a game where he could sucker him out of his money."

Kinstrey had already started to leave and then had turned back and asked, "Say, isn't this a new job for you—singing?"

"It's new. But only temporary till Wanda Hawley gets back. I wish it wasn't."

"Tell me. Can you cook?"

"Cook—me?" Bessie Talbot had laughed hoarsely. "Well, yes. But that was a long time back."

"There's a cook's job open out at my camp. How'd you like it?"

"Like it, mister? *Like* it? Why, I'd give my right arm to get out of this place!"

"I'll see you about it later," Kinstrey had told her. "Right now I've got some other business to look after—if it's not too late."

The wind seemed to be blowing from all four quarters of the compass and Kinstrey turned in at the next saloon with relief. It was the Crystal, and the crowd inside was dense, noisey and malodorous. Cass was not there, however, and once outside again, Kinstrey almost welcomed the clean, cauterizing bite of the wind against his face. In rapid succession he tried Lucky Nugget, Orndoff and McGee's and Café de Paris, all without result. Then as he was approaching Gardiner's Livery he saw Soldier Charley and on an impulse called out, "Charley? Wait a second, will you?"

The lanky Piute had just come out of the stable and was headed downstreet but at Kinstrey's call he stopped and turned, then came to a kind of grudging half-attention, recognizing Kinstrey, and solemnly saluted.

Kinstrey restrained a grin, saluting back. "You know Cass Calbraith, Charley?" he asked then. "You might have seen him at camp when you were there the other day."

Soldier Charley grunted, shook his head. "Me unload grub. See nobody. Just you and girl."

Kinstrey described Cass and explained, "I'm looking for him. I know he's in town. You haven't seen anybody around answering that description, have you?"

The Piute curtly waggled his head again. "No see um."

An idea seized Kinstrey. He said, "I might have a job for you, Charley—keeping track of some men for me. Eight bits a day. How about it?"

Soldier Charley's black eyes looked depthless, stonily meeting his glance.

"How you want um done?"

Kinstrey frowned. "I'm not sure yet," he replied, "but this young fellow I'm looking for may be with some sharpsters. If I smoke out the right men they may try and high-tail it out of town. I want you to follow them. I want to know where they go."

"Why you no go?"

"They know me. They might get suspicious."

"Me no got horse."

"We'll go into Gardiner's right now and hire one for you."

"You in *mucho* rush, huh?"

"I'd say we get started, if that's all right with you."

Soldier Charley stood immobile. Over his medal-bedecked gray shirt he was wearing today a kind of sleeveless jacket cut crudely out of an old horse blanket. He stared impassively at Kinstrey, his thin lips blue with cold.

"*Mucho* big rush, *mucho* big job. Cost um two dollar day."

Kinstrey stared into the Indian's imperturbable face, then with sudden helplessness blurted a laugh. "All right, Charley, come on then; but I'll never know why you don't just go out and hold up stages for a living."

Soldier Charley grunted. "Ketch trouble that way. Charley good soldier. Make um pay honest."

"Mighty respectable of you," Kinstrey said dryly.

They turned in at the livery, and some minutes and several saloons later, with the Piute leading a saddled sorrel, they halted in front of a large square-fronted building painted a brilliant turquoise blue. A sign over an impressively arched doorway spelled out in gilt letters: *Gentry & Crittenden Saloon.*

Frost and dirt had put a shield of opacity over the saloon's two wide front windows, but from within came the blended clink, clatter and low throb of voices that unmistakably suggested a house of chance. Breaths of horses huddled close at a crowded hitch rack were steamy in the below-freezing temperature. Kinstrey looked for the trigueno that Cass had ridden to town but didn't see it. His glance swung back to Soldier Charley's sullenly stoical face.

"Now remember," he instructed. "These men may spook and come out of here on the run. All you do is follow them; find out where they hole up—understand?"

Soldier Charley ceremoniously saluted. "Take um horse in alley. You no worry, Captain."

"That's the ticket. Keep it in the alley." Kinstrey gave back the salute a little absently, then wheeled and stepped up to the saloon's door. He opened it. Heat, smoke, noise and confusion whirled out of a huge room and seemed to gush at him like a rank breath.

Cass Calbraith was drunk, but not enough to have lost all of his wits. He had managed, slyly, he thought, to keep a single far corner of his mind open to the truth, and the truth was that this Red Danahy he had met a while back at Blue Chip Billy's had played him for a sucker right from the start. These two men Danahy had had him meet here at Gentry and Crittenden's were sharpers, no doubt of that. He'd dropped close to a hundred and seventy dollars to them in less than an hour—all the money he'd won in the game at Sportsman's Hall and then some. Still, he was no slouch of a player himself. Maybe he ought to hunt up Marna. If he could borrow a few dollars from her, maybe—

No, he thought foggily. These shysters would be gone by the time he could get back here. And anyway, Marna would loan him no money. To hell with her! To hell with everything, except having another drink. He reached for the bottle on the table, unsteadily filled his glass from it.

Danahy and Danahy's two friends paid no attention to him. They were playing now with his money, playing to see which of the three would walk off with the spoils. It wasn't going to be Danahy, that was sure. Danahy was out and the game had narrowed now to the other two, a thin, pale man named Frank Bell, who had slim, white, almost fragile-looking fingers, like a woman's, and a big clod of a fellow called Ike Waldo, with a blunt inexpressive face and eyes that seemed always to be watering.

I ought to get up and walk out of here, Cass thought, and then wondered if he could. He'd never got this drunk before;

had never felt any reason to until today. Until this morning when he'd surprised Boise and Effie Mannerheim together.

Damn Boise! And damn Effie, too! Apparently she could be trusted no further than any of the rest of her sex, and that was about the distance you could shake a stick.

Cass nursed his self-pity with bitter relish. No good. No damned woman was any good. Probably Boise wasn't to blame. Probably Effie had egged him on. And anyway, Boise was going to get his come-uppance, any day now. Boise was due for the heave, too—from Marna. Poor old Boise! Couldn't he see that this Lank Johnson was now the fair-haired boy? And Johnson had made his pile already. Close down the shop and ring bells the day dear, sweet little Marna would pass up an opportunity like that!

Cass finished the whiskey in his glass and suddenly knew he was through. His right hand slid away from the table and fell limply against the gun holstered at his side. The touch of cold steel against his hand prickled his fingers. He felt his head loll and jerked up straight in his chair, his glance sweeping the table with a look of affronted dignity. No one paid him the slightest attention.

Scallywags, he thought. Damned no-good tinhorns! He'd ought to show 'em where to head in. Could, too, if he wanted to be tough. Throw down with this old thumb-buster of Big Matt's and they'd draw in their horns. By thunder, he might just do that, too! Show 'em they'd better think twice before trying to sucker a Calbraith. Show 'em—

The suddenness of Red Danahy's jerking around in his chair pulled Cass taut. He saw Danahy grip Ike Waldo's thick arm.

"Ike!" Danahy breathed out. "Look—out there countin' heads at the bar. It's him!"

"Him?" Waldo glanced up with abrupt exasperation, then peered through reddened eyes in the direction Danahy had indicated. "Who you talkin' about? I don't see nobody. You must be drunk!"

A convergence of miners in the doorway to the gambling parlor was momentarily blocking a view of the bar, beyond it; but in the split second before Waldo's turning, Cass had looked and had had a startled instant in which to recognize Boise Kinstrey.

Cass's breath caught. He heard Danahy blurt, "I'm no drunker than you are. It was Kinstrey—I'm positive!"

"Positive, hell," Frank Bell broke in. He was a man of unhealthy indoor pallor with spindles of black mustache slanting down from a meager upper lip. His gray eyes had a cold impassivity moving over Danahy's drink-flushed face. "You'd need a telescope to pick anybody out of that bar mob. You're seeing things."

Blood congested Danahy's cheeks. "I know what I saw!"

Bell shrugged. "Suppose it is him? He's no fool. He wouldn't go against three-to-one odds."

"Make it two-to-one." Danahy's voice was thin. "I don't get paid to buy private trouble. I'm gettin' out of here."

Cass saw Ike Waldo flick a nervous glance toward the barroom as Danahy pushed back from the table and stood. Danahy threw a curt look at Bell. He said, "Right now; by the back door," and swung around.

Inside Cass's whiskey-fogged brain a thin voice pulsed. They're tinhorns, it said; a bunch of cheap tinhorns. It said, bigger and louder, *Kid*, am I? Don't ever call me that name again, Boise, you hear me?

Ike Waldo was looking anxiously toward Frank Bell. He moistened his lips. "Frank? You'd take the pot anyway. Let's go."

They ignored Cass. Bell frowned as his glance went to the doorway. Two faro layouts had just been vacated and the miners who had been at the portal were now jostling through a press of outgoing players to reach them.

Waldo was already out of his chair. Bell glowered at him, then grudgingly pushed back from the table himself. "Oh, all right!" he yielded. "But I take the pot—remember now!"

He got up, then as Waldo stood impatiently waiting, stooped to pick up his whiskey glass from the table and down what was left of the drink in it.

To Cass it seemed as if there was an invisible force pulling against his arm as his right hand groped toward the Root's Patent hinged to his belt. He lurched up as Bell and Waldo were starting away. The floor suddenly seemed to undulate under him. He threw his voice hoarsely.

"Bell—Waldo? Turn around! Damn you, turn or I'll shoot!"

By some impossible miracle he had the gun out of its hol-

ster as Waldo, and Bell behind Waldo, jerked around. Bell's
hand withdrew from his coat with fluid grace. The black little
derringer in his fist cracked flatly and kicked a puff of blue
flame.

Cass's impressions blurred. Something stung him under the
left shoulder near his armpit, and then with vague disbelief
he felt the Root's buck and roar, and simultaneously a gun
blasted from behind him, terrifyingly close. He reeled
around, clutching at the table, and then saw Boise Kinstrey.

To Cass's eyes, Kinstrey's face looked like the distorted reflection from a cracked mirror. Cass thought of a fish swimming up sluggishly out of murky water as Kinstrey moved
toward him. Kinstrey halted and, peering, Cass tried to focus
on him with bloodshot eyes.

"I got him," Cass muttered. "I beat him, Boise! You
saw—"

He felt a sinking in his legs and now was conscious of a
dull but angry throbbing in his left shoulder and armpit. He
heard Boise's voice as from a great distance murmuring,
"Better sit down, Cass," and then the sea of faces around him
seemed to blur and get cloudy.

A mist swimming in front of his eyes alarmingly thickened.
He heard a remote sounding bump and thought fatuously:
Dropped m'damn' gun! Suddenly he tipped.

His fall across the table had a kind of fluency, almost a
loose grace.

"Man," jocularly blurted a black-whiskered miner, "has he
got a load!"

Kinstrey angrily pivoted, spoke with soft, compressed fury.
"This boy's got a bullet in him, you lunkhead! Somebody get
a doctor—and hurry, for God's sake!"

19

BOISE KINSTREY came out of the room at the rear of Jules Mannerheim's store and found Marna waiting at the door to the adjoining room. She looked a little pale and overwrought, he thought, but not in a way of any great agitation or anxiety.

"Well?" she demanded tersely. "What does the doctor say? It's not going to be anything very serious, I take it."

Kinstrey looked at the dark, sultry beauty of her face and for a strange, frangible instant had a feeling of something going from him—something long held, long desired, but now slipping almost imperceptibly from him like a loosening garment.

He said quietly, "No, the wound's not too bad. Painful. But Doc says he ought to be up and around in a week or so."

"He'll have to stay here, I suppose?"

"Good Lord, Marna! He's your brother, remember?"

"I ought to—all I've tried to do for him. And now this!" Marna pouted, her budded, sensuous mouth giving a momentary sullen cast to her dark comeliness. "Well—" A shrug lifted her shoulders—"the damage is done, now. He wouldn't listen to me. Neither of you would."

"It wouldn't have made sense to sell the mill, Marna. Not when there's a fortune to be made out of running it yourself."

"I don't think it makes much difference now, Boise. You've ignored my wishes. What more is there to say?"

"Maybe a lot more," Kinstrey hinted. "If you'd listen."

It seemed to him that a suddenly irritated look crossed her face. Then it was gone and she said coldly, "How? The way you've listened to *me* in all this?"

Involuntarily Kinstrey reached out, touched her arm. "Marna, let's not quarrel again. Everything I've done has been for you and Cass. And because of Big Matt. I—"

"Now you're closer to the mark. Even father's ghost is

haunting you! He's dead now—and you still can't be your own man!"

Kinstrey flushed and jerked back his hand from her as if it had touched something hot. "All right! But the mill won't be sold, I promise you that! If I don't run it, Cass will."

Marna smiled coolly. "You have a temper, don't you, Boise? I'm glad I found out about it in time. Violent anger upsets me." She paused, then added spitefully. "As for Cass, I can't imagine him running anything. He's better at running away from things!"

"You've misjudged Cass, Marna. He'll run the mill and run it well, once he's got a few kid tantrums worked out of his system."

"Like his tantrum over that little blond hussy who chased him all the way out to your camp, I suppose?"

"Effie's not interested in Cass."

"Ha! I guess not! It's his money she's after—if by some freak chance you don't all get killed and the mill can keep running."

"You can believe that if you like. But ask her how she feels about him. She's quitting the camp. I've found a new cook."

Marna's lip curled. "How wonderfully convenient! Now she can nurse the wounded gladiator back to health. It will be a perfect romance!"

A coldness dropped over Kinstrey's face. He wheeled, saying in an inflectionless voice. "I'm sorry you feel this way. Good-by, Marna."

"Boise, wait! You haven't told me how this happened. Cass was gambling, you said. But who were the men, do you know?"

Kinstrey turned with a slow deliberateness, facing her again. "Cass gave me their names, yes. One of them—Ike Waldo—was still wearing a bandage on a burned arm. They're probably the same bunch who raided our camp and set fire to the wagons."

"Who was the one who shot Cass? You wounded him, didn't you say?"

"Let's give Cass the credit; it might do him some good. The man's name is Frank Bell."

"Bell!"

A sudden disconcerted look in Marna's eyes brought Kinstrey's sharp question. "Why, yes; do you know him?"

Marna's face was composed again. She said vaguely, "No-o. That is, I thought I might have. But—I guess not."

"He's a bad one."

"Unh!" Marna let out her breath with a sound of abhorrence. "All this brawling and skylarking and shooting. And you don't want me to get rid of the mill. I should think you'd at least look out for yourself."

Kinstrey's tone was meager. "I intend to."

"Fiddle-faddle! You'll wind up just like father did. You'll see!"

"Yes," murmured Kinstrey; "yes, I'll see," and then with neither a good-by nor a look back he wheeled and strode in rough anger from her out into the store.

He half-expected a conciliating outcry, a call for him to turn back, and he still half-wanted it, half-didn't. Did he only partly want her? Could a man ever think of such a woman in terms of limit, or any compromise whatever, when just the thought of holding her again could fire desire in him?

Kinstrey was almost to the front door when a hand touched his sleeve and he turned to be confronted by the craggy face and soft, melancholy eyes of Jules Mannerheim.

"A pity," said Mannerheim, "about the boy. The doctor is with him yet—*nein?*"

Kinstrey stopped, nodded. "Yes. Cass lost some blood. But he'll be all right now. I hope you didn't mind us toting him over here?"

Jules Mannerheim's bushy brows arched expostulatively. "Mind? Is best you do. Is all right. Tell me, *Herr* Kinstrey. How is my *liebchen?* I am an old one. I worry for her."

"You don't need to; she's fine." There was a quaver of huskiness in Kinstrey's voice, adding, "You'll see her tomorrow. I've found another cook for the camp."

"Ah! Is so? There is no trouble, I hope? Everything is good there, *ja?*"

"Everything's fine," said Kinstrey. "And thanks for taking in Cass, Mr. Mannerheim. It's good to know there's a place where he can rest and be safe."

"*Ach!* Is nothing." The storekeeper followed Kinstrey to the door. There, he said, "You tell *mein liebchen* I ask for her. You tell her Uncle Jules misses her. Good luck and good day, *Herr* Kinstrey."

"Good day," Kinstrey said, and stepped out into cold afternoon sunlight. Daylight would soon wane. He started with long, hurrying strides toward the livery. What had been good about this day? he thought with sudden, savage irony. First Effie. Then Cass. And now Marna. . . .

A wind whistling up the street slashed like an icy sword. Kinstrey tucked his head lower in the high, woolly collar of his mackinaw. He remembered now that he would have to get a horse for Bessie Talbot. He wondered how Effie would react when she saw her successor. The faintest of grim smiles played across his mouth as he hurried on.

Kinstrey had to wait for Bessie Talbot, a circumstance which annoyed him until he recalled the vagueness of his promise to come back for her. In his rush to go after Cass he had merely told her that he would be back "later" to see her about the cook's job and "later" could have meant next day, next week—or never. So after she had gone to pack her things he had a drink at the bar, champed at the bit and waited.

When Bessie Talbot finally appeared before him, dressed for the street and carrying a shabby reticule and pathetically small carpetbag he barely recognized her. Without rouge her face lost its hardened look and showed good bone structure and a soft, generously proportioned mouth. She was wearing a plain gray blouse, a divided gray riding skirt and an old, mangy-looking fur coat, too large for her and smelling strongly of mothballs.

He stared at it too noticeably and she said apologetically, "I had to borrow this from one of the girls. I didn't have a warm winter coat."

Kinstrey took the carpetbag from her, growling, "Looks all right," and led her outside.

At Gardiner's he had taken out Cass's trigueno as well as his own dun, and now he nodded to indicate his mount, telling the girl with him, "I'll take the brown; it might spook a little with a stranger."

She gave him a grateful glance as he gave her a hand into the saddle. He then tied her carpetbag to the horn of the trigueno and mounted.

"Going to be a cold ride," he warned. "Sure you're going to be warm enough?"

"I'll be all right."

"Might as well slope then. Be better if we can make it before dark."

She was going to be strange, he saw, and wouldn't be talking much until the feeling wore off. Well, that was all right. Everything would be all right—as long as she could cook.

Despite the piercing cold, traffic was heavy both in the street and on the walks. Espenshieds, Murphys, Studebakers rumbled in both directions, groaning under prodigious loads. Spring wagons and buckboards were everywhere, and in front of one wood and canvas saloon Kinstrey saw even a Red River cart, with its spindly box frame and tires made out of shaganapi. Anything on two wheels that could roll, did roll. Anything on two feet that could walk, did walk.

Gangs of miners from the early shifts, now up from the dank air of drifts and winzes, skylarkingly bucked their way through a knot of Chinese who had just left their halved barrel tubs in a wash house and now stood outside vigorously whacking soaked clothes against the boards of the building to clean them. A crew of Irish laborers headed for a cluttered lot wheeling barrows loaded with brick. Jewish peddlers shouldering huge packs moved doggedly through the street press hawking their wares in the lusty deep baritones of cantors.

Sun Mountain. Virginia City. Kinstrey felt a pulse of excitement beat through him. What would this raw new town be like in another year, two years? Already the Ophir was down two hundred feet and going deeper. Hygrade was becoming common. Carriages of the "nabobs" reputedly had silver stanchions and there was rumor of one team of thoroughbreds that had bits wrought from gold pieces. How far could it go? Where would it end?

Letting the trigueno pick its own pace on the crowded street Kinstrey frowned slightly. Not all on Sun Mountain was bonanza, he knew. When wind blew to the west, citizens of Virginia City had to close their windows. On such days the stench from a Piute camp below the Divide was too strong even for their hardy stomachs. Kinstrey had seen this camp: wigwams of dirty colored cloth patched with scraps of rusty tin; scrawny, unhappy-looking ponies hobbled near a stream. . . .

He came out of his wool-gathering with a start. A gangling, inordinately tall figure conspicuous in a fawn-colored jacket and white hat was just disappearing into a doorway some dozen yards ahead of him. Lank Johnson! Who else could it be?

The impulse that led Kinstrey to swing his horse to the right, in toward the gutter, was vague to him for an instant. Then he knew what had motivated his almost unconscious action. Maybe Johnson could tell him something about Frank Bell and those others. The promoter knew a lot of people. He might even know where the men hung out.

Kinstrey noticed Bessie Talbot's eyes tipped inquiringly up to him. He said, "There's a man in here I want to see. I'll only be a minute."

They were approaching a narrow frame building wedged tightly between a saloon on one side and an assay office on the other.

"Isn't this Mr. Lank Johnson's office?" Bessie said.

Kinstrey nodded as he pulled in the trigueno and dismounted. "Reckon it is. You know him?"

"Of him," replied Bessie shortly. "Everybody does, I guess."

Kinstrey pivoted, murmuring, "Be right back," and angled across the board walk to a weathered, unpainted door. He tried it, and with a jolt of surprise found it locked. Could he have made a mistake? Had Johnson gone into the assay office, next door? Or maybe the saloon?

Turning about slowly, he was conscious of a vague disturbance for which he could not account. He would have sworn Johnson had gone through this door, not more than sixty seconds ago.

The office had a single narrow window, so grimy as to be almost opaque. Kinstrey walked over to it and, peering through the frost-coated glass, could barely discern the figures of a man and a woman locked in embrace near a corner-set desk. The man's back was to Kinstrey, hiding any good view of the woman until she suddenly shifted slightly. Then he caught a glimpse of her hat—a fez-shaped red felt tilted dashingly over one ear—and shock pounded to his throat. The man was Lank Johnson. And the woman avidly inviting him with her mouth and body was Marna Calbraith. . . .

Kinstrey lurched around from the window, sickened. He felt Bessie Talbot's eyes fixed curiously on him as he stumbled up to the trigueno and swung into the saddle.

"Is—is something the matter?" she asked hesitantly. "You act like you'd just seen a ghost."

Kinstrey stared harshly at her, picking up his reins. "What do you call a ghost, Bessie?"

"Me? Why, I don't know. Sort of a demon, I guess. It's dead, really. But it's supposed to be able to come back and haunt you."

"Then it's the truth," Kinstrey murmured absently, and gigged the trigueno.

Bessie started the dun after him, asking, "What is?"

"That I saw a ghost," said Kinstrey, and something cold and frightening in his forward-staring eyes launched a little shiver up Bessie Talbot's back.

20

IT WAS well after dark when Boise Kinstrey and Bessie Talbot rode into camp. In the cook shack Effie Mannerheim was just finishing her after-supper chores when hoofbeats sounded outside. She went to the front window and peered out. Frost rime on the pane had been partially melted by the heat from her cook stove, and dimly she could make out two figures over by the wagons. A warm feeling of thankfulness sank through her. That must be Boise, back with Cass.

The glow she had felt quickly evaporated. She did not deceive herself as to her feeling toward Boise, for even self-deceit was foreign to her nature. At the same time, being the self-reliant and independent kind of person she was, it was not her intention to let herself be used by anybody. Boise had simply rebounded from his failure with another woman toward her. The attentions he had forced on her had meant no more than injured masculine vanity seeking to restore itself at the first available source.

Effie's lips firmed. One thing was sure. He'd find that good cooks didn't grow on bushes. Nevertheless he'd have to find someone to take her place. And the minute he did—

Her thought broke off. Out by the wagons, light flared up from a lantern. Then, still dimly silhouetted, two figures bulged out of the darkness, heading in the direction of the cook shack.

Stepping back quickly from the window, Effie with one hand jerked off her apron while with the other she tidied a curlicue of yellow hair that had wisped down over her forehead. She hung the apron on a wall peg beside the sink and had barely turned when a knock came at the door. She swiftly crossed the room and opened it. Boise stood there. Boise and a woman wearing a shabby fur coat that looked two or three sizes too large for her.

Effie's breath caught. Kinstrey asked, "All right if we come in?" and then without waiting for her answer stepped tiredly into the room. He walked to the door leading to her private

146

quarters and put down a limp carpetbag that he had been carrying. Then, pivoting, he nodded to the woman in the fur coat, now awkwardly standing beside him.

"This is Bessie Talbot," he told Effie. "She's going to cook for us. I'd appreciate it if you could fix her up with a place to bunk."

A light-cone shed by a coal-oil lamp hung from the center of the ceiling threw the sudden pallor on Effie Mannerheim's face into stark relief. Her voice held a strained politeness saying, "Miss Talbot is welcome. To a bunk—and to this job."

Kinstrey chewed his lip, then avoided Effie's eyes as he turned to Bessie.

"This is Effie Mannerheim," he said. "You'll be taking her place."

"Oh?" Bessie said. She gave Effie a troubled look. "I hope this ain't going to put you to any trouble," she said.

"It will only be for tonight," Effie replied. "You go right in and unpack. The light's on. Just make yourself comfortable."

"Thanks; I am awful tired. It's good to be where it's so warm—" Bessie Talbot's eyes hungered over the room—"and so cosy-like."

"You just make yourself at home," Effie said.

She and Kinstrey were like uneasy conspirators waiting for Bessie to disappear into the bedroom. They heard the door close gently behind her but neither moved nor spoke until sounds of muffled moving about came from the room and finally the creak of a bunk being tentatively tested.

"Well," Effie said then, her voice vehement but low, "you didn't waste much time, Boise."

"Did you want me to?" Kinstrey asked flatly.

"No, of course not!"

Kinstrey stared at her distraught face and felt a sinking remorse suddenly. "Effie?" he blurted. "I'm sorry for what happened this morning. It—didn't mean anything."

"I'm sure it didn't!"

Kinstrey flushed. "All right," he retorted stiffly, "stay mad! I'm only trying to tell you I didn't mean anything bad by it. Anything—wrong."

Effie said coldly, "If you're trying to explain *why* you did it, I know. Just by accident I saw what happened out here the other day between you and Marna Calbraith. So it's all quite understandable. This morning you were feeling very sorry for yourself. And here I was, handy and easy for a little sport—but only until you could patch up things with Marna, of course!"

Kinstrey's voice flared. "If it's any matter to you, Marna and I are through. For good."

"It *isn't* any matter to me, Boise. But if what you say is true I'm sure it's not because *you* want it that way."

"What do you mean? How do you know what I want or don't want?"

Effie's voice struck a soft, femininely wise note. "Don't you know? I thought your lady's interest in Lank Johnson had become pretty evident."

"That would be none of your business!"

"I think we had better say good night, Boise. I won't be troubling you after tomorrow. I can ride Bessie's horse back to town."

"All right!" Kinstrey's voice was harsh. "Any way you want it." He started to turn, stopped, swung around to face her again. "Damn it," he said. "Now you know I've got a temper, too. You know every damned bad thing about me. But I'll tell you one good thing. I'm grateful for your help out here. I guess I haven't shown it but I do appreciate it."

"Why, Boise. You don't have to—"

He had wheeled abruptly. gone to the door, and her voice trailed. The door closed behind him. Effie waited until his footsteps outside had faded. Then she turned to the wall. She laid her head against her arm, and muffled sobs shook her.

For two days Kinstrey sought to forget Effie, Marna, Cass—all of his harassing personal problems—by concentrating his full time and energies on the work of the mill. But with Joe LeBeau running the saws and Milt Mygatt dogging there was little for him to do but exercise general supervision and keep Pat Manogue and Geehaw Jenkins from tearing each other's hair out.

Despite the fact that the logs for the mine posts were sawed for grade, with each stick carefully "sawed around," the store of lumber being yarded outside the mill for air-drying had become so great by the end of the second day that Kinstrey ordered two wagons loaded and had Geehaw and Mike Cloona drive to Ophir with impressive cargoes. The result was that he was pleased and Philip Deidesheimer was pleased. That night, in fact, Geehaw brought word back from town that the Ophir superintendent wanted to see him the next time he came in. "Didn't say just whut about," Geehaw had enlarged knowingly, "but from the way he talked it'd be my guess he'd like to have you workin' for him at Ophir."

That night, stretched out on his straw tick in the bunk house, Kinstrey made up his mind to go in to town the first thing in the morning. But not solely to talk with the Ophir superintendent. No word had come to him yet from Soldier Charley, and he had now begun to worry about that. Charley might have run into trouble. If not, what was keeping him from reporting?

Tossing in his bunk Kinstrey tried to sleep and couldn't. Too many disturbing thoughts kept prodding him. The way Effie had looked at him the night he had come in with Bessie Talbot. His shocked discovery that Marna's dalliance with Lank Johnson had been far more than a mere innocent flirtation intended to arouse him to jealousy. And Cass. Cass had needed a good lambasting; but what had it done but bring the kid more trouble and drive him into deeper humiliation?

A pang of sadness infiltrated the bitterness in Kinstrey's mind. How differently things were working out from the way Big Matt had envisioned them! Cass kicking over the traces, and Marna having an affair with a Virginia City nabob. And he, Kinstrey, embittered by her betrayal, vainly attempting to salve his wounded pride with a girl who wisely suspected that he had just been using her on the rebound—and probably was right!

Kinstrey stared up moodily at the ceiling. Outside, wind soughed in the pines, a cold, mournful sound. If only he could get Cass straightened out, Kinstrey thought. Cass had good stuff in him. One of these days he'd wake up to himself. He should be able to manage the mill, given a little more seasoning. Especially if Joe LeBeau and Milt Mygatt stayed on, and somehow those two didn't strike him as short-stakers. And what, then, would be left to hold one Boise Kinstrey here in the Utah Territory?

Not a damned thing, Kinstrey told himself flatly—and knew that he lied. Abruptly, he flopped over in the bunk and turned his face to the darkened wall. But he kept seeing her brown eyes, hurt, staring, as they had confronted him the night he had brought Bessie Talbot into camp. Eyes that moved over you like a soft brush stroke. He remembered her face, stricken, dead-pale, in the lamplight. Why had she paled so suddenly? Was it because she knew about Bessie, had perhaps seen her around town?

Forget it, Kinstrey told himself. Forget it and forget her. But he couldn't forget what she had done for him. Not altogether. Things she did, she did so quietly, too. Like her finding Joe LeBeau and Milt Mygatt and sending them out here. And then, when there was no one else for the job, coming out here herself, to cook. He should be grateful. Instead he felt torn, angry, bitter. And was really going in to town tomorrow in hope of seeing her.

Be honest with yourself, man! That is it, isn't it? She's got you on a string, by God! Only she doesn't want any part of you. And can you blame her?

Kinstrey kept his face turned to the wall. But the eyes remained, grave, steady, accusing, staring at him out of the shadows. They didn't go until he sank, finally, into a troubled and restless sleep.

It was around nine the following morning when Boise Kinstrey reached the outskirts of Virginia City and presently swung his dun into a long upgrade course that was actually the vestigial starting point of C Street. For lack of a good night's sleep he felt surly and on edge, hardly in a mood to present olive branches to anybody. When he reached the main street, his eyes somberly began accosting the signs along the way: S. BLOOMFIELD—CIGARS, STATIONERY & FANCY GOODS; BLACK & HOWELL, PROVISIONS & HARDWARE; WILLARD & EILS, BLACKSMITHING; E. RUHLING & CO., ASSAY OFFICE . . .

Suddenly he started. A familiar lanky figure in a white Stetson and fawn-colored jacket had just stepped up to a doorway next to Ruhling's, and on a crabbed impulse Kinstrey gigged his dun in toward the walk and sang out, "Johnson? Hold it a minute, will you?"

Lank Johnson turned, his long face showing neither friendliness nor much surprise as he recognized Kinstrey.

"You get to town a lot these days," he said. "What can I do for you, friend?"

Kinstrey had the dun pulled down; he sat saddle slack-hipped, staring down at Johnson's rather prominent thin nose and impassive mild eyes. "I don't remember meeting you the last time I was in town."

Johnson smiled. "When an important business man is seen, the news gets around."

Kinstrey had expected to feel a blunt hostility toward this man, and now was faintly surprised when he did not. He said, "I'm looking for Soldier Charley. Wondered if you'd seen him around anyplace?"

"Charley?" Johnson thought a moment, then shook his head. "Come to think of it I don't believe I have. Not for a couple days anyhow."

Kinstrey shrugged. "No matter, I guess." Then, feeling a certain awkwardness from Johnson's manner of expecting fuller explanation of his inquiry, he tersely spelled out his reason for making it.

He thought the promoter had tensed slightly at his mention of Frank Bell's name and a second later was sure of it as he drove the question, "You wouldn't happen to know Bell yourself, I suppose?"

Johnson said, "No. No, the name's new to me," and with a nervous gesture took off his showy Stetson, cuffed his hand across the brim a couple times, then placed it back on his head. "Well," he said quickly then, "I've got to get along; appointment over at the Crystal. I'll let you know if I should run into Charley."

"Be obliged," Kinstrey said.

He watched the promoter launch his long beanpole legs into ground-consuming strides, thinking darkly: He *does* know Bell. And I'll bet a hat Marna does too.

Kinstrey gigged the dun, drawing it out from the walk and heading it back into the street. He was remembering how Marna, too, had reacted peculiarly to the name of Bell. What did it mean? And why had Johnson suddenly seemed in such a hurry to get on to the Crystal?

Uncertainty puckered Kinstrey's chapped lips as he nudged the dun again. He would have sworn that a bare moment before he had come along the promoter had been on the point of opening the door to his office and going in. Had something that he had said changed Johnson's mind?

Kinstrey rode on, preoccupied, almost missing C's intersection with Glory Climb. He swung belatedly down from the saddle and led the dun back to the empty hitch rack in front of Jules Mannerheim's. Then he strode long-leggedly across the plank walk and entered the store.

Inside, Jules Mannerheim stood alone in back of the counter. His sad eyes jerked up from a bolt of cloth he was folding as Kinstrey greeted him, then asked, "All alone today?"

The storekeeper nodded. *"Ja. Herr* Calbraith is getting a little sunshine; he and Effie are out, I am afraid. But *Fräulein* Calbraith—"

"Is *going* out. If nobody minds."

Kinstrey swung and saw Marna. "I'd like to talk to you first," he said.

Marna's eyes, clear, candle-flame blue, fixed on him coldly. "What about?" she asked. "I'm in rather a hurry."

"You don't need to be," Kinstrey said. "I just saw your friend Johnson. He's not at his office just now."

He felt a vicious satisfaction, seeing her start; then a meager smile replaced her startled look and she yielded. "Very well, Boise. What do you want?"

"I want to know," said Kinstrey, "why you lied to me the other day about not knowing Frank Bell."

This time he saw his shaft hit home with full impact. Marna paled, then in a provoked way bit at her rounded red underlip.

"Why should I lie about that?" she countered. "Frank Bell means nothing to me."

"No," Kinstrey said. "But Lank Johnson does."

He heard a door slam remotely and noticed that Jules Mannerheim had tactfully removed himself from earshot. A kindly and considerate man. Kinstrey's eyes forced Marna's. "Well?" he demanded.

Marna burst out, "How I feel about Lank Johnson is none of your business! Or how he feels about me! You had your chance, Boise. But you were blind to it. You—"

"I never had a chance," Kinstrey said. "Not after you'd met Johnson and found out he could build you a house with silver doors and gold doorknobs!"

The sudden sweeping up of her hand caught him by surprise. The bruising slap burned across his cheek like needles of fire and seemed to daze him momentarily.

Marna's cheeks flamed with anger. "There!" she said. "I don't like insults, Mr. Kinstrey, and now you know."

"At least I know where we stand with each other." Kinstrey's voice was cold, dispassionate, as he lunged suddenly and grabbed her by the wrists. "But there's something else I've got to know," he added with gritty flatness.

"Boise, let go of me!" She gave a furious jerk but his grip only tightened and she gasped with pain.

"Stand still!" Kinstrey rasped. "Now listen to me. You *did* know Bell, didn't you?"

"It's none of your business!"

"Where did you meet him, Marna?"

"You—you're hurting me!"

"Answer then."

"Well . . . it was at Lank Johnson's office."

"So! The man who shot your brother is a friend of Johnson's, is he?"

"No! He's not."

"Then what was he doing in Johnson's office?"

"Boise, you'll be sorry for this!"

"What was Bell doing in Johnson's office?"

Oh, what does it matter? He'd located a claim. He wanted backing from Lank to help develop it."

"Johnson told you this?"

"Yes."

"Where is this claim, do you know?"

"It's below the south end of the Comstock Lode. In Gold Hill. Somewhere near the Alpha Mine, I think."

Kinstrey's voice thinned. "Your friend Johnson picks himself nice cronies. One of them shoots your own brother. And you try and cover up for him."

"You're just stupid! You don't understand."

"Understand what?"

"I was only keeping a confidence for Lank. He didn't want it known that Bell had been to see him; that he even knew Bell. He was afraid that if news of the claim leaked out someone might beat his offer for an interest."

"How do you know Bell's lead is valuable?"

"Lank told me. Now will you let go of my wrists?"

Kinstrey ignored the request. He said with soft aversion, "Bell might have killed Cass. But you kept your mouth shut." His voice filled, thickened. "By God, I believe you'd have let him get away with murder! Just so that money-crazy dude of yours could get his itchy paws on another fat jackpot!"

The front door bell jingled as a man in miner's garb entered the store. He walked through to the rear, where Jules Mannerheim came out to wait on him.

"There!" Marna cried in a tense whisper. "Did you see how that man stared at us? Boise, you've got to stop this and let me go."

"Why? So you can slap me again?"

"You're out of your head! Is this the way you wrestle with that little blond baggage you've been sharing with Cass? If it is—"

Marna stopped. She was facing the front door and could see Effie and Cass as they entered, while Kinstrey could not. Kinstrey's face went white with anger as she suddenly stepped up against him and flattened her mouth to his. He was conscious of his hands falling away from her out of pure bewilderment; then her arms swept around him and for the time of a breath space she held him in a tight embrace, her bosom hard against his chest.

Kinstrey realized even as he jerked back from her that his action must have a guilty look. Dazed, he saw Effie flounce past him, her eyes set stonily forward. He caught a whiff of Marna's lingering perfume, heard a ripple of mocking laughter as she strutted to the door. She called from there, "Good-by, Boise—*darling!*" and then a man's voice was jabbering excitedly and someone was urgently pulling his arm. He wheeled and recognized Cass.

"Damn it, don't you hear what I'm saying?" Cass was demanding fiercely. "I saw him! I just saw Jack Raimo!"

21

THE SHIFT BOSS at the Alpha Mine told Boise Kinstrey, "Why, yes; there is a claim down this spur a piece, maybe a mile, two mile. Nothin' but a wildcat, though. Bound to be in borasca down there—location's too far from the main quartz ledge."

"I see," murmured Kinstrey, and crossed a knowing look toward Cass, standing beside him. "Would you know a man named Frank Bell?" he asked the foreman.

"Bell, Bell ... nope, can't say I do, mister. We're busy here. I don't get outside much."

"Well, much obliged anyway," Kinstrey said, and turned. His dun stood hipshot a few yards from the mine's hoisting house. Reaching it, he threw a deliberate long glance toward Cass's hired chestnut as he climbed into the saddle.

"Think that coon-footer'll last you on in?" he asked dubiously.

"This horse is all right." Cass was curt. He read Kinstrey's troubled look and added irritably, "And so am I, if you've still got any doubts about it. I told you Doc said I could ride."

"Tomorrow, you said."

"What difference will one day make?"

"None, I hope." Kinstrey blew out a resigned breath. "All right," he said. "Let's slope, then."

It was a moderately cold day—a degree or two under freezing, Kinstrey judged—but there was no more freshness or sweetness in the air here than there was in Virginia City. Gritty gray alkali from arrastras mingled with the swirling soot of smokestacks to smudge the sky and darken the sun. They crossed a low ridge where the raw earth bled from a trace of cinnabar and showed faint ocherous vestiges of sulphur. A jack-rabbit bolted from a clump of sage and from a hole in some rocks a spiny pocket-mouse peeped out, his beads of eyes bright with curiosity.

Kinstrey, with little conscious awareness of these sights and

155

sounds, drove his vacant gaze forward and down. The vestigial trace before them wound through rocky terrain from which most of the usable wood had long since been grubbed out, leaving only the perennial sagebrush and an occasional scrubby juniper or palsied pine. Were they on the right track? Kinstrey wondered. A few yards back he had noticed horse droppings that had looked fresh. But that in itself meant little. Only that a horse and rider had been by here, perhaps fairly recently.

Kinstrey took a covert cornerwise glance at Cass, riding tight-lipped and stony-eyed beside him. Cass looked pale, sickly. The kid had taken some hard licks but Kinstrey sensed a change in him. It wasn't a definable change, just something one felt. And in Kinstrey the feeling was that the change was for the better. Cass looked older and wiser somehow. But something lay latent in his dark eyes—something inscrutable and puzzling to Kinstrey. A kind of grimness. Or was it simply the old sullen stubbornness and defiance, gone masked and ingrown under the hard batterings of experience?

Kinstrey's thoughts back-tracked. A while after their start from the City Cass had told him, with startling unexpectedness, "Sorry about that trouble between us out at camp, Boise," and he had curtly replied, "Forget it."

But Cass hadn't wanted to drop it. "I guess I made a pretty big fool of myself," he continued doggedly. "You know—over her."

"You're not the only one."

"She's really a fine girl, Boise."

"Sure, sure."

"I think she's in love with you," Cass said.

Kinstrey's breath caught and he twisted around, startled. "You're crazy!" he jerked out.

Cass shook his head. "You can't ever tell."

"I can tell." Kinstrey's voice was ragged. "You're the one she goes for walks with."

"She just felt sorry for me. I can't talk to Marna any more."

"Listen," Kinstrey said. "Why don't you wake up and learn about women? They don't show that much interest in a man just because they're sorry for him."

Cass stared bluntly at him. "When are you going to wake up about Marna, Boise?"

"I already have."

"It didn't look like it back there at the store."

Kinstrey explained that, watching Cass's face slowly darken. "The tricky little tart!" Cass exploded, when he had finished.

Kinstrey turned in the saddle, startled by the venom in Cass's voice. "I'll say this," he returned mildly. "Marna's welcome to Johnson if she wants him."

"She's wanted him all along," grumbled Cass. "I told you what she was."

"Sure." Kinstrey had dismissed it. "Sure, you told me," and then had gigged the dun, sending it into a brief canter which had shot him ahead of Cass's horse.

A few minutes after that something had happened which had given him an unexpected reprieve from the gloom into which he had sunk. He had met Larsen Petersen and the flume gang returning to town in their wagons and Petersen had given him the surprising news that the flume was finished and would be ready to operate as soon as he and Philip Deidesheimer could give it a final inspection in the morning.

Kinstrey's hopes had soared after the meeting with Petersen. But now, as he and Cass rode deeper into the bleak wilderness below the Alpha, they sank again as he bleakly considered Jack Raimo's sudden reappearance on the scene. But wasn't it possible that Cass had been mistaken in his identification? He had admitted that Raimo had looked "different." The gunman had been sporting a fancy mustache, for one thing, and for another had been dressed to the nines in a new suit and hat. If Raimo had been forced to lay low for so long where had he suddenly found the money to get himself spraddled out like that?

Kinstrey's eyes became remote, canvassing the barren brown slope before him. Maybe Cass *had* been mistaken. When he had spotted Raimo—coming out of the Crystal—the gunman had been moving fast, and with the crowd milling in front of the saloon and all, it was just possible that he'd been deceived in—

The Crystal! Kinstrey jerked taut suddenly. How could he have forgotten that? More, how could he have possibly overlooked tying that in with the rest of it?

Shock brings a clarity to the brain, like an abrupt surging of light into a dark place. Now, almost as if in clairvoyance,

Kinstrey's thoughts raced backward. The Crystal was one link; now others sprang to his mind. Links of suspicion. Links that alone meant nothing. But tied together, they forged a naked and unmistakable chain of guilt!

Cass's voice impinging on Kinstrey's abstraction startled him alert.

"Anything the matter, Boise?"

"Matter?" muttered Kinstrey. "No; what makes you think that?"

"I don't know," answered Cass. "The way you looked, I guess. Just for a minute."

Kinstrey frowned. "I had a brain storm. It's probably crazy. Let's get more work out of these nags."

They speeded up the horses a bit. After a time Cass grumbled, "I don't see a sign of any damned tunnel, do you?"

"No," Kinstrey replied. "But we haven't made two miles yet."

"Close to it, I'd say."

"We've been up, down and around," Kinstrey pointed out. "Makes it hard to judge."

They rode on, silence again falling between them. Kinstrey took off his gloves and blew on cold-numbed fingers. Overhead the sky hung out clouds that resembled forbidding gray tumors. Before them the tan belt of the trace rolled on in endless undulations.

Kinstrey's uneasiness sagged into worry. Suppose he'd just been playing a wild guessing game suspecting that Bell's claim might be the hideaway for Ganahl's gang? And believing that Jack Raimo had headed this way? For that matter, how did he know but what Cass had mistaken someone else for Raimo, back in town?

Kinstrey gnawed fretfully on his chapped underlip. If Bell and Bell's cronies *had* high-tailed it out here it seemed reasonable to suppose that Soldier Charley would have notified him before now. Unless, of course, something had happened to the Piute. And in that case—

"Look!" Cass cried abruptly.

Kinstrey's eyes jerked up. Cass had taken a few yards' lead on him and now sat his horse on a boulder-ringed ridge, from which the terrain appeared to slope sharply downward once more.

Kinstrey prodded the dun. At the same time he called in a tense undertone, "What is it?"

"Keep in back of these rocks," Cass warned as he worked the dun up the rise. He was pointing as Kinstrey reached the top. "And look down there."

A crack between abutting boulders afforded Kinstrey a meager peep hole as he ranged his horse between them. He peered out and gave a low whistle. Downward and to his left a tunnel ran into the side of a rocky bluff. The entrance was boarded up except for a narrow opening covered by a length of tarp, and some ten yards to the right an empty corral of flimsy poles showed up lonesomely. The front gate bars were down and Kinstrey noticed that the ground in front looked freshly churned.

"Guess our birds flew the coop," he murmured.

"Wha'd you expect?" growled Cass. "If Raimo did come out here, it wasn't just to say howdy. Maybe this place had gotten hot. Maybe he came to warn Ganahl."

"Maybe." Kinstrey spoke absently. He was staring down, vaguely watching the tarp as it flapped desolately under the slaps of an icy wind. Straight west of here, barely five miles as the crow could fly it, lay their sawmill mountain, with its great wooden vein through which would flow shortly an unending stream of dressed timbers for the bowels of Ophir. The flume; finished. And not too far from here. Suppose Ganahl had been keeping tabs on the job, knew that Larsen Petersen and his gang had quit early today? And what if Petersen had failed to notify Pat Manogue of his early departure?

Kinstrey's violent spinning of the dun sent Cass's chestnut into a startled buck.

"Hey, easy!" Cass gasped out. The chestnut quieted, but now was blocking Kinstrey's horse as Cass hitched around in the saddle. "What's the rush?" he asked Kinstrey. "Don't you want to look the place over down there?"

Kinstrey sat rigid on the dun. "No! We're heading for camp. Must be a trail they've been using. We'll pick it up."

"But why—"

"You ask too damned many questions!" Gnawed to fury with impatience Kinstrey drove his dun against the livery mount. The chestnut gave ground with a protesting whinny and started crow-hopping as Kinstrey's angry working of the

dun forced it on past. He heard Cass blurt angrily from behind him, "Still have to be the Big Britches, don't you,
Boise?" and then at an unexpected sound from his right he
tightened the dun's reins with a jerky suddenness.

The fretted horse reared as a twig snapped and brush
crashed startlingly. Kinstrey had his Walker skinned from
leather and was fighting the dun, now crawfishing wildly,
when he saw the sorrel slog out of a thick tangle of brush
and simultaneously heard Cass's frenzied yell, "Boise! Don't
shoot, for God's sake!"

Kinstrey slid from the dun in a reckless drop and then was
dog-trotting across the hummocky ground toward the yel-
low-reddish horse. Soldier Charley sat the sorrel's saddle, his
long torso tipped a little forward, like a tilted statue.

Kinstrey noticed that the Piute's manner of saluting him
seemed labored. Anxiety exploded into exasperation with his
question, "Charley, what the devil happened to you? It's been
three days now!"

Soldier Charley's black campaign hat rested askew at the
back of his head and his ordinarily alive black eyes seemed
sunk in apathy as he nodded stolidly to his right. Kinstrey,
following the nod, saw a brushy bluff which commanded a
view of the tunnel entrance.

"Me watch," grunted Charley. "Me up there."

Kinstrey waved impatiently. "All right! Then you must
have seen them when they lit out of here. What time was
that?"

Stoically, Soldier Charley shook his head. "No see," he
said.

"But Charley, you were up there watching! How could—"

"Man come. Surprise Charley."

"Raimo!" Cass, down from the chestnut now, came hurrying to where Kinstrey stood tracked beside the sorrel. "He
must mean Raimo, Boise!"

Kinstrey was starting to turn when he noticed the red drop
fattening at a corner of Soldier Charley's mouth. He stopped
his swing and stared at it, chilling. Suddenly the sphere burst,
daubing the Indian's bronze skin with a streak of scarlet.

Shocked realization dried Kinstrey's voice as he blurted,
"Charley, for God's sake! What happened up there?"

A greenish pallor tinging Charley's cheeks was suddenly

more noticeable as he bent and gripped his saddle horn with both hands.

"Charley—work—three day," he mumbled in jerky gasps. "You—you pay um—six—"

"Boise!" Cass cried. "Look out!"

Soldier Charley's right hand had slued out from the saddle horn, palm extended. His coppery skin became ghastly as he tipped.

Kinstrey's arms already were up. He caught the frail body and lowered it tenderly to the frozen ground. Then, remaining hunkered down, he worked at the pinned folds of the crude blanket coat. As it came open he gasped.

The row of gimcrack medals fastened to Soldier Charley's shirt swam in a soup of bright vermilion from his hemorrhaging lungs. Suddenly a spongy cough shook him and he twitched convulsively. A shuddering breath started, stopped.

"Boise?" Cass said. "Is he—"

"He's dead." Kinstrey's voice was hollow. For a moment he remained rigid, staring down at the still, waxy face in shocked immobility. Then he reached slowly into his mackinaw pocket and took out a rumpled bandanna. His jaw muscles ridged as he spread it gently across the starkly upstaring eyes.

"It's a wonder he lasted this long," breathed Cass.

Kinstrey straightened heavily. He said, "Come on!" and strode to the dun, his brusque glance barely brushing the man with him. His teeth were clamped as he swung himself violently into the saddle.

He realized that Cass, still motionless beside the body of the Indian, was staring back at him with cold disapproval.

"Look!" he grated. "Don't think I like leaving him here. Nobody could owe that poor redskin any more than I do."

"Then why don't we take him?" argued Cass. "We can pack him in on the sorrel."

"No!" Kinstrey was emphatic. "There's no time. We'll have to send back later."

Cass walked with stiff huffishness to his chestnut, then wheeled as he came beside it and angrily met Kinstrey's flat stare. "Maybe you can tell me," he flared, "why we're in such a bloody hurry we can't—"

"Damn it," exploded Kinstrey, "can't you figure anything for yourself? Suppose Ganahl's had a man watching the mill?

Petersen's gone. This may be just the chance he's been waiting for."

"Well, why couldn't you have mentioned that before?"

"There's been too much gab already. Satisfied now?"

"I'm ready." Cass tongued a boot in his stirrup ring and swung into the saddle. He stared around then at Kinstrey's stiff-set face. "They'd have a pretty good start on us," he asked, "wouldn't they?"

"Too good, would be my guess." Kinstrey's voice was flat. "But maybe Manogue had guards out." He waved Cass with him and started the dun, afraid even for that slim hope, now.

22

IT WAS lively curiosity, rather than any thought of precaution, that prompted Pat Manogue to stroll out of camp that afternoon for a look at the new flume. Guards, he had decided, need not be set out until it was dark. He had been given notice of Larsen Petersen's early leaving but a certain innate thriftiness in him shrank from wasting man power in profitless and probably unnecessary vigil.

There was another thought at the back of Manogue's mind as he crossed the yarding area to the right of the mill and for a moment feasted his eyes on an imposing pile of freshly sawed posts, smelling richly of bleeding pitch. When Boise got back from town tonight he wanted to be able to brag of a record day's production, and judging from the way that little Frenchy, Joe LeBeau, rassled with a saw, the record would be set. Manogue smiled in pleased anticipation.

A short distance from the yarding lot a fork of Washoe Creek maintained a brisk flow of water through an ice-bordered channel. Manogue crossed the stream where the banks pinched in and a small bridge had been thrown up by Petersen's men. Reaching the farther bank he glanced briefly at the gate by which water could be diverted at will from creek to flume, then went on a little farther to where the shelf of level terrain abruptly ended and the mountain pitched sharply downward again.

Manogue had come to look, but not to exert himself unduly, and now he took from his pocket a pair of binoculars that he had rummaged out of some junk in one of the wagons. He adjusted the lenses to his eyes and the flume's slanted sides sprang into focus. Moving the glasses very slowly he began following the course of the big conduit down the shank of the mountain.

Suddenly he stiffened. Three-quarters of the distance down the stump-checkered slope, the glasses sharply limned the figure of a man. Manogue's breath froze, then gushed out in relief as he observed that the man was merely tying up bundles of dried slash and roping them together. Probably someone Petersen had left behind, he decided, to clear the slash away from the flume and burn it.

"Swith!" muttered Manogue in annoyance. "Th' big Swede might've told a man."

He continued angling the glasses on downward, stopping with a jerk of breath as the eyes of the lenses caught suddenly on two new figures.

"Well, God give me patience!" he blurted, staring. "Two more! And all that fussin' an' flutterin' around f'r th' sake of a few bundles av faggots!"

Holding the glasses steady he watched the men pull several small rolls of the slash into a heap and tie them together. Then joining a maguey to the tie rope they began dragging the huge bale into an underpocket where the flume trestled over a low gully.

"Thorns av Calvary!" burst from Manogue. "Now why w'ud they be doin' that unless—"

Suddenly it was clear. Manogue whirled. He ran very fast and lithely for a big man, back toward the mill.

Boise Kinstrey and Cass Calbraith brought their horses up to a high knoll and unexpectedly came into a full view of the road skirting the easterly flank of the mill mountain.

"Boise, look!" Cass called in sudden surprise. "You can see where the south trail starts up the mountain from here."

Kinstrey nodded without removing his eyes from the road curving around the mountain's east slope. The flume was north on that road, a mile, maybe less. He brought his glance back on Cass and noticed the drawn look on his face. "Rest a minute," he suggested.

"Rest if you need it," Cass said. "I don't."

Kinstrey showed rancor only in his abruptness in gigging the dun. "All right! Let's slope then."

They started down off the knoll, Kinstrey's mouth compressed. Cass's face too had become hard-set, and making his covert glance toward it Kinstrey despairingly thought: He's got to prove he's hell on wheels if it kills him.

They came out on the road and pointed the horses north. The animals were still capable of an occasional lope but Kinstrey could feel the dun tiring under him. His mind retreated into fatalism. What's the difference? he thought gloomily. By now Ganahl's probably been there and gone.

Kinstrey's eyes pinched. But suppose delays had occurred? Ganahl, for example, might have discovered guards posted and decided to wait for darkness. Or he might still be reconnoitering the slope. The possibilities renewed a faint hope in Kinstrey.

They came onto a steep upgrade and the horses bent to a dogged plodding. Kinstrey felt a reviving sense of urgency as he began recognizing landmarks. Another long swing, at the crest of this grade, and the flume would be visible, plunging down the mountainside like a mammoth wooden spinal column. Suddenly new impatience gnawed at Kinstrey. And then the mountain stillness was shattered by percussive blurts of sound.

Cass's head jerked up. "That sounded like gunfire!"

Kinstrey went taut, then discounted, "Or maybe just a skinner up ahead somewhere, snapping his bullwhip." He didn't want Cass going off half-cocked again but his hand nevertheless slid down unobtrusively and made verifying contact with the stock of his Winchester before withdrawing.

The hill's final hump was sharp and he roughly fought the dun up over it, then swerved abruptly in ahead of the chestnut which Cass now was furiously attempting to whack back into life. A ratatat drumming beat at the stillness again as Kinstrey made a grab for the coon-foot's bridle reins and gave a restraining yank.

"Slow down!" he barked at Cass.

"Why?" demanded Cass tensely. "You heard it—those were shots! And look ahead there. Isn't that smoke?"

Kinstrey looked, and felt his stomach sink. Interlaced with the overall atmospheric grayness ahead were smudges of darker gray which could be smoke. He said with deliberate self-restraint, "There's a ridge at the head of this bend. Simmer down now. We'll have a look when we get there."

"Like to give the orders, don't you, Boise?"

Kinstrey had to bite down on his lip to restrain a sharp retort. "I'm older; I've had more experience. Let it go at that."

They had the horses trotting gently. Ahead and to the right of the road loomed the ridge, a rocky, flat barren fringed with sagebrush.

"Sure, let it go at that!" mimicked Cass. "You're the big augur. I'm just the kid who's not dry behind the ears yet!"

"Whatever you say, Cass."

"Why don't you spit it out, Boise? Say what you really think about me?"

Kinstrey twisted in the saddle. "Goddamnit, will you quit this? I've told you before I owe you more than I can ever pay back. But I want you as a live friend, not a dead hero."

He was aware of a sudden uncertainty in Cass's eyes, then a kind of odd wistfulness, "Oh, to hell with it!" Cass repudiated abruptly. "I guess I am just a sorehead, Boise. But sometimes—"

He broke off as Kinstrey suddenly stiffened. The sound was a vague muffled tattoo at first, then was more distinct, expanding into the unmistakable swift detonations of shod hoofs flailing a frozen roadbed.

"Quick!" Kinstrey motioned tensely to the right, where a slab of high rock offered protection at the edge of the road. "You take that side," he told Cass. "I'll fort up over here."

"But whereabouts? I don't see any good place—"

"Damn you, *move!*" Kinstrey swept off his hat and in the next split second had swatted the chestnut across the rump with it, sending the startled animal into a bouncy canter toward the rock slab.

Approaching hoofbeats now sounded alarmingly near as Kinstrey dropped from the saddle and flogged the dun into a nervous trot toward the side of the road. He heard it crash into some brush as he ran for the only cover he could see—a cairn of small stones heaped into a ditchside pile some dozen yards ahead of him.

He didn't run far. The ground was rough and hummocky and he had taken only a few hopping strides when his right leg sank in a pothole and he was thrown sprawling. The fall smashed the breath out of him and he was dizzily starting to rise from his hands and knees when two riders came into sudden view around the bend ahead of him.

He could only gape as the lead rider recognized him; then in the miracle of a breath space Al Moss brutally rechecked his paint and with a fluid shift of his right hand cleared his gun.

Moss shouldn't have missed at the distance. He fired three times, the kicks of the bullets in the frozen ground following

Kinstrey as he rolled. Kinstrey's subconscious retained memory of a shallow ditch to his right. As he flung himself into it he heard gunfire crash from the rock where he had left Cass. He looked gingerly up over the lip of the trench.

Beside Moss a big claybank was rearing violently, and as Kinstrey breathlessly recognized Frank Ganahl on it the horse abruptly swiveled and slammed against Moss's paint, throwing it into a vicious bucking.

Then, suddenly, the paint seemed to go wholly berserk. There was a frenzied snort as its back warped and it savagely sunfished. Moss was hurled from the saddle at the instant Ganahl was yelling, "Al, the rock! Watch that rock!" and then Kinstrey was almost sick seeing one great hairy hoof of the claybank smash down on the head of the man pinned under it.

There was no sound but an eggshell crunch; Ganahl's horse was still dancing as Kinstrey saw the shank of blue steel slanting down at him from the rider's right hand. He lunged up out of the ditch as Ganahl's first bullet struck earth warmed by his body. A second chipped flints from a rock beside him and ricocheted with a vibrant whine. A third never came.

Cass firing again had apparently creased the claybank. The terrified animal reared, and then as it started a spin a section of Ganahl's gray wampus shirt was fleetingly broadside to Kinstrey and he squeezed off three shots in stuttering sequence.

The first slug shattered the right elbow of the blond-haired rider and dropped his arm slackly to his side. A second and a third both entered the gray cardigan, stitching it with contiguous black buttonholes.

Ganahl's broad frame slanted out from the saddle, then, over-balanced, somersaulted loosely down as the claybank shied from the body and trotted delicately aside with its stirrup leathers flapping.

Kinstrey glanced only briefly at the two corpses sprawled in the road as he climbed to his feet and shook the stiffness out of his legs. Then he walked to where his dun stood hipshot, opposite the slab of rock that had sheltered Cass. He rocked up into the saddle before calling, "Cass? All clear now. Come on out."

Cass Calbraith's face was a chalky white as he stepped

from behind the rock, leading the livery chestnut. Kinstrey looked at him and was touched to tolerance.

"Messy, all right," he said, with a backward nod toward Moss. "Look the other way if it turns your stomach."

Cass piled into the chestnut's saddle, hitched around fiercely. "Think I'd puke over a son of a bitch like him?"

Kinstrey answered mildly, "I could have, easy enough. So calm down. I only thought—"

"I know what you thought! So stop covering up. You thought I was cold-footed in that fight."

"Cold-footed!" Kinstrey stared with honest astonishment at the tight, tormented face of the man forking the chestnut. "Are you loco?" he breathed then. "Your first shot spooked Moss's horse and helped put him out of business. Then you pinked the claybank. If you hadn't—"

"Ah, don't give me that bellywash!"

"But it's true."

"Sure. And while I had a nice big rock to hunker in back of, you were out there throwing gravel in their boots. Who got Ganahl?"

"I did—with your help. And don't forget I was the one put you in back of that rock. You did all right, I tell you."

"Sure," said Cass with bitter softness, "sure, I always do all right when somebody else wrastles the calf before I come out and rope it."

"You're making a mountain out of a molehill, kid."

"Kid! That's what I am, all right! Just a kid who needs some calking up his backbone."

"You need a swift kick in the pants maybe."

"What about those bodies?"

"I'll have Manogue send back."

"Come on then! There must've been more in the party than just these two. Let's find out what happened at the flume."

Cass gigged the chestnut with a waspish kick, then, as he came abreast of the bodies stretched out in the road, looked deliberately down and spat.

Kinstrey let out a sighing breath, starting the dun. He understood Cass, and, understanding, feared for him. One of these days the kid would bid too rashly for the homage he craved, the affection and understanding he needed but had never known. Then Heaven help him! thought Kinstrey, and worked the dun into a grudging lope.

A few charred boards of the flume were still wisping smoke as Boise Kinstrey and Cass Calbraith reached the point of its runoff and dismounted, leading their horses in off the road and tying them to a whip of juniper. Kinstrey then felt a relaxing relief as his gaze anxiously reconnoitered the slope. Where the mountain ledged broadly some hundred yards up from the road, members of the mill crew were at work drawing off bundles of smoldering, soggy-looking slash from under the duct's burned areas. But even from here it was apparent that the damage was minor. A dozen or two charred boards would have to be ripped out and replaced. Beyond that, the big trough appeared intact.

Beside Kinstrey, Cass stood sullenly mute. Kinstrey said, "Looks like we got off lucky."

"Maybe."

"What's that mean? You've got eyes."

"We haven't talked with Pat yet."

"Come on, let's talk to him then. Somebody up there's looking down at us with a pair of field glasses. Maybe that's Pat."

The grade was abrupt at the start, and Kinstrey was aware of a sudden drawing tiredness in the calves of his legs as they began to climb. Halfway up, a huge deadfall had torn a great round crater out of the earth, and they were circling this when a shout drove their attention upward. From a bluff to the right, Pat Manogue waved. Then he was tilting, sliding, scrambling down a shaley embankment to meet them.

"Swith!" he panted, and then before he could utter a word more Kinstrey curtly motioned him toward a flat rock at the rim of the excavation. "Squat and catch your breath," Kinstrey said tersely. "Then let's have it. Short and sweet."

The voluble wagon boss didn't wait to get his breath. He gasped out what he had to tell in a few jerky sentences. From up on the ridge he'd spotted the skulkers with a pair of field glasses, then had alerted the crew. By that time the raiders had set torches to the dried slash heaped around the flume, but Geehaw Jenkins' opening of the flume gate to full width had sent water spilling down in such over-volume that the flames had been extinguished before too much damage could be done.

Meanwhile the raiders had been caught in a cross-fire of the mill crew's guns. One had managed to flee to cover and escape, but of the two others, one, a man named Ike Waldo, had been killed, and the third, who called himself Red Danahy, had been shot painfully and perhaps seriously through the leg. The raider who had got away he had been able to view through the glasses, galloping northward, toward Virginia City. The man's name, Danahy had told him, was Bell.

"Frank Bell," Kinstrey supplied grimly, when the wagon boss had finished. "And there were two others you never spotted—Ganahl, and Al Moss."

Pat Manogue's eyes bulged disbelievingly. "Ganahl an' Moss? Sure, ye're joshin' a man now!"

"They were here all right," affirmed Kinstrey. "But it's my guess they stayed behind the scenes just to watch things, and then lit a fast shuck when your boys sprang their surprise."

Excitement flared in Manogue's voice. "Ye crossed trail with th' spalpeens!" he surmised, and reading confirmation in Kinstrey's eyes demanded, "What happened, in the name av God?"

Kinstrey told him, Manogue listening without interruption as he added a brief recital of antecedent occurrences. Then as he concluded the wagon boss whacked his knee and blurted, "Bucko, ye've done it! Ganahl, be God! There'll be a fast witherin' on th' vine now av what's left av th' gang!"

"Raimo's still loose. And what if there was—" Kinstrey stopped. There was a sudden bleakness on his face, a quick wonder in his thoughtfully pinched eyes. "This man Danahy said was Bell," he brought out abruptly. "Could that have been Raimo, do you think?"

"It c'ud not have been. Bell's tall. Raimo's a runt."

Kinstrey stood. "I'll have a look at the flume. Then I've got to get back to town." He turned, looked blank for an instant, then suddenly wheeled again to stare back at Manogue. "Where the devil's Cass?" he fumed. "He was here a minute ago."

Manogue rose. "So he was. But actin' restless, I noticed. He probably wint up to talk with th' boys."

"Come on!" Kinstrey said. He walked to the shale slide.

Manogue started after him like a great ungainly bear as he began climbing with quick, angry bursts of speed. He reached the ledge and saw that Cass was not there. Alarm stabbed him.

"Let's see those glasses a minute." He seized them roughly from Manogue, peered through the lenses down to where the horses had been left. The dun was still tied to the juniper. The chestnut was gone.

23

C STREET's sharp-angled buildings were beginning to blur and soften in dusk as Boise Kinstrey led his wearied dun to the hitch rack in front of Jules Mannerheim's mercantile and wearily looped its reins over the tie bar. He had searched every saloon and gambling dive on the street without luck. He had cut no sign of Cass, nor any of Jack Raimo and Frank Bell. Had he been a bigger fool than he thought Cass was—expecting to find Cass prowling the town on a lone-wolf hunt for Raimo?

Kinstrey slowly released a breath as his peering eyes foraged the street one last time, up and down. He felt bushed. But he had to be sure about this. And there was still the possibility that Cass might have come here to the store first, to see Effie.

Kinstrey frowned as he stamped his feet to work the numbness out of them. It was going to be very cold. With the sun down the air had taken on a bitter metallic taste that was somehow remindful of the copper in the town's drinking water. The tip of Kinstrey's nose showed flanges of crimson, and his flat cheeks had a slack look of tiredness and seemed faintly bluish. He stretched four long strides to cross the board walk and reach the entrance to the mercantile.

The small bell hung inside gave its warning tinkle as Kinstrey pushed against the door and stepped into a domain of warmth, dimness, and tangy overall redolence of fresh leather and calico smells. Effie Mannerheim was behind the counter, stacking some empty boxes. Her face had a momentary inquiring look as she swung around; then as recognition came it seemed to Kinstrey as if impersonal dark veils had suddenly been dropped across her eyes.

"Oh!" she exclaimed with surprise. Then her voice cooled into evenness, saying, "Marna's in her room. But before you go, Philip Deidesheimer was here. He left this note for you."

Kinstrey picked up the envelope she had thrust across the

counter toward him and stuffed it into his mackinaw pocket without glancing at it.

"Thanks," he said. He was aware of his voice sounding flat and harsh. He said, "It's not Marna I want to see, though. It's Cass. He been here?"

"Why, yes!" Effie Mannerheim seemed agitated suddenly. Kinstrey stared as her face blanched and she blurted, "Have *you* seen Cass? Is he—all right?"

"I've been looking for him; I didn't find him." Tension ran back in Kinstrey. "What's the matter?" he demanded. "What makes you think he wouldn't be all right?"

Effie said, "Do *you* think he is? Is that why you were out looking for him?"

"What do you know about this, Effie?"

"Only what Uncle Jules told me. Cass *was* here—about an hour ago. I wasn't in at the time but Cass came to buy a gun and Uncle Jules sold him one. A new model Colt that we've just stocked."

Kinstrey's ejaculation had a fierce vehemence. "The gristle-heeled young fool!"

"Boise, what happened? You didn't find Raimo this afternoon, did you?"

Kinstrey's voice was vibrant. "No. But I wish to God we had. Or I had."

He told her of the afternoon's occurrences, bluntly finishing finally, "I downed Ganahl but Cass was a big help to me. He can't believe that, though. He's got a bee in his bonnet that he's gunshy. And now he's going to prove he's a heller if it kills him." Kinstrey's voice flattened. "Which it probably will."

Effie's manner was disquieted, murmuring, "I suppose I'm to blame for part of this. Cass knew I'd looked on him as—well, as a little too young to be serious about a woman three years his senior." She paused, glancing troubledly at Kinstrey's set face, then went on, "But after the fracas at Gentry and Crittenden's, I thought I noticed a change in him. He really seemed to be a stronger kind of person—until Marna let it out that it was you who wounded Frank Bell and not him."

Kinstrey froze. "Marna did that?"

"Why, yes. Didn't Cass tell you?"

"No. But I might have guessed. Damn her!"

Effie stared at him in surprise. "I didn't tell you this out of spite, Boise. I really thought you knew."

A savage bitterness welled in Kinstrey. He said tensely, "I told her to let Cass have the credit. He needed that boost." Anger pitched up his voice. "But kind-hearted Sister had a grudge to work out!"

Effie said gently, "I'm sorry. I wouldn't have mentioned this if I'd known you'd be so upset."

"Upset? Sure I'm upset! But it's not for the reason you're thinking!"

"It's no use, Boise. I saw you with her in your arms this morning."

A last frayed thread had been holding back Kinstrey's temper. Now it snapped. "You didn't see any damned thing of the kind!" he ripped out. "What you saw was an act—put on for your benefit. She doesn't care anything about me! But when she spotted you coming through the door with Cass—"

"Effie knows what happened then. You kissed me."

Kinstrey whirled. Marna Calbraith stood at the far end of the counter, looking glowing and desirable in a dark velvet dress stitched elegantly with creamy rickrack braid. She came up to him at an easy saunter and halted.

"Well, why don't you go on, Boise? I'm dying to hear the rest of it."

Kinstrey sucked in a breath between his teeth, staring at her. Her marble-smooth skin was tinted delicately pink and a warm scent of violet was in the room suddenly.

"All right!" He jerked out the words tightly. "You'll hear it. And right from the horse's mouth."

She rested a hand negligently where her dress molded one slender hip. "Don't you mean jackass's, Boise dear?"

"By God, yes, I do! Because that's what I've been as far as you're concerned—a blind, stupid jackass!"

"Stop blatting nonsense. You remind me of Cass."

"That's what I intend to do! If anything happens to that boy tonight, his blood's going to be on your hands."

"Blood! What on earth are you raving about now?"

Kinstrey's words came in a crescendo of violence. "I'm raving about your telling Cass that his bullet never touched Frank Bell! I'm raving about your wrecking his chance to have a little more pride and respect in himself. I'm raving about your selfishness and meanness and spite, whittling on the kid till he's not sure he's good enough to be third assistant water boy to a whistle punk!"

"Well, is he?"

Kinstrey's wrath boiled over. "Thank God he's not the miserable self-centered thing you are! And maybe you'll understand what he's good for when somebody carries him in here on a shutter—with Jack Raimo's bullet in his guts!"

"Raimo!" For the first time something almost like fear flickered briefly in Marna Calbraith's darkly blue eyes. Then scorn flooded back in her voice. "Nonsense! Now I *know* you're raving. Cass would never have the nerve to—"

"Ah-h, save your breath!" Kinstrey pivoted around from her and faced the girl in back of the counter. In the store's deepening gloom, with no lamps lighted yet, the taut clean lines of Effie Mannerheim's face were shadowed by pallor. "Tell me something," he requested. "Does Lank Johnson have any kind of interest in the Crystal?"

Effie gave him a surprised stare, then glanced uncertainly toward Marna Calbraith before answering, "Why—why, yes. I believe he owns the controlling interest. There's the Belonger brothers, and a man named Wilson Burrish—"

"That's all; thanks." Kinstrey turned to Marna. "Johnson owns about everything but our mill, doesn't he, Marna—including you?"

Marna answered with low-voiced fury, "Nobody owns me! But now I'd marry Lank if I didn't care a fig for him—just to spite you!"

"Then I'll try and not kill him," said Kinstrey, "so you can. That ought to give him all the worst of it."

"Worst of—" Marna gasped, stopped. "*Kill* him!" she blurted out then. "Boise, have you gone stark raving *mad?*"

"No, I don't think so." Kinstrey turned roughly from her to face Effie again. Even in the dingy store light, Effie Mannerheim's clean-limned face had a kind of appealing freshness and winsomeness. Kinstrey's voice was hollow. "Maybe I'll be lucky and find Cass," he told her. "In case I do, I'll say this now. Good luck to both of you."

Effie Mannerheim's large brown eyes seemed to go oddly blank suddenly. She started to say, "Both of us! Boise, you don't think—" but by then he was moving away and her voice trailed away futilely.

He reached the door. He heard Marna cry out with fretful

vehemence, "He *is* crazy!" and then he had the door open and a blast of icy air slammed at him. It felt tingling, revivifying. The night was clear and crackling cold. The snow squeaked under his boot soles as he stepped outside and launched into his long swinging gait, heading upstreet.

Cass Calbraith was beginning to feel a first gnawing fear and uncertainty after he left Jules Mannerheim's and went to Mackwood's Dining Room. The new gun seemed a prodigious weight at his right side; the new holster smelled freshly tanned and creaked with stiffness when he touched it. It's as good a gun as money can buy, he told himself, and knew he was whistling in the dark. A gun had to be backed by something. It had to be backed by a human hand, and the hand in turn had to be backed by quickness and guts. . . .

In the dreary cavern that was Mackwood's he ate a dreary meal of burned steer meat flanked by a splatter of greasy fried potatoes, but tasted nothing. He rose from table with a queasiness in the pit of his stomach that he realized had nothing to do with the dinner, poor as that was. He touched a hand to the squeaky new holster and had a feeling every eye in the room was pinned on him. That was bad enough; the voices were worse. The voices that really didn't speak, yet did. The voices that jeered and taunted: *Mighty purty shootin' arn ya got there, young fella. Whut's it fur—t' fancy up yore pants? Har, har, har!*

They could tell that he had no guts. He could see it in their eyes, the amused, sly glances they seemed to give him. Nobody noticed him or spoke, however, when he rose and walked to the door. He paid his chit and went out. The night air was bracing, and he felt a little of his thin-worn purposefulness coming back. Oddly, however, it wasn't the thought of Raimo—his father's murderer—that goaded him. It was the remembrance of Marna's gibes and insults, Boise's thinly screened protectiveness. And wanting to make a good impression on Effie. Even now. Even when he knew it wasn't going to get him anything.

He started down the street. I'll have a drink, he decided. Just one, to loosen me up a bit. A little ahead, the lights of Orndoff and McGee's flashed through the darkness. Suppose Raimo was in there? At the door Cass faltered. Maybe he'd ought to forget the drink. Take a little more time to think this over.

He stared down at his hand hesitating on the door and an inner voice warned: Don't think. Don't stop. If you stop now you'll never get started again.

He went in. The first two drinks didn't seem to touch him. The third did. After it, he bought a cigar and lighted it with a flourish, unaware of the amused smile of a tall, cadaverous-looking man standing next to him. A pleasant enervation had begun to spread through him as he strolled to the door.

Outside, he found it necessary to concentrate, trying to remember something. Then he did remember. The Crystal. Jack Raimo had been coming out of the Crystal when he'd spotted him this morning. Maybe that was where he'd find Raimo now.

The Crystal was a block from Orndoff and McGee's. In exhilarated preoccupation, Cass almost passed it. He giggled out, "Hey!" and lurched around. His first lunge at the door handle missed, but he caught it the second time and grinning at his cleverness swung open the door and took a feathery step across the threshold.

Standing just inside the doorway he looked around him with awe, blinking against the iridescent light shimmering down on him from a huge chain-hung cut-glass and silver chandelier. A broad crescent-shaped alcove to his left was unfinished and darkened, but the opposite long cherrywood bar gave off a rosy glow, and a drowsy hum of voices ran steadily above sounds of clinking glasses and shuffling feet.

For a minute, trying to get his legs to steady under him, Cass stared with befuddled admiration at the four wide separate sections of backbar mirror, each encased glitteringly in its own solid silver frame. An oil painting of a reclining nude, with Titian hair draped artfully across her loins, occupied the large vacant space between the two center sections of glass. In the smaller panels there were prints of mustached prize fighters in sparring tights and photographs of prize-winning mine crews, stripped to the waist.

Cass moved from the doorway. Light from the big crystal chandelier filtered down through billows of cottony smoke. He started his tour along the bar. His legs felt a bit steadier, and suddenly he was appalled at himself. Strutting along this crowded bar with a gun at his hip, peering into faces. Hunting a man. Him, Cass Calbraith!

He went on. A knot of men was blocking his view of the end of the bar. As he swerved to circle them his attention was diverted. A door was swinging open forward and to his left, where the alcove ended against a partitioning wall. Cass stared at the door, marked OFFICE. Then the person who had been intending to come out seemed to change his mind suddenly. Cass swerved his glance to the right as the door swung halfway shut. Then he saw Jack Raimo.

Raimo stood at the heel of the bar, alone. And Raimo had already seen him. Cass felt the impact of eyes that had the immobile fixity of a snake's.

"Keep away from the alcove, kid."

Cass had started toward its sheltering darkness. Raimo's evenly spoken command halted him. Raimo was at an angle to his right; the office door at an angle to his left. Cass felt his heart lunge to his throat, pound, then loosely drop.

"Come a little closer, kid," Raimo said.

Shock sobered Cass, but he was aware now of a loss of breath, a sudden and continuous pounding in his chest.

"This suits me," he answered.

Raimo had on a new black broadcloth suit, the pants stuffed into new, lustrously polished shin boots. His sliver of a mouth twitched.

"Who're you lookin' for, kid?"

Cass swallowed, said, "I don't see anybody here but you."

Raimo stepped out from the bar. He said, "Get out of here, kid. Get out fast, you crumby little punk."

Cass took a step. There was a dry humming in his ears, an abrupt, tense gathering of readiness in his whole body. In another moment his hand would feel that involuntary nerve-impulse that would send it plunging to a draw. He was going to be hurt; killed maybe. But at least—

"Pull, you red-handed son of a bitch!" he sobbed.

A startling, entombing stillness came down on the room suddenly. Men at the bar turned with a finicky slowness. Talking ceased. Simultaneously a voice said soothingly from the office doorway, "Easy, Bub. You don't want to get hurt, now do you?"

With a gasp, Cass jerked his eyes from Raimo. Frank Bell stood in the doorway, his bandaged left arm hung in a sling, but his right negligently extended, tilting up a gun. Behind Bell the spare, gawky figure of Lank Johnson towered strikingly.

Cass froze as Johnson slid past Bell and came toward him, affable, smiling, covered by Bell's gun.

Johnson stopped as Bell moved out carefully from the doorway. His long arm circled Cass's shoulders. "Come on, Cass," he said quietly. "Let's go in my office."

"Get your hand off me!" Cass snapped. He saw Bell on one side, Raimo on the other. And suddenly he knew. This had been a trap. But not for him; for Boise. They'd stationed Raimo there at the end of the bar for bait. Boise wouldn't have seen Bell, hidden behind that shut door. But Johnson! How did Lank Johnson fit into the picture?

The promoter's bland voice impinged on his ear. "Come on, Cass. Don't make trouble. You'd only get hurt."

Cass glowered at him. "Some chance I've got to make trouble!" His heart was jerking with loose, thumping wallops as he split a quick glance between Bell and Raimo. He had to get out of here and warn Boise or Boise would be finished. But how could he? If he tried anything like that—

Johnson was saying condescendingly, "I knew you'd be sensible about this," and then the promoter was nursing him toward the office door and he was letting himself be led to it, nearer, nearer. "You won't be to blame for what happens," Johnson's voice droned on soothingly. "Kinstrey's been asking for this. He's had plenty of chances to—"

Cass drove forward savagely. Raimo had been indolently turning to lounge back against the bar, and Bell, smugly smiling, had been sliding his gun back in its leather. Johnson was catapulted violently against the slimmer, more delicate Bell as Cass hit him, the collision staggering both men. Cass somehow slid between them before either could regain balance, and it was at this moment that Raimo stepped out from the bar in sudden alarm.

Raimo's light, swift draw was a gesture of futility. A furious meleé in progress before the office door offered him no target. Soft footsteps drew toward the gunman, unnoticed until a voice flatly stated, "Here's your target, Raimo."

Boise Kinstrey's hand was at the butt of his Colt as Raimo spun.

24

CASS CALBRAITH had managed to hook his fingers in under Lank Johnson's pants belt. Johnson's panicked push had sent him slamming against Bell, crushing the gambler's frail body to the wall, as Jack Raimo's gun was abruptly changing trajectory. The gunslinger's weapon twice wickedly spat blue breaths before Boise Kinstrey squeezed off a single answering shot.

The effect was like two ear-splitting drum wallops, a pause, then a great resounding third wallop, *Pom!*, that seemed to shake the room in successive concussions. But Raimo had spun and fired too fast, Kinstrey had laid his one shot with dispassionate concentration, aware of a curious disembodied sensation after feeling his left sleeve twitched, then a burn across his left thigh, as if a hot branding iron had suddenly been brushed over it.

Jack Raimo seemed to be lifted up off the floor as Kinstrey's slug struck just above the cervical rib and tore out through the back of his neck. A gout of crimson jetted from his cleaved jugular. Then as he rocked back, his little eyes bulged as if squeezed by some hidden hand, his right foot caught against the brass rail and he was thrown like a sackful of loose bones.

Kinstrey vaguely was aware of the gunman's weapon clattering on the floor and spinning away in blue dazzle, but he wasn't watching Raimo now, or needing to.

His glance shifted to the left, where Cass and Lank Johnson now were rolling and twisting on the floor together, struggling with the furious concentration of a pair of mountain cats. Frank Bell, his face contorted with pain, was just rising groggily from beside the doorjamb where Cass's jerkback had pounded the breath out of him. He saw the spearhead of Boise Kinstrey's long shadow driving across the room toward him and bent in a cowering crouch.

Kinstrey hadn't quite reached him as he freed his gun but

before he could raise it Kinstrey's right leg swung and kicked it out of his hand.

Bell crumpled with a whimpering cry as Kinstrey turned and picked up the fallen gun. Wheeling around, he stared down without pity at the gambler's broken wrist. He pocketed the gun and said, "Up off your butt, mister!"

He felt a grim elation seeing Cass now on top of Johnson as he stooped and gathered slack from the seat of Bell's pants. He heaved and set the spare-framed gambler on his feet in one easy motion, then roughly spun him to face the front door.

"Now get out of here," he said, and giving Bell a shove provided emphasis with an added last word, *"fast!"*

The gaunt, black-mustached gambler had the look of a cringing hurt animal weaving his way to the front door. No one in the room spoke or gave him any acknowledgment whatever as he opened the door and went out.

Kinstrey had resolved to interfere in Cass's fight with Johnson only as a last resort. Now he saw that interference would be necessary only to save Johnson's life. Cass's face had a crazed contortion above the promoter's, and Johnson's cheeks were turning mottled from the thumbs Cass held wedged at his throat.

Cass was sobbing and at the same time hissing through set teeth, "Big bastard, big bastard, big bastard!" as he thrust his thumbs savagely deeper and deeper in Johnson's purpling neck.

Kinstrey leaned down and caught him under the armpits. He gave a tug and said, "Get up, Cass." When Cass made no response, his voice sharpened. "Do you hear me?" he clipped out. "I said get up!"

Slowly, Cass twisted around and stared up at him with a look of vague stupefaction. At the same moment his fingers slid slackly from Lank Johnson's neck, and almost as if this had been a signal for the release of tension, men lined in frozen rank along the bar suddenly began to stir. A glass clinked. Then feet shuffled and a first voice lifted tentatively out of the taut silence that had drawn down on the room.

Cass now made no resistance as Kinstrey hauled him to his feet, dragging his lax legs across Johnson's. He wobbled as Kinstrey let go of him.

"Is—is he—dead?"

Kinstrey looked down. A first tinge of color was creeping back in the promoter's leaden-hued face.

"No; he's not dead. But he would have been in another minute."

"You—you should have let me alone," Cass said.

A bartender and a swamper walked over, looked stiffly down at Lank Johnson, then at Kinstrey.

"We'd better get him in his office," the bartender suggested.

"Go ahead," Kinstrey said. He touched Cass's arm. "I don't know about you," he said, "but I'm falling off my feet. Let's find some place where we can rafter for the night."

They were fortunate to obtain a double-shotted bunk at the Indication. Kinstrey drew off his mackinaw and boots, then glanced at Cass. "Your choice," he said. "Upstairs or down?"

"It's no never-minds to me."

Kinstrey climbed into the upper bunk and in luxurious relief stretched out. They talked for awhile in sleepy monotones.

"I know you got Raimo," Cass said. "What happened to Bell?"

"I just had to shoo him away. You'd pretty well fixed his wagon before I joined the party."

"Son of a bitch."

"He won't bother us again. I'm certain of that."

"Boise?"

"Yeh."

"I'd never have gotten Raimo, would I?"

"I'll tell you this much. I never would have, if you hadn't got there ahead of me tonight."

"You know something, Boise? I'd never have got there at all without three hookers of gut-warmer in me."

"You'd have got there," Kinstrey said.

Below him, he heard a long-drawn sigh. Then Cass's voice floated up again.

"Boise? I really blew up tonight. I'd have killed Johnson. What made you stop me?"

"He never had anything to do with Big Matt's murder."

"No, but he hired men who did."

"Greed's Johnson's worst sin. That and his vanity. Greed's made him a wealthy man and wealth's made him proud.

doubt if he can stand to fail at anything, and now he has. It may just about finish him around here."

"You knew this afternoon that he was behind all our trouble at the mill, didn't you?"

"I'd begun to add things up, yes. When I ran into Johnson this morning I told him about putting Soldier Charley on Bell's tail. I could see right away he was upset and anxious to get away. Said he had an appointment at the Crystal. Then a little later you spotted Raimo rushing out of the Crystal. I began to get suspicious then. Maybe Raimo was running to warn Ganahl and the others. Then I began remembering other things. One especially."

"What was that?"

"Remember the day Philip Deidesheimer gave me that five hundred dollar advance? Well, I met Johnson right after that; him and Marna. And I told him about the money. There's no doubt he set up that trap for me over at Blue Chip Billy's. He didn't want us getting any help out of Deidesheimer."

Cass's voice was drowsy. "Well, I still say Johnson's as bad as the rest of them. Maybe he's no killer, but he hired killers."

"He's money-mad," Kinstrey said. "That blinds a man."

"You almost sound sorry for him."

"I am. He's going to marry Marna, isn't he?"

A sleepy chuckle came from Cass. "By God, yes! I almost forgot about that infliction."

"Well, do forget it. Let's get some sleep."

"I was a fool tonight, Boise."

"You were." Fervently, Kinstrey added, "But if you hadn't been, I wouldn't be here to tell you so."

"Hogwash."

Kinstrey's bunk creaked. He called down softly, "Good night—partner," and in a minute they were both asleep.

It was past eight-thirty the next morning when Kinstrey woke. Last night a fire had been going in a big sheet-iron stove in the center of the bunk room, but now it was out and the room held a dead chill and preternatural quietness. He thought with vague disturbance that he must have overslept and swung his long legs out over the bunk. He dragged his boots and mackinaw down with him as he dropped to the floor and glanced into Cass's bunk. He was not surprised, finding it empty. Cass had gone out for breakfast. Or maybe over to Effie's. . . .

Effie's. An obscure pain threaded Kinstrey as he pulled on his boots and shrugged into his heavy sheep-lined mackinaw. Then he put on his hat and circled the big, barracks-like bunk room with a forbidding glance. This was a room for drifters, casuals, such as he. Family men made their own homes. They had a reason to. . . .

Kinstrey ate a depressing breakfast in Mackwood's and was selecting a cigar at the cashier's desk on his way out when a dry voice from behind him said, "Try one of these. They beat Mackwood's."

Kinstrey turned and saw Philip Deidesheimer. The Ophir superintendent held a well-used cigar case which he was smilingly extending. Kinstrey said as he took a cigar, "How are you, sir? Beat Mackwood's? Would that be hard?"

Philip Deidesheimer merely smiled. "Heard there was quite a fuss last night over at the Crystal."

"News travels fast."

"Yes. So do some people, when things don't go just as they like."

Kinstrey's glance searched the superintendent's square-jawed face but there was only the usual inscrutability in those shrewd gray eyes as he bent forward to accept the lighted match Philip Deidesheimer was holding out to him. "Meaning?" Kinstrey said, drawing tightly on the hard-wrapped Havana.

"I'll be direct," Philip Deidesheimer said. "I had a visit from Lank Johnson this morning. He owns two sawmills Ophir's always wanted, as well as a big timber tract."

Kinstrey nodded, puzzled. "I know."

Philip Deidesheimer said, "Well, now Ophir has what it wanted. We'd bid on the properties before but Johnson never would sell. Until now."

Surprise flaring briefly in Kinstrey's blue eyes was superseded by an amused glint. "I wonder what could have changed his mind."

"I wonder," said Philip Deidesheimer. He pulled at his neat spade beard, added, "You're quite a detective, young man. A lot of people in this town never cottoned to Johnson but they never suspected him of skullduggery. They'll be glad to see him go."

Kinstrey gave a start. "Go?"

"I got an impression that Mr. Johnson was planning to dispose of all his holdings and leave town."

"He's a sensitive man."

"Vain is the word." Philip Deidesheimer extracted a cigar from his worn case, lighted it. "Well, I've got to get over to the office. Let me know as soon as you can about the job."

Kinstrey stared blankly. "Job, sir?"

"Oh! Then you didn't get the note I left with Miss Mannerheim. I want you with me at Ophir, Mr. Kinstrey. As assistant superintendent. I think you will find the remuneration satisfactory."

"Why—why yes, sir, I'm sure of that. But I may not be staying—"

"Think it over. Take plenty of time." Philip Deidesheimer swung open the door, a dry smile touching his broad mouth as he looked back. "Take till tonight," he said.

Then he was gone and Kinstrey stood gaping at a closed door.

Kinstrey walked. He lost track of time, place; sights and sounds and smells of the City seemed elusive, unreal, as if he walked alone in a vague and microcosmic world in which all sense of identity with the veritable real world was cut off.

He walked, and he thought of Philip Deidesheimer's offer. And felt the pitiless irony of it. He had wanted to prove himself: prove that he could do something, be something, without Big Matt's help. And now he *had* proved it. But to what end?

The day was mild; there would be a slight thaw by noon. The dark hoof-churned earth of the street gleamed moistly and by slightly exercising the imagination one could almost catch a whiff of spring in the air. Almost. If there was any hope in a man.

There was none in Kinstrey. He walked. He passed people without noticing them, only shifting course to avoid collision. His breakfast didn't set well. He felt a dull gnawing, a kind of naked heaviness within him. It was in his belly and it was up in his throat. And he knew what it was and what he would have to do about it. *Get out of town. Get out of the territory.*

Cass could manage the mill all right now. He was younger

than Effie. But he was no longer a kid. He'd proved that. Even with a couple of drinks in him it had taken guts to do what he'd done last night. Effie could do worse. A lot worse.

Kinstrey thought of Big Matt. *Remember this, Boise. The world bends its knee to just one kind of people—those who demand it. Never be scared to walk heavy and make a big noise. It's the squeaky wheel gets the grease. . . .*

Words. Just words. Words of some truth for some men. But not for all. Each man had to find his own words, make his own rules to live by. Each man had been cast according to his own mold and had to live unto himself.

A man was influenced by another man, and then the influence was cut off and there was a change, maybe for worse, maybe for better. Maybe a certain man had thought he could hold life in the palm of his hand like a chunk of clay and squeeze it to any shape he desired. But the clay never stayed in one shape. Big Matt had tried to be God. He had tried to make things come out his way. Things came out God's way. Because there was no other way for things to come out.

A sudden commotion on the street roused Kinstrey from his abstraction. A spooked horse had just run from Willard and Eils' blacksmith shop but had been caught outside by two men, who were trying to pull it down as it reared and fought savagely against their crouched weight on its bit rings.

Passersby on the opposite side of the street, their way blocked momentarily, stood watching, and suddenly Kinstrey froze as his glance fell on a man and a woman who had just stepped up to the edge of the crowd, then were mingled with it.

For a moment he wasn't sure. Then a flash of blue cape caught his eye and at the same moment Effie Mannerheim half-turned to look up at Cass and, smiling, slid her arm under his as the crowd jostled and threatened to fall back.

With a sharp intake of breath Kinstrey stepped into the doorway of Bloomfield's Cigar Store, out of sight. But in another minute the excitement was over. The horse, finally subdued, was forced back into Willard and Eils' and the flow of pedestrian traffic started moving again. Kinstrey waited until he could be certain which way Effie and Cass were going. Then as they started upstreet toward Mackwood's he abruptly reversed his own direction and turned downstreet.

He knew he would have to face them later. But right now

he wanted a breathing space; time to prepare himself. And tomorrow he'd pull stakes. Philip Deidesheimer's offer was a strong temptation even now. But he'd be too close to Effie if he stayed in Virginia City. He'd have to get out. And the sooner the better. . . .

He didn't remember swinging around the corner of Mannerheim's store or seeing the bearded face of Jules Mannerheim at the window peering curiously out at him as he started the steep ascent of the short street called Glory Climb. At the top a rimrock commanded a view of the City and a sweep of lonely, far hills. Kinstrey found a flat rock and sitting down pulled makings out of an inside pocket and began building a cigarette.

A feeling of bitter emptiness pressed upon him as he presently lighted the cigarette and stared moodily away. Consciousness of time again left him. He smoked three cigarettes down to his fingertips and was absently starting to make another when he heard the footsteps, then a lilt of voices. He jerked around and felt his breath stop.

Cass Calbraith and Effie Mannerheim were walking toward him, breathless from climbing. Effie approached tentatively, Cass with reaching, angry strides as he surged ahead of her. He gusted an exasperated breath, halting before Kinstrey.

"So, Jules was right! It *was* you he saw headed up here."

Kinstrey slowly stood, letting the tobacco of the unfinished cigarette sift between his fingers as he crumpled it. He swung a wavering glance toward Effie, then said, "I didn't see Mr. Mannerheim. I was just taking a walk."

" 'Just taking a walk!' " Cass mimicked fiercely. "Great jumping catfish, don't you know what's been happening down here? Lank Johnson's quitting town, and Marna's packing up to leave with him! And Philip Deidesheimer was at the store. He wants to see you. He—"

"I know," interrupted Kinstrey. "I met him at Mackwood's."

"So you know about that," Cass said. "Well, I'll bet there's one thing you *don't* know."

"Cass, please!" Effie chided.

She stood a little to one side and, staring at her, Kinstrey suddenly felt a warm rush of tenderness. She looked slight and appealing with the blue cape billowing around her and the gold-braided black turban slanted jauntily across her swatch of smooth yellow hair.

Cass was asking with clumsy irony, "Can't I just tell him he's the biggest damn fool in ten counties?" and then he said, "No, I guess not," and turned.

Kinstrey had barely any consciousness of his leaving. Effie's brown eyes turned up to him had a wistful earnestness, her voice had a tight fervency, as she said, "I tried to tell you last night, Boise, before you went rushing out. I've felt sorry for Cass. But that's all."

"But you kept talking of how changed he was!" Kinstrey blurted. "I thought—"

"You big dunce!" Effie said.

Her face was up to him then, eager, waiting, and as he bent over he felt his heart lurch suddenly and knock hollowly against his ribs. Then his arms were around her, and with the warm, sweet pressure she put against his mouth it was a long time before he was finally able to tell her, "I'm starting a new job tomorrow."

"I know. Mr. Deidesheimer told us." Effie's body was like an arrow. She looked up at him with her brown eyes shining. "And isn't this a coincidence?" she said, laughing. "I expect to be starting a new job myself—any day now!"